DEVILSKEIN
&
DEARLOVE

Alex Smith

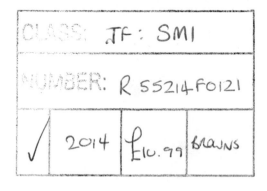

This Edition published in UK 2014 by Arachne Press Limited
100 Grierson Road, London SE23 1NX
www.arachnepress.com
© 2014 Alex Smith
ISBN: 978-1-909208-15-5
The moral rights of the author have been asserted

Printed in the UK by TJ International, Padstow.
Cover image © Ed Boxall
Chapter heading images © Cherry Potts

Thanks to Muireann Grealy for her proofreading.

CONTENTS

For my baby boy and his wonderful dad

1

Grumpy Girl

When Erin Dearlove arrived at Van Riebeek Heights to live with her reluctant Aunt Kate, the neighbours all said she was an obnoxious brat, too thin, spoiled, wild-looking, and with a habit of speaking like she'd swallowed a dictionary. They were pretty spot on. Her face was scrawny, her sandy amber hair unbrushed, she used convoluted vocabulary with spite, and she never smiled because she had no parents. Apart from Aunt Kate, who had been sworn to secrecy, nobody quite knew what had happened to them. Erin relished shocking people by telling them her mother and father had been eaten by a crocodile. 'Can't undo it, can't forget it,' she'd say, then add, 'I found bits of them on the shaggy white carpet of our designer home.'

Some people's jaws dropped open in horror. Erin liked that.

But the truth of her parents' demise was even uglier than a crocodile.

In the first few days at Van Riebeek Heights she found it impossible to avoid being cornered by overwhelmingly chatty grown-ups endowed with a blur of names like Nozizwe, Ebindenyefa, Zibima Oruh, Granny Wokoya, Aunty Talmakies, Varsha Lalla, Tekenatei, Ayodele, Boitumelo and Jaroslav

Chudej, and when their unwelcome geniality forced her into conversation, Erin would boast how her dad had been an important and very corrupt banker. 'Mr Dearlove, my father, was a splenetic, abusive man,' she'd say. 'He had many enemies, but even he did not deserve the horrendous fate that befell him and his wife and their irksome dog.' After telling the story a few times, she'd added that yapping terrier, but she never once mentioned the brother she had lost on that same unspeakable morning.

Her bad reputation at Van Riebeek Heights was sealed one Tuesday in the hour before twilight. 'Of course,' she said to Mrs Puoane, a flabbergasted neighbour from upstairs, who was seven months pregnant with twins, 'I was fascinated by their fabulous parties, their beautiful clothes, and famous friends who often appeared in glossy magazines and international newspapers, but the Dearloves were hard to get close to.' About this, Erin just shrugged. 'There was no warmth in that architecturally astonishing house. It's almost a relief that those Dearloves are gone.' But as she said the words, her heart constricted; it ached and so she added with venom, 'Parents are so overrated. With the way science is advancing, they'll soon be superfluous.'

Ping!Ping!Ping! went the Company Soulometer and Devilskein regarded the scurrilous contraption on his kitchen table with satisfaction. The Tuesday sun had sunk and night was on its way and the device alerted him to a quarry on another continent. The contraption was something like a GPS, except it dated back almost four thousand years, back to the early days of Babylon, and instead of directing a Companyman to a place, it gave the longitude and latitude of any living person who had, with true intent, thought or uttered aloud some variation of: 'Oh, I would sell my soul for/to…'. Of course, the Company did not buy souls, nobody can buy a soul: it is priceless; it has to be pledged. In order to procure these most precious of commodities, the Company dangled all manner of carrots and smidgens of hope in the way of desperate would-be traders: 'Your soul is not sold, it is pawned, and it is security for your debt to the Company; it is redeemable on certain terms. So if you or somebody you know can muster the wherewithal within a reasonable amount of time, there is a chance you can have it back. Until such time, it will reside in a locked room in our Indeterminate Vault. And like gold bullion for a government, its great treasury of souls made the Company a universal superpower. Exactly the nature of the said 'wherewithal', the specifics of the certain terms and the length of the reasonable time were all things never made obvious. Company policy was never obvious. Its magic was too shadowy and despicable for any such contractual transparency. However, betwixt the hot air and subterfuge, trading in souls did in fact have very definite rules. And every room in the vault of endlessly nested doors had a key.

Erin smiled cruelly at Mrs Puoane, her pregnant neighbour. 'I do not miss Mother and I do not miss Father, but nor do I relish the ridiculously small size of my Aunt Kate's apartment on this filthy Long Street.' She sighed. 'I suppose I have to face the fact that I am well and truly poor.'

As night absorbed any remnants of that Tuesday, Erin went on to plunder her imagination and further regale Mrs Puoane with how having always been rich and given everything she ever wanted, she assumed that living with Aunt Kate was a temporary measure until the complications with the bank were sorted out and she would have her four-poster double bed and the private forest, vineyards, peacocks and rolling lawns of the estate back again.

Two doors down, a boy who had already heard most of the blah about the mansion with the glass stairs was surprised when he happened to open one of his mother's old copies of *Garden & Home* to see an article about a convicted fraudster, a banker who boasted that he was out of prison before he even went in, and who happened to live in a mansion with glass stairs. His place was so big it required a staff of five gardeners and five housekeepers. But his surname was not Dearlove. 'And look!' muttered Kelwyn Talmakies to himself. 'There's a peacock in the vineyard.' On reading the article Kelwyn learned too that the tycoon who owned it despised anything cheap, bohemian, homemade or crafty; he wore only Armani clothes, Italian bespoke shoes and Rolex watches. Kelwyn frowned, but his thoughts were interrupted.

'Rover 1, come in, Rover 1, come in,' crackled a voice from a walkie-talkie lying beside Kelwyn.

He rolled over and picked it up. 'Rover 1, here. What's up, Rover 2?'

'We have a situation,' said the fuzzy voice named Rover 2. 'Need back-up on the corner of Church Street.'

'Be right there. Over and out.'

Duty, in the form of his sidekick, Sipho, aka Rover 2, who lived on the first floor with his grandmother, had radioed in and Kelwyn, unsure what to make of the article, stashed the magazine under his bed. In doing so he was chuffed to discover one of his favourite penknives: an Opinel with a carbon steel blade and a comfortable hand-carved wooden handle; he'd saved up to buy it from 'Serendipity' a musty, resin-scented antiques and oddments shop in Long Street. He collected penknives and had a particular soft spot for Opinels – 'the peasant's knife', his father had told him, before vanishing back to France – and Kelwyn owned three of them.

*

Rubbing his hands in anticipation of a deal, Devilskein, a Companyman with a formidable reputation, noted the co-ordinates of a middle-aged actor in an apartment in Istanbul. The fellow in peril fancied he was a theatrical genius waiting to be discovered. 'Honestly, I would sell my soul for a good part,' the actor said to a confidante as they sat smoking on a roof-top terrace with a view of the Bosphorus.

The first law of soul trading is that of 'Ask and You Shall Receive', like easy credit (but in the small print on any contract with the Company, the crippling interest rate on borrowings runs into several thousand percent).

Erin flickered her eyelashes and made a final bid to push all those terribly friendly people at Van Riebeek Heights away for good: 'It's no wonder I ignore the children around here,' she said to Mrs Puoane, whose ankles were starting to swell from having to stand for so long. 'They're rather dirty, low-class and uncouth. And besides, most of them are boys and I have nothing in common with them or anybody else on this noisy street where my aunt lives.'

Mrs Puoane rubbed her belly and groaned: one of the twins' small feet was kicking eagerly and its sibling was thumping its mother-to-be right under her ribs.

And so it was that after only a week at Van Riebeek Heights, her petulance earned Erin a nickname: 'Grumpy Girl'. It was Kelwyn Talmakies, owner of the walkie-talkie and the exceptional penknife, eldest son of Leilene Talmakies (who was Aunt Kate's friend and favourite neighbour) who started calling Erin that name first. He was a stocky teen with caramel skin, blond hair and a fighting spirit. His nails were usually full of mud, and his T-shirt often streaked with earth – despite Leilene Talmakies' best efforts to encourage her son to bathe twice daily, he frequently smelled of pungent kelp. He always kept a penknife in his pocket. To his mother's chagrin, Kelwyn had a tattoo of a gecko on his right calf, for shortly before abandoning his family, his zoologist father had instigated the inking of this reptile on his son's leg. What's more, Kelwyn seemed to relish goading Erin with his friendliness. But his greatest crime was being the same age as her dear, dear brother who was no more. For that alone she detested Kelwyn from the moment she laid eyes on him.

'You stink,' she'd said to his initial 'How do you do?'

'It's called "Seagrow",' Kelwyn said, sniffing his shirt happily. 'It's liquid fertiliser for plants.' Then he ventured, 'Do you read *Garden & Home*?'

Her face crumpled with disdain. 'Don't be absurd.'

She had, until he interrupted her, been reading a book, just as she'd done every afternoon of her life when it was still normal. The only difference was, instead of being propped up on a cosy sofa, surrounded by a great pile of checked and striped and floral cushions made and lovingly down-filled by her Mama, she was sitting on a flight of gritty concrete stairs in the dismal stairwell of Van Riebeek Heights; her mother was gone forever and eternally hurt in a way that no person should be hurt. Erin could pretend all manner of things (she was very good at that, indeed), but no matter how desperately her heart wished it, she could not erase the truth, nor undo what had been done.

A heatwave had hit the town, that January was fast becoming the hottest in recorded history. At least it was cooler there on those concrete stairs. And it should have been suitably lonely, for it was one of the higher floors; Erin aimed to escape detection and the attentions of the children in the lower floors, but alas, Kelwyn, who smelled of seaweed and asked silly questions about magazines, had found her out.

Kelwyn wiped sweat from his brow, leaving a smear of potting soil on his forehead.

'So this is where you hide,' he said, deciding to let the *Garden & Home* thing go. He tilted his head, trying to see the cover of her book.

'Go away.' Erin turned her back and dipped the book to obscure the cover in the hope that he couldn't see the title.

But he'd recognised it immediately, as a zillion other people would have done too. '*Harry Potter and the Prisoner of Azkaban*,' he said, triumphant. 'I loved that series. Hey, I've got them all, so if you'd like to borrow number four…'

'*Why* would I want *your* books?' she said, scathingly, as if he and his books were diseased. 'They probably stink as much as you do.'

But as much as she was angry, Kelwyn was equally jovial: they were perfect opposites. 'Well,' he said, unfazed. 'Books are expensive and maybe you don't belong to a library around here, being new and all.' He noticed a small brooch pinned to her shirt. 'I like your owl.'

Mention of the precious owl unsettled her and that made her loathe Kelwyn all the more. He had no right to like the brooch.

Along its four kilometres, Long Street below jangled with cars and coins (paid to parking marshals, tips left for waiters, currency exchanged for curios), and women in high heels who smelled of sun cream and coffee as they passed by brightly repainted and restored French, Cape Dutch, Victorian, and Art Deco buildings.

Higher up in the sixties block known as Van Riebeek Heights, which at six storeys towered over the street's mostly historic architecture, Devilskein was making notes in the Company ledger. And like any master of deception he made sure to include some error. The Company's contracts, and their deals, were laced with falsehood and equivocation. The truth of the matter was that once pawned, a soul was almost certainly lost because the Company books were fiddled and riddled with cunning sub-clauses and impossible to fathom appendices; who knew what keys opened which doors? On the kitchen table beside Devilskein was a heap of rather exquisite keys. And the walls of the kitchen were lined with shoeboxes, each one filled to the brim with a clatter of 'lost' keys.

The second law of soul trading was that of 'Compound Interest', an ugly cunning triumph of usurers across time. But there was some honour to the business – the Company never took souls that were contractually signed away with any unwillingness by their owners. And of course, the Company, never spoke of 'taking' a soul; souls were pledged to them. They were merely brokers, and happened to make use of the souls in their indeterminate possession like a bank might use its clients' funds to speculate in other markets. And keys were never thrown away, why that would be unjust; the keys were always somewhere, in some box or other, but with so many keys the chance of finding any particular one was slimmer than a cat's whisker.

Erin narrowed her eyes. 'Before the crocodile bit him in half, my father was a millionaire. So I certainly don't need your charity or your stinky old books. Leave me alone, stupid.'

Kelwyn was a bit hurt by her rejection – briefly he contemplated a mean retort relating to that article in *House & Garden* – but he brushed that impulse aside; it was not in his nature to be petty, he was a generous, warm, good-humoured soul. But fifteen-year-old Kelwyn, the saviour of all manner of damaged frogs, snakes, insects and plants, did have a naughty streak. 'Lighten up,' he said with a laugh, and poked her and started to tickle and tease her in a bid to lift her from her gloom. He started to sing: '*Erin is a grumpy girl! Erin is a grumpy girl. Grumpy, grumpy, grumpy, grumpy, grumpy—*'

'Stop it!' she swatted him. 'Go away, get away!'

A fat and crispy cockroach slipped out of a drainpipe and scuttled along the ridge of Erin's step.

She didn't make any kind of girlish squeal, which impressed Kelwyn, and he smiled, which she took the wrong way.

'Go away, I said!'

Kelwyn didn't go, and nor did the roach, so Erin got up and started away down the stairs, first walking and then running, with Kelwyn following, singing the 'Grumpy Girl' song and tugging at her ponytail, which made her all the more infuriated. On the way down, they were spotted by several other children – Duduzile, Celine, Ishara, Tutu, Sipho (aka Rover 2), Olanma, Max, Lauri, Dajana and Malika – whose ages ranged from four to thirteen and who thought it a great sport to join in the singing.

They followed her to Aunt Kate's front door, which was locked, and Erin had forgotten her key. She banged on it loudly and called to be let in.

Steam billowed inside the apartment; music blared; Aunt Kate frothed soap and put a razor to her leg.

It had become too much for Erin. Kelwyn realised she was close to tears and so he called the choir of bullying children to a hush.

'Come on, Erin,' effortlessly affectionate, unusually so for a boy of his age, he put an arm around Erin's shoulder. 'We're just playing – let's all be friends.'

Pricklier than an angry porcupine, she pushed him away. 'Never. Not in a thousand years. I don't need friends.'

'If you keep on being grumpy,' said Kelwyn, 'you're only going to make yourself miserable and the only friend you'll have here is Mr Devilskein,' he made a whooo-whoo ghost-type sound, 'the creature who lives on the top floor.'

The younger children thought that a great joke and fell about laughing.

Mirth jingled and mingled with the stairwell heat. On the top floor a kettle boiled and a poodle yawned. Mr Devilskein dipped a quill pen into a pot of Sabbath black ink made from the bones of burned witches. The label said: *A.P. Jones Hellstain. Fine Unholy Ink for Turncoats, Tax Collectors, Lawyers, Snake-oil Salesmen and other Malefactors.* It amused Devilskein, who had purchased it once on a trip to Salem, the town infamous for its 1692 witchcraft trials. Whenever he used the ink, it made him smile.

'Well, quite frankly, I'd rather be Mr Devilskein's friend than yours.' Erin was incensed, so added haughtily, 'In fact, I'm due to have tea with him this evening.'

Something about that impressed the children around her. Eleven-year-old Duduzile whistled.

'Tea with the monster,' whispered six-year-old Ishara, agog.

'I don't believe you,' said Kelwyn. 'You're fibbing, Erin Dearlove.'

'What you believe, boy, is of absolutely no interest to me,' said Erin, with all the scorn her thirteen-year-old self could muster.

'I'll know if you're lying. I'll follow you to see.'

'Do whatever you like. Mr Devilskein and I are having tea and scones at six p.m. tonight.'

'That's a strange time for tea and scones,' said Kelwyn.

In the heavens above, a cloud moved. A shaft of blinding sun burned at the creases in Erin's brow.

'You know nothing about time,' she said, trying to be superior and enigmatic.

'What do you know about him?' Kelwyn asked. 'Nothing, I bet.'

'It's none of your damn business!'

Kelwyn also knew nothing other than the second-hand embroideries of rumour. 'Have you even seen him? His scars? His nails? He is a monster and he's grumpy just like you. He'll probably eat you for tea after you've eaten your scones.'

'Rubbish.'

Fortunately, Aunt Kate opened the door just then. Water glistened on her shoulders; her legs were streaked with cocoa butter moisturiser.

'I'm so sorry, love,' said Aunt Kate, still wrapped in a towel, 'I was–'

'At last!' Erin turned her back on Kelwyn and pushed past Aunt Kate.

'–in the shower,' said Aunt Kate, finishing her sentence.

Apart from Kelwyn, the children scattered, as they did not want to get a scolding for being bullies.

'Enjoy your tea, Grumpy Girl,' called Kelwyn after Erin. 'It may be your last. I'll be waiting to see if you're a liar as well as a grouch.'

Erin's bedroom door slammed shut; Kelwyn winked at Aunt Kate and gave her an angelic grin.

She ruffled his hair and said, 'You're naughty, Kelwyn, for teasing her like that. She's had…' Aunt Kate's tone became serious and sad, '…the worst experience imaginable.'

'What, in the mansion with glass stairs?' said Kelwyn.

In a whisper, Aunt Kate, who could no longer bear the burden of knowing what she knew, said, 'Promise you will never ever tell anyone at Van Riebeek Heights what I am about to tell you?'

'Why?' Kelwyn asked.

'Because Erin wants it like that, but – well, it's hurting

her. I think at least one of you should know. But only you.'

'Then I promise,' he said earnestly.

Aunt Kate's whisper was almost inaudible. 'Her family did not live in a mansion with glass stairs, they were farmers.'

'Rover 1, come in please,' the old walkie-talkie in Kelwyn's back pocket hissed.

Kelwyn grabbed it and said into it, 'Not now, Rover 2. Am busy.' He shoved it back into his pocket. 'Sorry about that, Aunt Kate. Please go on.'

She smiled, a bit sadly. 'They did have a rambling farmhouse and hundreds of hectares of grazing for cattle.' She paused, as if recalling the place in her mind's eye, 'But they weren't rich, the house was run-down. Their only wealth was that land and those animals.' She frowned. 'Then the cattle were poisoned, thousands of them. And as for the land, no buyer will touch it after what happened to the Dearloves… so Erin, the only survivor, is penniless.'

Ping!Ping!Ping! went the Company Soulometer. Devilskein paused from his work with the ledger and placed the quill back into its pot of awful ink. A new set of co-ordinates gleamed on the machine's grid. This one was connected to a past date – the brokering of souls did not conform to usual laws of linear time and fixed place; it was an inter-dimensional business. So it could be that a Babylonian concern was able to produce a contraption that made use of round-earth geographical norms established dozens of centuries after Babylon vanished. Devilskein raised his brow: the quarry was a master artist of the High Renaissance. He was a genius sculptor, whose overwhelming ambition was matched only by the pungent stench of his body that was never washed; he was poor as can be, never changed his clothes, but what talent that soul possessed! And yet the artist was suffering from a debilitating spell of gloom in the form of artistic block:

His prodigious imagination had gone blank and he wanted it back at any price. Devilskein's delight was perhaps too much for his ancient heart, which constricted so painfully he thought he might faint. When the moment passed, he rubbed his chest and said to his French poodle (who was asleep), 'The arteries of my wretched heart are clogged something awful. I suspect it's going to pack up soon.' He sighed and lamented again, 'I suppose we should stop eating the fat on our lamb chops and having clotted cream with our pudding.' He heaved a sigh of great disgruntlement. 'We should give up whisky, cigars and foie gras. Pah! Never! But I suppose some day soon I will have to visit my Physician.'

Even though Erin had said she didn't care what Kelwyn thought about her, she actually did; Erin cared about a lot of things she tried not to, and she hated herself for that. In her room, with the door locked, she tried to read more of her Harry Potter book, but she couldn't stop thinking about the so-called monster, Mr Devilskein. When it was just before six, she when into her aunt's kitchenette and reached up high to the back of the cupboard for the new packet of biscuits: Lemon Creams. A jar of honey fell over, rolled sideways, and crashed onto the counter, but didn't crack.

Her father had liked honey.

Her father? Not the mean one who got eaten by a crocodile, but the real one, who wasn't rich, but who was her dad. Erin stared at the jar and thought she must be in a dream – this can't be real life, it's not meant to be like this, is it? Her limbs felt heavy with a deeply horrible realisation. She touched the silver owl brooch she always liked to have pinned on her shirt – it had been her mother's brooch. Then suddenly as it had come, the moment passed, and once again she was just a grumpy girl who'd been orphaned by a crocodile.

She unlatched the front door and, biscuits in hand, she marched up the stairs to the top floor.

Kelwyn was waiting for her. He looked at the biscuits.

'I thought you were having scones?' he joked, awkwardly. He wanted to say something else, something better, more comforting, but what could he say? There weren't any right words for things like what happened to her family, those things just shouldn't happen. Besides, what could he say without letting on that Erin's aunt had told him what she, and now, he, had sworn not to tell.

'I changed my mind. Anyway, I prefer biscuits.' Erin stuck her nose in the air and passed him.

'It's the last door at the end,' he said, still at loss for the right words. 'In case you didn't know.' He could have kicked himself.

But she was oblivious and undeterred. 'I knew that.'

Nobody Kelwyn knew of in the block had ever been brave enough to venture into the creepy flat because the monster that lurked there was said (variously) to be evil incarnate, a face-eater, an eyeball collector, a tokoloshe, a fleshless ghoul, a Satan worshipper, a creature with blades for fingers. None of it could be true though – Kelwyn thought the monster was probably just a vivid conglomeration of nightmares, books and horror films and maybe in part the invention of parents in the block who didn't want their children playing around in a dirty, abandoned flat. Still, the Devilskein myth was too fearsome for anyone to tempt fate by actually going into the infamous apartment 6616 – after all, everyone knows that where there is smoke there could well be just a little fire.

Kelwyn sighed, and gave up trying to dissuade her, thinking Erin would find out soon enough. 'Well, I'll be waiting out here,' he said, then he thought of something better to say: 'If you need me, scream, and I'll come and save you.'

She gave him a withering look and said, 'This isn't a trashy romance novel. I don't need to be saved, thank you very much.'

With that, she knocked on the door of the apartment. Her hand holding the Lemon Creams was trembling.

Not far away, a luxury cruise ship blew its horn, signalling its departure from the safety of the harbour at the end of Lower Long Street.

Even if there was no monster, Kelwyn admired Erin's courage. And he liked her fair amber hair that made wisps and waves around her pale face.

'I know you were making it up about the tea and scones,' he said, quite gently, thinking not about tea with Devilskein, but about the other things, including the *House & Garden* article.

'You know nothing,' she said with venom. 'Now, for the last time, GO AWAY! You're like a stray dog. I've got no scraps for you, dumb dog, so scram!' She gave him another scowl before knocking again more loudly. Irritation made her confident; she was very curious to see this infamous man named Devilskein. Was he really a monster? No, probably just a recluse, maybe he was disfigured, burned in a fire. Whatever he looked like, she doubted anything could out-monster her hidden-away grief. Since she disliked everybody else in Van Riebeek Heights, perhaps he could be her friend, or better still, she thought, if he really was a proper monster (not just a hideous recluse), perhaps he could swallow her and her stupid sad heart up. *I'm all yours, monster.*

She knocked again and called, 'Hello!'

'You may not have been making it up, but I was,' Kelwyn said, he turned and sauntered away, kind of hoping she would follow. 'This floor is deserted. The monster is just a story the kids around here scare each other with.'

Erin ignored him and knocked a third time.

A meat supply truck rumbled down Long Street; it had a delivery of lamb, beef and crocodile carcasses for a restaurant called Mama Africa.

The wind gusted and in a sweep, the door to Devilskein's apartment opened with a creak.

Kelwyn stopped and turned, thinking the lock on that derelict flat must have been faulty, causing the door to fall open. But he was too far off to see anything.

What Erin saw made her want to run, but she would not allow Kelwyn such satisfaction. She thrust the packet of biscuits forward towards the horrifying being in front of her. 'I've brought biscuits for our tea, instead of scones,' she said loudly, so that Kelwyn could hear.

'What on earth are you?' said Devilskein, taking in the skinny girl with scraggly hair and a green T-shirt the same colour as her big, terrified eyes. 'What manner of ugly human thing?'

'I could ask the same of you,' Erin said in a scathing whisper. 'Now are you going to let me in or not?'

He narrowed his lashless lids and cocked his hairless head; he could see into her soul and was intrigued at how it shimmered, but still, Devilskein was unprepared for a social event like tea and biscuits. 'Really, you wish to come in? Are you sure, little girl?' An antique gadget on his belt, like a compass crossed with a calculator, pulsed with an ominous red light.

In the near distance, the cruise liner edged out into Table Bay, followed by seals, which were being watched by sharks.

Erin peered into the gloom beyond him – from ceiling to floor the walls were lined with shoeboxes. 'But of course, I'm sure,' she said, snippily. 'Otherwise I wouldn't be here, would I?'

Again her soul caught his attention.

She has a living soulmate! Devilskein thought, calculating possibilities. Soulmates were in fact rather rare. And, unless he was mistaken, when joined and transplanted, then, *ahhh!* The twinned hearts of soulmates made a sum of immortality, or at least another thousand good years for a Companyman like Devilskein. *What uncommon luck! I must speak to the Physician immediately.* He growled softly, but she pretended not to hear. In a strong voice, especially for Kelwyn's benefit, Erin added, 'Our arrangement was for tea at six. Have you forgotten?'

Excited, but still perplexed, Devilskein suggested his place was untidy. 'Far too untidy for a visitor.'

'Never mind that. You can tidy up and I will put on the kettle.' Taking a deep breath, Erin summoned all her courage and pushed past Mr Devilskein. For the first time in one thousand three hundred years, Devilskein was shocked. He closed the door behind Erin and for the briefest moment the light bulbs faltered and darkness engulfed them.

Kelwyn's jaw dropped.

'What is this place?' asked Erin, looking about at the shadowy gloom with a vaulted ceiling. 'It's like something out of an antique book.' A pair of eyes beneath a flop of brown curls watched her from the kitchen door. The creature's brown nose twitched.

'The kettle is this way,' said Devilskein, indicating a door. 'You will boil it, as you said you would, and we will have tea as you said we would. You will not expect me to talk to you, and you will not go into any rooms other than the kitchen. And when you are in the kitchen, you will not poke about in any of the boxes or cupboards.'

'Why would I want to poke about?' Erin said. 'I am not domestically inclined. What could your kitchen possibly contain that is more interesting than any other kitchen on the planet?' And with that she went off to find the kettle.

On entering the kitchen, she frowned at the towers of

shoeboxes, but didn't dare comment on them.

There was a gaping maw where a stove should have been (Devilskein enjoyed eating but not cooking; he was not a creator) and in its place there was a large French poodle nestled in a basket.

'Dammit,' said Devilskein, remembering an important piece of equipment left out on the kitchen table. It would not do for the scrawny girl to see the Company Soulometer. And besides he wished to make contact with his Physician. He tapped the gadget on his belt and the pulsing red light turned purple; it gave out a soft sigh of pernicious gas.

Erin filled the kettle with water and turned it on, and only then became aware of mist (not kettle steam), a peculiar sweet-scented greyness that grew thicker and made her eyelids heavy. She noticed the fat digits of a clock offering six minutes past six and yawned.

Devilskein caught her as she fell asleep.

2

Across Time

It seemed to Erin that she had been sleeping for an age, but when she opened her eyes, the kitchen clock was still showing the same time. Water from a leaky tap dripped into the metal sink; a dragonfly hovered near the moisture. Devilskein had made a pot of tea and set out the biscuits on a turquoise platter. The teapot, a nicely fulsome round one, was turquoise too. There were no windows, but she could hear cicadas singing thickly in some distant garden. Remembering her fearsome host's instruction not to make conversation, Erin took a biscuit and ate it quickly and in silence. In fact, she was ravenous, so she ate five in succession and washed them down with the tea, which was excellent, neither too milky nor too strong.

Devilskein watched over the steam of his cup, tapping a long fingernail on the delicate porcelain. His Physician had confirmed the unique value of the hearts of soulmates, one heart was good, but to have them both, now that was a prize. There was a catch, however, they needed to have found each other in order for their uniquely powerful bond to imbue their hearts with immortality. It would require some plotting, he mused, in the wispy steam of tea.

Erin tried not to stare at the tiny foreign words carved on Devilskein's scarred face, nor to look at the place where his ear should have been.

All of a sudden, the gadget on his belt emitted an unnerving wail.

Yeeowl-whaawheeeee-whaaaaaaa-yeeeowl!

The kitchen shuddered like a locomotive leaving a station. 'Are we moving?'

Devilskein frowned. *How absolutely inconvenient.* He clutched the device, deactivated the irksome siren and, with a tap of his finger, made it issue forth a second dose of that pernicious gas.

Erin supposed it was sleepiness that made it seem as if she was in a train carriage. She yawned again and, feeling oddly content and cheerful, rested her head on her arms. Her legs dangled; her shoes were no longer on her feet. The clock ticked with metallic, somnambulant precision: one weighty tock followed by a lighter tick.

The contraption on Devilskein's belt had indeed moved the kitchen in time and space.

In walked an irate man in a robe embroidered with palm trees. He glanced at the sleeping girl. 'I'm here for my key.'

Devilskein tapped the hole where his right ear should have been and pretended he couldn't hear.

The robed man repeated his request.

As a Companyman, there was nothing more important to Devilskein than maintaining control of his hoard of keys. It was immeasurably displeasing to be faced with the possibility of having to give a person back their soul.

'My key,' said the robed man. 'I have fulfilled my side of the bargain and I DEMAND MY KEY!'

Devilskein grunted and pulled a wooden stepladder out from under the table. He used the ladder to access the most precariously positioned shoebox at the top of the tallest of the towers. He climbed down, opened the box, and placed it in front of the robed man. The box was full of keys, hundreds of keys.

'It might be in there,' said Devilskein. He rummaged in the box. 'No, not in this one.'

The man scowled. 'You haven't looked very hard.'

Devilskein narrowed his lashless eyes. 'I tell you it is not there, but there are six thousand thousand other boxes in this place.' He checked his watch. 'Unfortunately, I have other things to do right now, and according to your contract you are obliged to find it yourself. So, if you will step this way I will take you to the sorting room and you may look to your heart's content.'

The man was outraged; he bellowed an expletive in Arabic and thumped the kitchen table with his fist. 'What do you mean, I am obliged to find it? You are the broker, it's your vault, they're your keys, you must find it!'

'No. You should have read the small print,' said Devilskein with a mirthless smile. 'But none of you ever do. This way please.'

The next thing Erin knew, Devilskein was shaking her. His hands were icy.

'Wake up, scrawny child!' he said. 'You fell asleep and now you must go. Your people downstairs will start looking for you and I have a long night ahead of me.'

Erin got to her feet. Outside, stars had long since pushed the sun from the sky. She frowned when she saw that the time on the clock had not changed. Devilskein shoved the remaining Lemon Creams back into the packet, which he twisted at the top and handed to her. 'Away with you!' *And find your soulmate little one! My immortality depends on it.*

She was too drowsy to protest, even though she wanted to tell him to keep the biscuits, and more than that, she wanted to know how it was she had been sleeping all this time, which felt so terribly long. She realised her feet were bare.

'Go on then.' He handed her her shoes, ushered her out of the kitchen and towards the front door. 'Go home and don't come back.' *Or not until you've found that true love of yours.*

Having slept, her eyes were accustomed to the dark and she could make out more of the entrance room than when she first came in. It was a small room, with uneven floors and six internal doors and it had a curious habit of expanding and contracting. 'Is this room breathing?' asked Erin, watching the walls rise and fall. It seemed as if they were standing inside the lungs of some beast. Erin rubbed her eyes. 'No, of course not.' She shook her head. 'A room doesn't breathe, does it?'

Devilskein said nothing, though he thought of a Japanese man who once said: 'The body is the outer layer of the mind, as the cover is the outer layer of a book'. He smiled.

'I don't know why I feel so dizzy. I'm sorry I fell asleep.' She slipped her feet into her sandals, struggling to fasten the buckle of her right shoe. 'You really like shoes, don't you?' she said, finally unable to resist making at least some remark about the towers of shoeboxes.

Jerking his head at the front door, Devilskein grunted. 'If you don't leave now, I will become angry.'

'No need for that,' Erin said, abandoning the faulty clasp. She was going to reach for the door handle when she remembered something. 'I had the strangest dreams. I was in a museum and then it became a train.' She looked about disconcerted. 'But it wasn't exactly a train; it was rather like this room with six doors. And there was a different view from every door.'

'Out!' He pointed at the exit. 'I have things to do.'

'What things? What do you do?'

In the corridor a cat stalked a pair of pigeons.

Another growl gurgled in Devilskein's throat. 'Did I not say there would be no conversation? If you change the rules, I cannot be blamed for the consequences.'

Feeling more awake than before, Erin, who had never been timid and was by then quite used to Devilskein's fearsome appearance, put her hand on her hip and asked, 'What on earth are you talking about? What rules are you talking about?'

He clenched his fists behind his back. 'Your friend warned you, and I warned you, but you are an insolent child.'

'What friend? I have no friend, and quite frankly you are a very rude man.'

'Man? What gives you that impression? My clothes – yes perhaps, they do bear a resemblance to the clothes of men.' He smiled a ghastly smile and laughed a dreadful laugh. 'Go before you see too much, before it is too late.'

Erin lost her courage, and with it the urge to ask questions. Without looking left or right again, she opened the door and departed from Devilskein and his strange world. The hunting cat in the corridor hissed; the pigeons flapped and scattered. Outside it was dark, much, much darker than when she'd gone in. The passage lights cast rays upon the cement floors of Van Riebeek Heights. A little distance ahead a heap moved, jolting mosquitoes and sand flies from their blood-rich drinks. As Erin approached, she realised it was Kelwyn. He looked up and rubbed his eyes. The predatory cat bared her teeth as Erin passed.

'What were you doing in there?' Kelwyn sneezed.

'That's none of your business.'

He stood up and rubbed a cramped muscle in his neck; he'd been sleeping at an awkward angle. 'I thought I'd never see you again.'

'Well, sorry to disappoint you.' She marched past.

'That's no way to say thank you.' He sneezed again – Erin was covered in dust.

'I have no need to thank you.'

He scratched bites on his legs and scrambled to follow her down the stairs to their floor. 'Oh yes you do,' he checked his watch. 'In half an hour I would have come in there to rescue you from the monster.'

'He's not a monster.' She turned her startling eyes upon him: her irises began with a rim of black and progressed through emerald to all shades of green ending with a pale, dreamy jade around their pupils. 'Mr Devilskein happens to make excellent tea and I was in no need of rescuing.' She recalled Devilskein's laugh and shuddered, but decided she would return to his apartment the following evening. 'In fact, I'm meeting him again tomorrow and I'm going to bake scones. I promised I would.'

'You're insane!' Kelwyn grabbed his fifteen-year-old head in exasperation. 'You can't go back there, that creature will kill you.' And he didn't want that, because even though she was infuriating, Kelwyn's heart ached a bit for Erin and her proper posture, long neck and pale face garlanded over the cheeks and nose with a scattering of freckles, but what he wanted most was to fold her in a hug and tell her everything would work out, that she didn't have to tell stories. He had a feeling about her, he couldn't explain the feeling with any exactitude, but somehow he knew they were more than just unlikely neighbours.

Eyes blazing beneath fair eyebrows, Erin turned and glared at him. 'Don't call me that and don't tell me what I can and can't do.'

Kelwyn shrugged. 'Okay, grumpy, if you must go back, I suppose you must, but I don't think it's a good idea.'

The luxury liner cruised further away, into the shark-filled waves; lamb sizzled in the cooking pots on the stove at Mama Africa. There were sirens in Long Street and music and laughter and cigarette smoke floated up from the bars and clubs.

Erin's face contorted with fury. 'What you think is irrelevant. You're just… a stupid boy.'

He smiled, lopsided. 'Is that the best you can do, Grumpy?'

She roared with frustration and pushed him aside. 'You're such an idiot.' She ran to her aunt's door and when Kate opened up, for the second time that day, Erin pushed past her unceremoniously, just as her aunt was saying, 'I've been worried about you!' and ran into her bedroom, slamming the door behind her. She threw herself down on her bed.

Kelwyn lingered outside. His legs were covered in bites, and mosquitoes followed eagerly for more of his sweet blood.

'Where on earth have you two been?' asked Aunt Kate.

Cockroaches scuffled; a full moon took possession of the sky; Kelwyn's bare legs itched.

'I saved Erin from a monster,' Kelwyn said.

And Erin vaguely heard, and would have argued the point, but with her head on a soft, clean, but poorly ironed pillowcase, she was unable to fight the exhaustion that pulled her towards sleep and dreadful dreams.

Aunt Kate was saying something Erin couldn't quite hear.

'Everything is fine now,' Kelwyn said, and it was in that moment that he realised he definitely had a crush on the girl with a traumatic past.

Their voices and conversation travelled along the concrete to several floors up, where Devilskein and his poodle, Calvados, were listening.

'Remember your promise, Kelwyn,' Aunt Kate said.

Kelwyn nodded. 'I'll never tell.'

'Good,' she smiled. 'Night then.'

With that, the corridors of Van Riebeek Heights became

the domain of night insects. Back at home, Kelwyn gave his mother a kiss hello. She was enthralled by a pastry and chocolate challenge on Masterchef.

'Sipho left this for you.'

Barely looking away from a developing tower of éclairs, she handed Kelwyn a photocopied page.

Kelwyn nodded. And once in his room he took his walkie-talkie out of his bedside drawer: 'Rover 2, come in please.'

'Rover 2, ready for action. Did you get the poster?'

'Affirmative, Rover 2. I see the subject answers to the name "Ramon".'

'Affirmative, Rover 1. Subject has been missing for fifty-six hours. Subject's human says she fears subject will starve or be run over if he doesn't come home soon. My mother won't let me go out looking now.'

'No. But we must act quickly, Rover 1,' said Kelwyn. 'We'll do a dawn sweep. Meet me at ground level, at six a.m. tomorrow morning.'

'Affirmative, Rover 1. Good night.'

Ping!Ping!Ping! For the second time that day the Company Soulometer let out its unsettling wail. From an ivory box, Devilskein took a pinch of snuff. He checked his watch. It was a few minutes before midnight. 'I suppose, Calvados,' he said, tickling the dog's ear, 'after the night's work, we will have to procure jam from our friend at Versailles and cream from the all-night shop, if that silly, scrawny girl is coming back tomorrow with scones. She has no idea what she is getting into.'

3

Aunt Kate

Erin slept until noon the next day and dreamed non-stop; her last dream before waking was of a towering curtain, upon which sat a shiny black spider with sharp fangs and wings like a wasp. The creature had already sucked the blood out of her parents and her brother, leaving them crumpled, and before she could escape the curtain, the spider-wasp fell upon her neck and sank its spiny talons into her voice box. She woke with tears in her eyes and discovered Aunt Kate noisily vacuuming the carpet in her room.

Erin screamed like a woken baby, 'What are you doing? Can't you see I'm sleeping? What's wrong with you, you crazy woman?'

Aunt Kate had her back to Erin and was engulfed in the suction roar of the machine; she could hear her niece's tantrum, but decided to ignore it on account of the fact that she felt it was high time Erin started getting up at a decent hour.

Erin looked about the room that had become hers and felt a second surge of unfathomable rage.

'This room is the size of the walk-in cupboard in my previous bedroom,' she shouted over the roar of the vacuum.

Aunt Kate ignored the comment.

'It's awful,' Erin said, more loudly. 'Not only does it overlook the refuse area, but it's tatty. This is what Mr Dearlove would have called "bohemian".' She sniffed disdainfully. The room smelled of sandalwood incense. The curtains were always closed on account of the inauspicious view. In one corner was a rolled-up yoga mat and a squashy Tibetan cushion embroidered with bells and silver thread.

'Mr Dearlove hates bohemian things,' Erin said. She looked around and pulled a face at what she saw. The walls of the room were covered in a mural: a savannah, arid and rocky, with a single tree reaching for a velvet sky of clouds and stars. It was hyper-real and very deftly done. Aunt Kate had painted it.

'Yes,' said Erin. 'Mr Dearlove would despise this dump – he likes expensive objects branded with famous names.'

'Is that so?' said Aunt Kate, unconvinced – she had known Erin's father to be quite the opposite and yet Erin actually seemed to believe this fabrication. A psychiatrist friend had told her that in response to the extreme trauma she had suffered, Erin had created an alternative reality for herself. The psychiatrist said it would be temporary, but as far as Aunt Kate could see it was becoming more elaborate and more entrenched by the day.

In spite of, or perhaps because of her worries, Aunt Kate made an effort not to react and not to take the bait when Erin goaded her.

Erin upped her game. 'If you were a better artist, you wouldn't be so poor.'

For the first time since she had been there, Erin noticed that the mural contained creatures; they were well camouflaged though, so only with careful looking could they be spotted. Erin got out of bed to inspect a rather lovely lizard she had spied on one of the branches of the tree.

'It's a rock monitor,' said Aunt Kate, turning off the

vacuum cleaner. Immediately the sounds of Long Street cluttered the air: big trucks rumbling, old chugging cars, new speeding cars, taxis hooting, refuse vans grumbling. Aunt Kate put her arm around Erin's shoulder. 'Cool, isn't it?'

Erin shrugged off her affection. 'No, it's not cool. I despise reptiles.'

'But some of them are real beauties,' said Aunt Kate. 'You know, we should go camping sometime.' In a bid to deal with Erin's rages, unprovoked rudeness and general cantankerousness, Aunt Kate had decided to put into practice what she learned about inner calm from an ashram in India where she'd lingered in her twenties.

'Quite frankly,' said Erin, looking down her nose at her aunt, 'I couldn't think of anything worse than camping, except camping with you.'

Aunt Kate exhaled and managed a smile. 'Ah, no, camping is great. I bet you'd just love it. Tea around the fire, marshmallows on the braai, showering beneath the red skies of sunrise, and sleeping with nothing between you and heaven but stars. Good food, good wine, the occasional joint – not for you of course. Fresh, sweet air, wild and wonderful and rare creatures, like bat-eared foxes.' Aunt Kate's eyes glittered. She thought of a man she had almost loved. She'd seen her first real bat-eared fox with him.

Erin listened, then said as if perplexed, 'Why would anyone want to sleep on the dirt with the creepy crawlies?'

'In fact,' said Aunt Kate, pretending she hadn't heard, 'there's a bat-eared fox in this mural. Have you spotted it yet?'

Erin shook her head. 'Why are your eyelashes green? You're so weird.'

'Thank goodness for that. ' The only make-up Aunt Kate wore with any regularity was the green mascara a friend had sent from Tokyo; she liked it for dull days in need of perking up and nights out, because it was funky and matched her eyes. She was plainer than her deceased sister, Erin's mum, but Aunt Kate was tall and strong with high cheekbones, boyish short hair, strong shoulders, a fulsome smile, and a grand sense of humour. Her body was lean from surfing and diving and her teeth were stained from cigarettes. She had a cherry blossom tattooed on her wrist; she'd had it done in Kyoto. In her life so far, she'd lived and worked at odd jobs in India and Jamaica and Cameroon and Japan and Thailand and Croatia.

A telephone started ringing in a neighbouring flat.

Aunt Kate's jovial reply made Erin freshly angry.

Chairs scraped over the floor in the flat above them. Somebody was bouncing a ball: *thud, thud, thud.*

'Why are you vacuuming, and anyway when is your maid coming back?'

Aunt Kate laughed again. 'Back?'

'I'm assuming she must be on holiday or something.'

Aunt Kate gave a bemused snort. 'What makes you think I have a maid?'

'Everyone has a maid. We had three maids in our mansion.'

'Well, Erin, not everyone has a maid; some people do their own housework.'

'So who is going to wash and iron our clothes and make us food and clean the toilets?'

'We are.'

'You're joking!' Erin was indignant. 'The maids did that in the mansion with the glass stairs.'

Aunt Kate frowned, but not because of Erin's snotty tone – she was wondering if Erin would ever actually remember her real home on the farm, her real parents and her brother, all of which she seemed to have erased from her memory and replaced with a strange cast of unlikeable characters.

'I've never ironed a thing in my life,' Erin continued, 'and certainly never cleaned a toilet. How disgusting.'

'Well,' said Aunt Kate, undaunted by Erin's impudence. 'It's high time you learned, it'll do you good. And you can start by pulling off those sheets from your bed. You've been here for three weeks now and they can more than do with a wash.' Aunt Kate winked. *Thump, thump, thump* went the ball upstairs, where a child was batting a cricket ball against a much-dented lounge wall. 'And since you're new to the washing thing, I'll help you this time, but in the future you must take the initiative and wash your linen once a week. Monday is the day I do my washing, so perhaps you can have Tuesday for your washing? How's that?'

Something crashed in the flat above. The bouncing of the ball ceased.

'Thanks for nothing,' said Erin.

Kate gathered a pillow and pulled off its cover, then tossed it to Erin. 'Do the same. Strip the duvet and the mattress.' The pillow had fallen at Erin's feet. She stood there, doing nothing.

In the flat above there was screaming: a mother lambasting the child who had smashed the TV screen with the cricket ball.

'Come on then, Erin, it's not difficult. It'll keep you busy and maybe it'll even cheer you up to do something for yourself for a change.' Kate picked up the pillow and placed it in Erin's unwilling hands. 'Later, I'll teach you to cook a Thai green curry and steamed jasmine rice.'

'I don't like spicy food.'

In the flat above the reprimanded child was crying.

'But you've never tasted my Thai green curry. You might just love it.'

'No, I won't.' But it occurred to Erin that perhaps this cooking thing could come in handy. 'Can you make scones?'

'Sure. And muffins, delicious bran and date muffins.'

'I don't want muffins. Only scones. Today. Will you make them today?'

One floor up, a door slammed shut.

'Please… do you ever use the word "please", Erin?'

'Please will you make them today, before six? I need them.'

Kate frowned. 'Okay, WE can make scones together, but only after YOU'VE done your laundry.'

Erin rolled her eyes and pulled the cover off the second pillow.

There was silence above, but next door the phone was ringing again.

'Excellent,' Aunt Kate rewarded Erin with a happy smile. 'We have a deal. Get dressed, bring the laundry through and I'll show you how the washing machine works.' With that, she picked up the vacuum cleaner and left, humming a song by one of her favourite rock bands.

'Crazy witch,' muttered Erin. She struggled to undo the buttons on the cover. As she did, she cursed and grumbled: 'Never in my life have I ever been asked to do anything; in our mansion with the glass stairs we had five gardeners and five housekeepers and I spent my days reading and I never had to eat Thai curry.'

By the time she had won the battle with the buttons and disrobed the duvet, removed the sheet and gathered up the pillowcases, Erin was feeling less angry and so the tone of her grumbling had softened. 'I suppose, not everyone can live in a mansion like ours. I might learn quite a lot about the lives of "common" people here and about the ordinary things that such people do.'

She pulled on a pair of shorts and T-shirt with a little alligator motif.

Then, with her vision obscured by the pile of laundry, Erin staggered into the kitchenette where Aunt Kate was waiting with a box of detergent and a bottle of aloe-scented fabric softener.

She showed Erin which compartments of the washing

machine drawers used powder or liquid. It was a second-hand machine bought off Gumtree and the compartments for the detergents were stained and caked with soap that hadn't washed away.

'Why aren't you married?' asked Erin. 'Apart from your short hair, you're not so ugly.'

Kate chortled and knelt down. 'Well, thank you. I'll take that as a compliment.' She pointed at the dials. 'It's always set at quick 30-degree wash. More environmentally friendly and economical. Just leave it like that and press the Start button.' Aunt Kate did that and lights came on, the drum whirred into action and water swished into the machine. 'Actually, I was married once, for your information.' Aunt Kate stood up. 'So, now you've done part of your side of the deal let's make those scones. Why do you need them before six? Have you got a date with Kelwyn?'

'Absolutely not!' Erin was appalled.

'Nothing wrong with Kelwyn, he's sweet.'

'He's vile. And he's poor. And he's a boy.' The washing inside the second-hand machine sloshed in loud, lumbering circles.

'Oh come on. You need friends.'

'I have a friend upstairs.'

'Who?'

Far below a car swerved, tyres screeched, glass broke, metal crumpled and then shouting started.

'Mr Devilskein, in apartment no. 6616,' said Erin. 'On the top floor.'

'Somebody lives up there?' Aunt Kate was incredulous. 'In number 6616? Erin, is this some kind of a joke?'

'No,' said Erin, pertly. 'And the scones are for him.'

'How old is he?'

'Ancient.'

Aunt Kate had no idea how accurate that statement was.

'But he makes excellent tea.'

'Which flat is it, exactly?' asked Kate.

'The one at the end.'

A warning wail of sirens began, and grew louder with urgency, as an ambulance sped up from the bottom of Long Street to the scene of the calamity.

'Are you sure? The entire sixth floor's been empty ever since I've lived here,' said Aunt Kate. 'And that's ten years. Besides, how would anyone live up there? As far as I know, the roof is still broken and that's why some of the apartments have damp problems.'

'I don't know about damp problems, but the roof isn't broken. And Mr Devilskein is definitely on that floor.'

Pensive, Kate took out cake flour, murmured, 'Sounds like there's been an accident down there,' as she gathered the sieve, salt, butter and a measuring cup. 'You must remember to be very careful when you cross that road, Erin, there are some crazy drivers out there.' She unfurled the flour packet; a puff of white wheat particles dusted the air. 'What does he look like, this Devilskein?' Aunt Kate asked.

'A monster,' said Erin, trying to get a view of the accident from their kitchen window, but failing to see much. 'He's hideous. He's got one ear missing and his face is all marked with tattoos and scars, and the skin on his hands is scaly like the water monitor lizard you painted on the wall in my room.'

'You're pulling my leg.'

Erin shook her head.

Under Kate's direction, flour flumped into the measuring cup, then flumped again into the sieve. Aunt Kate showed Erin how to tap the sieve without making too much mess. So together they made scones, but all the way through the baking lesson, Erin wondered about the floor that was supposed to be vacant and Aunt Kate decided that the mysterious Mr Devilskein was another manifestation of her niece's fertile imagination. Still, she gave Erin a bit of a talk about stranger-danger and said, 'If you feel uncomfortable leave immediately. If you feel trapped, scream! And if necessary, kick him in the balls and poke him in the eye.'

Erin's face crumpled at what seemed to her to be unnecessary meanness. 'You're mad: he's very old and harmless.'

At that very moment, Mr Devilskein was making his favourite journey: a circuit through his vault of beautifully ordered keys. The library-sized safe was located in a crease of time between the top floor of Van Riebeek Heights and a prehistoric burial ground. The feeling he got ambling between the floor-to-ceiling aisles of keys was very much how a bibliophile would feel when wandering in the British Library. Each key, like a book, held a story, and though most Companymen were too ice-hearted to be sentimental, Albertus Devilskein was different: though thoroughly cruel, he was also most thoroughly cultured, and as much as he was lethal, he was equally a romantic. And so he cherished the key vault and whiled away a happy afternoon contemplating its contents. *Keys are such pretty little wonders!* he thought. In his kitchen was a myriad of shoeboxes filled with keys yet to be catalogued – as was expected, Devilskein had made sure to mix the keys up, so that there was never any way of tracing which key unlocked which room. The Company frowned upon keeping keys in any order that might be fathomable by a claimant coming to retrieve his or her precious soul. But Devilskein could not resist the poetry of classifying his keys according to the Dewey decimal system.

Six floors down, the accident that might have been avoided by wiser driving was finally cleared and Long Street had returned to normal.

When Erin left the flat just after six armed with her tray of scones, Aunt Kate felt quite tempted to follow her up to the top floor, but thought better of it – her psychiatrist friend had advised her to allow Erin to work through the fantasies in her own time.

(Special Agent) Kelwyn (Talmakies, of the Avid Animal Search and Retrieve Squad) did follow though. He trailed behind Erin, in a wake of fresh, hot-scone smell.

'Can I have one?' he asked.

Erin was doing her best to pretend he wasn't there.

She did not reply.

'They smell awesome.'

Up and up they went, following the concrete stairs to the top floor of Van Riebeek Heights. Although the sun had not set, and the sky was still blue between racing grey clouds, a nearly full moon was visible in glimpses. The traffic was thick; and workers were on their way home or stopping for beer or white wine with ice and cigarettes. Waiters in street cafés decanted recycled peanuts into dishes, lit candles, turned up music, replaced thin toilet rolls in washrooms with fat new ones, all in preparation for the parties of the night.

'Oh, hello,' said Kelwyn, who loved all animals. 'Haven't seen you before.' At the top step, a large curly-haired poodle was waiting. Kelwyn reached out to pat the dog, but just as his hand made contact with Calvados's curls, the dog bared his teeth and backed off. A voice from the corridor said, 'My dog never allows strangers to touch him.'

'Mr Devilskein?' said Erin.

Kelwyn stopped walking and stood watching as Erin continued on to number 6616. But Devilskein who had more than one pair of eyes, not in the back of his head, but in the bodies of the insects all along the passageway, was most deeply delighted to see into Kelwyn's soul, for it told him a secret he thought he would not so easily uncover.

'I baked us scones,' said Erin.

'You're late,' said Devilskein, grumpily, from within. 'It's ten past six.'

The door was open, so Erin followed the poodle into the flat. Devilskein closed the front door behind them and all sounds of the life in the street below vanished.

Kelwyn was left lingering at the far end of the passage. His stomach grumbled; those scones really had smelled good.

'Sorry I'm late,' said Erin, looking about her, wondering what lay beyond the six coloured doors.

'To the kitchen, child.' Devilskein shooed her out of the murky vestibule. 'And just because you have scones, don't expect obsequious niceties. If they taste awful, I won't eat them out of kindness; don't expect any of that.'

On a table covered by a fine white linen cloth there was a trio of tiny spoons and dainty silver dishes containing berry jam – it happened to have come fresh from the sixteenth century, from the Court of Versailles, unsalted butter, and whipped cream (these last two were more locally and recently procured at a 24-hour mini-market). Two throne-like chairs, two porcelain cups and saucers with matching side plates, and two silver knives also awaited the commencement of the tea party.

The silence was so dense the poodle's moist breathing was audible. He settled and closed his eyes.

Since she had been late, Erin observed the 'rule' of no conversation and instead of talking she occupied herself with slicing open a scone and slathering it with jam and cream. Her knife clinked with horrible loudness against the porcelain plate when she set it down. She was mid-bite when Devilskein cleared his throat and said, 'You're a brave child.'

'Not really. Apparently, I'm grumpy and spoiled.'

'Nothing wrong with being grumpy; friendliness is

overrated. I have in my time been possessed with the skill of telepathy and it is no surprise to know that more than half the smiles people offer hide decidedly unfriendly thoughts. Civility is naught but a cunning mask. A tool for getting ahead in the human world. People are nice while they need you in their lives.'

Erin shrugged. 'Well you're not nice at all, so does that mean you don't need anyone in your life?'

'Maybe, maybe not.'

'You're full of secrets, aren't you – like what's behind all those doors in your entrance?'

'Zoos, gardens, an infernal limbo and time-traps, mostly. And now that you know, I will probably have to kill you.' Although he said that, and could have done it with the greatest of ease, Devilskein was not yet ready to kill Erin. And surprisingly, too, he was enjoying her company; for although he was an esteemed Companyman, company, for him, was in fact a rarity. And perhaps it *was* needed.

The poodle whimpered in his sleep before he began to snore softly.

'Whatever,' said Erin, oblivious to the immeasurable power of the Companyman sitting across the table from her. 'Can I go inside one of them and see? I used to have a huge garden where I lived before and now there is nothing but concrete, tar, shops and nightclubs. It's sordid.' Her feet dangled; on that grand and imperious chair, her legs were not long enough to reach the floor.

Devilskein frowned, startled – and amused – by her lack of trepidation. *What could it harm to let her see*, he thought. Now that Devilskein had pinpointed the whereabouts of her soulmate, the boy in the corridor she called Kelwyn, the grumpy girl was not much longer for this earth. 'Go in at your own risk, if you dare, but there is nothing at all to see, unless you happen…'

With half a scone in her hand, Erin stood up and wandered back into the gloomy entrance where the claustrophobia of shoebox towers continued. She chose to open the third door; it was yellow. As Devilskein had said there was not much to see but six more doors in an empty chamber.

'Clearly this is not a zoo, nor a garden,' she said. In the centre of the room the marble tiles made a circular pattern. 'So it must be a time trap. And where do those other doors go? And what is that sound?'

Halfway to the centre of the room, she spied a cricket and stood still, listening to the insect making his stridulations. Usually she would have avoided it, but something about this creature seemed lovely to her, so she kneeled down and put out her hand, inviting it to climb onto her palm. Its spindly legs tickled her as it did so and Erin giggled for the first time in far too long. She did not feel at home at Van Riebeek Heights and she had few memories of the mansion with the glass staircase, but sitting there in Devilskein's strange, middle-of-nowhere room, with the singing cricket in her hand, she felt uncommonly content.

'You are a sheer delight,' she said, imagining that the cricket must have been into all the rooms of Devilskein's lair and so would know everything about them all. 'Maybe you can show me the secrets of this place.' She held the cricket up closer to her face. She liked him. 'And we can be friends, if you fancy?'

The cricket chirruped and flew up into the darkness of the ceiling. She walked out of the room and closed the yellow door behind her. Back in the kitchen, she found Mr Devilskein dolloping Versailles berry jam onto a scone.

'I went into the room with the yellow door,' she said, triumphant.

'It is not difficult to twist a door knob.'

'I walked to the centre of the room.'

'Nothing special about that, either.' He smacked his lips, or rather the scar where lips would have been. 'You put too much baking powder in your scones.' Despite his complaint, however, Mr Devilskein had already eaten two and was on his third.

'It was a time trap, that room, wasn't it?

Briefly, Devilskein paused from chewing to observe the glimmer of her soul; it truly was most uncommon and valuable. He could see into her heart's secret, most subconscious, desires: she wanted to undo time at any price, she hankered to be a hero – to come out of the cupboard where she had hidden, and save the people she loved from their most gruesome fate; swirling inside her he saw talent tainted with fury of volcanic proportions. *Her heart will fit my chest most splendidly.* 'No way of knowing what a time trap really is,' Devilskein said, nonchalantly doing some calculations in his head.

'But I found a cricket, a singing cricket, and I'm sure he has a way of knowing.'

To Erin's great surprise, Mr Devilskein's hideous face was suddenly transformed by a smile. His eyes twinkled. He looked completely different to his usual sour self. And then he whistled something of a tune. The next moment, with an arpeggio of chirps, a cricket, surely the same cricket, came circling through the air of the kitchen and landed on the lid of the tea pot.

'That's him!' Erin was thrilled.

'Wondered where you'd got to,' Mr Devilskein said to the cricket. 'Off chasing girls as usual, I suppose.'

The cricket stopped his song and wiggled his feelers. He seemed to be listening to Mr Devilskein, as if he were a person, not an insect.

'Do you know this cricket?' she asked.

'Yes, we have been acquainted for a very long while. I saved him from an apocalypse once, and in return his true love saved me. Now he's as precious as my dog, this cricket.'

Devilskein smiled again and addressed the cricket. 'Not so, young fellow? We've shared a lot, haven't we?' Devilskein's tone was almost fond, which Erin thought most out of keeping with his fearsome reputation at Van Riebeek Heights and definitely at odds with his often surly demeanour.

'His name is Zhou. He was an envoy from the time when Genghis Khan ruled China. Isn't that so, Zhou?'

The cricket replied with a single chirrup. That gave Erin a strange feeling in the pit of her belly – something like a memory squirmed inside her: a boy, her brother, Joe, reading Chinese fairy tales to her when she little, before she could read for herself. Fiercely, she crushed the memory with some other kind of reality check: it was one thing having tea with a disfigured old grinch, and playing make-believe zoos, gardens and time-traps (surely that is all it was?), but it was another thing completely when the monster began conversing with insects.

'Does he always come when you whistle?' she asked, suspicious.

'Used to, but he has been lost some while. Did you find him or did he find you?' Devilskein cocked his head and appraised the skinny girl afresh. 'It could be significant. It could herald some great change.' He rubbed his chest in the area of his heart and Erin couldn't help gawping at his long, sharp fingernails.

'But how can he understand English?' she asked, forcing herself to avert her appalled gaze.

'Oh, that took several decades. When we first met, he knew only Chinese, but we have since taught each other our languages. Now he knows Babylonian, Persian, Pashto, Arabic, Latin, Greek, and the Queen's English, and I know the Emperor's Chinese.' As if to prove it, Devilskein said something in a language that Erin did not know. The cricket replied with a trio of chirrups, which seemed to delight Devilskein into a gale of laughter. It was all most peculiar and Erin began to suspect that the monster was making a fool of her, because how on earth could he really be talking to a cricket?

'So you're saying he was once a Chinese man?'

'That's the sum of it, but not the whole of it.' Devilskein tipped tea into his saucer and placed it before the cricket. 'Drink up, friend, if you don't mind red tea.'

'Why do you call it red?' asked Erin. 'It isn't rooibos.'

'Because, my dear,' then Devilskein uttered something she did not understand, 'the Chinese characters making the word "black tea" literally translate as "red tea".'

Apparently the cricket did not mind the redness of the tea. He clambered up onto the saucer and sucked at the tea therein.

'It must be lonely to be a man living as a cricket,' Erin said, leaning down towards the little creature. 'You cannot make friends with other crickets and you cannot make friends with men.' It replied with a chirrup.

'Aye,' Devilskein nodded, 'he says it is.'

'I am probably lonely too,' she said. 'My family is dead, eaten by a crocodile.' Thinking about it, about her parents, the mansion with the glass stairs, and how mean most children seemed to be, she felt an uncomfortable sense of violent irritation. She scowled.

'Let us drink to loneliness, then,' Devilskein said. 'It is not the worst of all afflictions, I assure you. And having family doesn't prevent it either; as with everything, loneliness is a state of mind.' Devilskein topped up her cup. 'So, lonely girl, you have not yet told me your name.'

Without taking her eyes off the cricket, she said, 'Erin Dearlove is my name.'

'Well, Dearlove, I think you and I, apart from age and appearance, are very similar: both of us sour and friendless, and I bet you have an ugly temper, just like me. We are both thoroughly unpleasant to be around.' He grinned. The cricket made a comment in chirrups. Erin did not much like hearing that she was a 'thoroughly unpleasant' person, but thinking about it, she realised that Mr Devilskein could be right.

'Zhou, the cricket, says he will be your friend.'

'Really?' Erin lost all her usual bristles. 'I would like that very much, cricket, I mean Mr Zhou.' That memory of the dear brother who read her Chinese fairy tales resurfaced and as if to stamp it out once and for all, Erin thumped her fist on the kitchen table, causing the delicate porcelain to jump and clatter.

Chirrruppichee! The cricket was knocked from his perch on the saucer and leapt across the tabletop and out of the kitchen. Erin ran after him, but couldn't catch him before he disappeared under one of the six doors, this time the brilliant turquoise door. She tried the handle, but it was locked.

Devilskein and his poodle appeared in the shadowy vestibule. His face was back to being surly. 'What are you doing?' he asked sharply. *Just because she is going to be my heart donor, doesn't mean she has any rights around here.*

'The cricket has gone in here. I bet it's a garden.' She was rattling the handle to no avail. 'I want to see it. I miss having a garden. Let me go in. Unlock it.'

'Absolutely not! You are a meddlesome brat. What is beyond those doors is none of your business. Be off with you!' He shooed at her like she was a pesky fly. 'Out! Out of my home, this instant!' He flung open the front door, yanked her by the ear, and pushed her out, slamming the door behind her without even so much as a goodbye.

4

A Demon Howls in the Stairwell

It was mid-summer and hot, and Long Street smelled of fermented garbage, roasting coffee, wet cigarette butts floating along in gutter water, truck fumes and incense burning at a nearby Indian emporium. Every day at Van Riebeek Heights seemed the same. Every dawn Erin woke up and ambled through to the kitchen-dining-room-lounge area of Aunt Kate's flat to find her aunt with her bottom in the air and her hands on the ground doing 'downward dog' as part of her daily yoga workout, which Erin learned was a sun salutation. By now, Erin had learned to make tea for herself and she had taken to making it for Aunt Kate as well. She would set out two striped mugs of tea with two homemade coconut biscuits – she'd been shown how to make biscuits as well as scones. Then she would perch on a barstool at the kitchen window with a view of Long Street and gaze out at the black road that went on forever and which would in the hours ahead fill up to a frenzy of traffic and people in funny clothes (it was a street of wild and wonderful fashions). One biscuit, slowly nibbled, and two mugs of tea would pass in that way – staring out at the difficult world getting ready for a day of work. Aunt Kate had stopped making light conversation in the morning because Erin only replied with a grunt. Erin had four choices every morning: to pull the blanket over her head and die of sadness; to get up and do nothing other than read; to go out onto the street and amble about aimlessly in the sweltering, noisy turmoil of the city; or gather all her courage and return to Mr Devilskein and to the possibilities beyond those six doors in the vestibule of apartment 6616. He had been a bit more monstrous than she'd quite bargained for though, so in spite of her curiosity and hankering to see one of the gardens or zoos he'd spoken of, she was reluctant to go back.

Meanwhile, Devilskein, though possessed of unnatural strength, was finding his chest pains increasingly worrisome. It irked him that the smelly boy who was supposed to be the soulmate of the grumpy girl spent most of his time gardening or pretending to be some kind of Undercover Animal Rescue agent and had made no headway in terms of sweeping Erin off her feet. As a result, Devilskein made an emergency appointment with his highly esteemed Physician, also a Companyman, in the old city of Kabul, in Afghanistan. Thus it was, one Wednesday in mid-February, that Albertus Devilskein found himself trudging through the mud of an alleyway in a bazaar filled with soothsayers, DVD hawkers, goldsmiths, stone-carvers and tea merchants. After a long cup of black tea at one such merchant, he made his way to a door studded with eyes made from lapis lazuli.

'Salaam,' said the famous Physician, ushering Devilskein through his apothecary and into a consulting room. 'It has been quite some time since you were here, Companyman. I was expecting you to come bearing a pair of fresh young lovers' hearts.' A rabbit hopped from under a workbench and into the arms of the physician. 'But I see no such thing.'

'They're taking their time,' said Devilskein, and he went on to explain why.

At length the Physician prescribed a rainbow of tablets that Devilskein would have to take twice a day until he procured the necessary hearts. 'If you fail to take the tablets, you will die,' said the revered Physician.

'I thought I was immortal,' said Devilskein, quite petulantly. He hated taking medication and was already thinking that he would only take half the prescribed dose.

'Not quite, old fellow. We're super-genarians, but not invincible. Only our CEO is immortal.'

Devilskein grunted. *Her.* Immediately he regretted the resentful thought for, fearsome as he was, any mention of Her made him anxious. What if she heard his thoughts? 'She is a wonder,' he said, trying to sound adoring, yet feeling a surge of complex emotions in his ailing heart. Once, disguised as a mere human, she had tricked him most terribly.

For two weeks Erin stayed away from Devilskein and his vestibule of doors. But, unlike other people of her age, she still wasn't going to school. And with all that time on her hands she became bored, and that made her glummer than ever.

'Why don't you try surfing or go swimming at the Long Street Baths, or even just take up walking,' Aunt Kate suggested to Erin, because her psychologist friend had said that physical exercise helped to prevent depression.

Usually Erin would roll her eyes heavenwards at Aunt Kate's suggestions, but one day she realised that if she didn't do something, she would always do nothing. Also, somewhere hidden deep in her mind was the memory of a woman, her mother, who was vibrant and active and full of joie de vivre, a woman who wouldn't have liked to see her daughter in this sorry apathetic state.

Because Erin hated walking along Long Street, she decided to take up jogging and asked Aunt Kate to wake her when she got up to do her yoga. And so, one morning before the rush hour, when the air was still cool in Long Street and the breeze still distantly scented with the mountain on the left and the sea on the right, Erin took to racing up and down the very long road, nearly an eight-kilometre round trip. In fact this was the best thing she could have done – she found there was great anger in her muscles and that by pushing them to go faster and faster she could force it out of her. As days went by, the more she ran the faster she became. Her blood and body were invigorated and she grew stronger and fitter. Sometimes the wild South Easter blew, but even though she detested this wind, she did not allow it to deter her. She raced the wind in one direction and fought it and all the debris and obstacles it hurled at her in the other direction. At first she could only just complete one length of Long Street, but as February neared completion, her lungs became powerful and her stride became long, and she even took to greeting a homeless man who padded about in sheepskin slippers and skinny jeans. Soon she was easily able to do two and a half lengths of Long Street. Then she would return to Aunt Kate's flat, full of energy and conversation and ravenously hungry. A single butter biscuit would no longer suffice for breakfast. So Erin took to making scrambled eggs or French toast instead.

On the first day of March, she made a beautiful omelette.

'You've become quite the cook,' said Aunt Kate, enjoying the tasty fare. 'And developed quite an appetite too.'

'Food tastes nicer these days,' said Erin, surprised at the truth of it.

'It's all that running. You're looking fantastic. You've even got a tan.' Aunt Kate thought of the scrawny, pale, cantankerous child she had taken in almost two months before. 'We seriously need to think about school, though.'

Erin had simply refused to go to school when the new term started in January and Aunt Kate felt her niece could do with a hiatus from school-type pressures. However, she had not intended this to be permanent.

'School! I don't do school. In the mansion with the glass stairs I had home tutors.'

'Really?' Aunt Kate sighed, disappointed. She thought she'd heard the last of that wretched mansion, she thought the jogging was making all that stuff right, that Erin had progressed.

'I hate children and teachers,' Erin said. 'They're all mean and what can they tell me that I can't read for myself in books?'

Far below a red motorbike roared down Long Street. In the kitchen in the flat directly above them, chairs scraped along the floor.

And in the apartment two to the right of Aunt Kate's, Kelwyn's mother was pouring mugs of tea for each of her five children. Her two youngest, the twin boys, Max and Milos, took theirs straight to the lounge to drink while watching TV. Her two daughters, Lilly and Sabine, both still in their pyjamas, took theirs to their bedroom to have in bed. 'Get dressed, you two!' called Mrs Talmakies, who was in a hurry to get to work at the decor shop where she earned good commission selling sofas and beds to very rich people.

'Thanks, Ma,' said Kelwyn, taking a mug of tea and then stirring in a large spoon of sugar. Next to the mug was the latest edition of *House & Garden*, which Kelwyn's mother always bought for him because he loved the features about gardens. It was open to an article about water-wise wall gardens and seated to the left of the magazine's middle fold was a fat leopard toad. This was the latest of Kelwyn's rescues; he had run into Long Street and swept it up just before a van flattened the poor creature.

'Can I keep him, please?'

Kelwyn's mother sighed, but she knew the creature was already part of their family as far as her son was concerned. In spite of herself she smiled because into her head flashed a memory of the day Kelwyn was born, of how tiny and helpless her baby boy had been when the doctor placed him on her chest minutes after his first breath of the world. He had weighed 3.1 kilogrammes then, and now – she smiled again without realising it – there he was, a tall young man, taller than her and stronger by far. Perhaps a bit scruffy and sometimes quite smelly (and thanks to his father he had that wretched gecko tattoo), but he was a son to make any mother's heart proud. She would never have guessed that life with him would grow to include all manner of creatures and plants; he was always saving things: mole snakes, frogs, lost dogs, stray cats, chameleons and all manner of plant life. In particular, he had a way with orchids, the most temperamental of beauties. Nevertheless, Kelwyn's mother really wasn't keen on adding a toad to their home menagerie.

'Please, Ma,' said Kelwyn and he gave her a look that she could never resist. Again the image of him as a newborn curled up on her chest came to her. 'I'll think about it. We'll talk about it after school,' she said, trying to sound stern, but they both knew the toad had found itself a happy home. 'Now then, Kelwyn, hurry up with that tea and toast or you'll miss the school bus.'

His nose crinkled and he grinned at her, a bountiful smile of pure happiness. 'Cool,' he said.

She tried to remain stern (she didn't want him to think her a pushover) and simply said, 'Are you going to work at Joy Café after school?'

Kelwyn nodded, took a last bite of toast and spoke while he chewed: 'Mrs Chen has brought a new orchid.'

Two apartments to the left, Erin was eating her breakfast in a leisurely fashion, with no intention of ever catching a school bus.

'In the age of the Internet, school is pointless,' she declared, even though they didn't have an internet connection at Aunt Kate's flat.

'No, school is essential,' said Aunt Kate. 'It's just the way it's done, Erin. Everybody has to go to school. A home tutor is not an option either. There's no money for that. And there are some good schools within walking distance from here.' Aunt Kate pulled a face; she'd been investigating the matter. 'Only problem is they're very oversubscribed. With waiting lists.'

'That suits me just fine. I'll do home schooling. You can mark my work.'

'I don't have time Erin. If I don't do another exhibition soon, we'll be broke and then we won't be able to pay the rent or buy eggs for omelettes.'

'Mr Devilskein can be my tutor. I bet he does nothing all day.'

And before her aunt could object, Erin was half way to the bathroom. Aunt Kate followed. 'Ah, Erin...' she said, in the troubled teenager's wake.

'I don't want to discuss it anymore,' said Erin, closing the bathroom door and locking it.

Ping!Ping!Ping! cried the Company Soulometer on Devilskein's kitchen table. He studied the co-ordinates of a man named Michael Gauntlet who had sworn he'd sell his soul to be the next British Prime Minister: he wanted to change the world.

'Come along, Calvados,' said Devilskein. Devilskein popped two fat heart-pills into his mouth. 'Duty calls us to

London.' He changed his mind about taking the pills. Spat them out. *Once a day is quite sufficient*, he decided, in spite of what the Physician had advised. *I'll take one tonight again… or maybe even just tomorrow morning.*

And so Devilskein and his poodle set off, going down the stairs and then along Long Street. Anyone who was watching them might have been stunned to observe that halfway along the road, the poodle, like a shadow, entered his master's body. Then, shortly after that, Mr Devilskein climbed into an inauspicious looking Toyota and vanished. The car, a 1995 model, had dark-tinted windows and no engine. It was perpetually parked in that spot and yet, by some enchantment, it never fell prey to parking fines.

After rolling his eyes at a Nietzsche quote (from the bane of his university life, *Thus Spake Zarathustra*: 'the devil himself is perhaps skin') in the object gallery, Michael Gauntlet had moved on from the etchings of bodies flayed and exquisitely rendered, walked swiftly through diseases of the skin, passing a display of ceramic eating bowls textured with syphilis and acne, and then stood, captivated in the Hall of Marks, looking at a photograph of a prisoner whose body was covered with tattoos. He was in the Wellcome Museum at an exhibition called 'Skin'.

'The ghost of Christmas future,' said a voice.

Michael turned and said, 'What?' He shivered at the same time; it had become uncommonly cold in that vicinity.

Beside him stood a lean man in a fine suit, jacket with tails, which was in opposition to the crude tattoo marking his face and an ugly gash where an ear should have been. On his lapel was pinned a lapis lazuli rabbit. Mr Devilskein stared into Michael Gauntlet's eyes: beyond the pupils, deep into the secrets of the ambitious young man's cerebellum. Devilskein snorted. 'I see you are a man of great ambition.' He tut-tutted.

'What?' Michael curled his lips. He'd been in a bad mood even before this stranger arrived.

Ignoring Michael's scowl, Mr Devilskein focussed on the picture Michael had been looking at and said: 'How curious to see him here.' Devilskein stepped back from reading the description relating to the artwork and said to Michael, 'I've met that man. It is … unsettling to see him turned into a work of art.'

Taking in the suited man's extraordinary face – creased, scarred, inked with strange words – and the lapis lazuli rabbit again, Michael said, 'Who are you?' He took a step sideways to create distance; the man was one of those who impinged on one's space.

'Oops, careful where you tread.' Mr Devilskein caught Michael's arm as if saving him from a pothole, but as far as Michael could see there was no visible danger.

'Why? Why must I be careful?'

'Traps. There are traps everywhere and it is not yet your time.'

Michael rolled the 'Skin' exhibition programme into a scroll. Then he unrolled it and stared at the word skin on its sheer, tracing-paper cover. 'Who are you?'

'I'm a Companyman.'

'What do you mean?'

A murmuring group on the scheduled morning tour came through to the dimly lit Hall of Marks, and a guide, taking his cues from the programme, introduced the area by talking about deformity, illness and ageing. He went on to personal and cultural decoration, as a form of communication.

The group stopped some distance away from the two men contemplating a cabinet containing the dried, tattooed flesh of deceased sailors and prostitutes, purchased sometime during the nineteenth century.

'What is the one thing you most desire?' asked Devilskein in a languid tone.

Michael Gauntlet did not have to voice his reply; Devilskein could hear his thoughts.

'You won't remember meeting me or the agreement that we are about to make,' said Devilskein. 'You have a need, I can fulfil it. In return I need to make a small remittance to the Powers That Be, to raise funds for the payment. You will pawn your soul to the Company for a limited period; however, after that limited period, for every day that your soul remains pawned, the cost (currency or value system as yet unspecified) of buying it back increases to the power of two. In other words: your wish is my command. Do we have a deal?'

'Yes.' Michael was uncommonly confident.

'Excellent.' A puff of noxious mist plumed from the lapis rabbit on the stranger's lapel, hitting Michael between the eyes.

Devil's Breath! Product of the beautiful belladonna plant, a favourite among Companymen.

From a pocket in his jacket, Devilskein whipped out a fine calligraphy pen and thrust it into Michael Gauntlet's hand.

Feeling woozy, Michael Gauntlet, the future Prime Minister of Britain, laughed and his tightly furled exhibition programme unrolled considerably.

That same instant, somewhat tentatively, Erin ventured back to the top floor of Van Riebeek Heights. A wind had blustered all night before and the corridor was full of old boxes and leaves and plastic bags. It was deserted, neglected and felt empty of life. She called out to Devilskein as she picked her way around the boxes, but there was no reply from the far end of the passage. Still uncertain if it was wise to return to the temperamental old man's abode, she paused and peered over the corridor railings to look at the street below. She hung over the bars, mesmerised by the traffic and the throng of tourists and locals going to and fro by foot, by car, on bicycles, some on skateboards too. Skateboards seemed to be the ultimate cool accessory for boys on Long Street, that and tattoos on their legs. She hung over even further, so that she was completely bent at the waist and her head was upside down and her hair dangled down towards the street. Blood rushed to her skull and made her eyes practically bulge. She was rather enjoying the sensation of it, but when she heard a dazzling arpeggio of chirrups Erin righted herself immediately and was momentarily quite dizzy as the blood flowed back down to her heart. There on the railing was a cricket.

'Zhou!' she cried. 'Is that you?' She held out her hand. 'Zhou, the cricket from China?' It did not occur to her how odd it was to be talking to a cricket; she was too thrilled to see the creature.

He answered with a chirp and scuttled up onto her hand. He chirped more and she heard words in those sounds. Zhou was speaking to her. It seemed he was saying, 'Would you like to learn to speak Chinese?'

Erin had tears in her eyes, she was so happy to see him. 'Don't be silly! Why would I want to learn Chinese? Whoever will speak to me in Chinese?'

'I will,' the cricket seemed to reply. 'I will tell you stories in Chinese and I will take you to a Chinese garden.'

The cricket scuttled up and down Erin's arm and she giggled and for an instant looked quite pretty. 'A garden! One of Devilskein's gardens, one of the gardens behind the doors?'

A triple-length truck laden with jangling soda bottle empties revved and rumbled along the lumpy tar of the street below. It skirted around orange cones marking off an area of works where the road had been eviscerated and its clay-earth innards lay scooped out in piles around a troublesome system of old pipes.

The cricket flew in circles, stridulating as he went, and

Erin followed him in great spirits down the corridor towards number 6616. When the cricket disappeared under the door, without thinking about what she was doing, Erin simply turned the handle. The door wasn't locked, it opened easily. The place was deserted. The cricket hopped across the dusty entrance and went under one of the six coloured doors, the one painted turquoise. But just as Erin twisted that knob and pushed the door open, she spotted a giant bunch of elaborate keys on a demi-lune side table in the vestibule. They were all shapes and sizes, unlike any she had seen before. One key had a pair of dolphins at its head. Before she could study them properly, she heard footsteps and the clicking of a dog's claws on cement; Mr Devilskein and Calvados were coming up the stairwell and she realised she was trespassing. She had already experienced him angry when there was no reason to be so, but now there was a real reason for him to be cross and she didn't want to see what kind of a rage that would induce. Without remembering that the turquoise door was left ajar, she dashed out of the apartment and headed for the fire escape on the far side of the building. Just as Devilskein and Calvados arrived at the top of the stairs, she leapt onto the ladder and made it down to the floor below. Breathless, she could smell hake frying at the fish-and-chip shop diagonally opposite and the fumes from the empties truck that stopped at every bar and restaurant, gathering more bottles.

She clambered off the ladder, and ran back to Aunt Kate's flat with a lot to think about. Erin's mind was so full of thoughts that, in spite of the wind that had picked up again and the grumbling traffic of midday, she put on her running shoes and spent the afternoon slowly jogging from Long Street to Sea Point, along Beach Road and over the hill to the start of Camps Bay.

When finally she returned home that evening, she was

exhausted, elated and very hungry. There was a lovely Thai vegetable curry for dinner.

'Ooh, that smells so good,' said Erin, who a couple of months before might have said just the opposite.

In the past, Aunt Kate's chattering about art, surfing, and life and men (who seemed a big problem in Kate's life), irritated Erin, but it didn't that night. She listened as she chewed her food and she even complimented Aunt Kate on the delicious meal.

The jangle of a TV soap opera theme tune drifted from the windows of almost every apartment in the block and the gathering South Easter swept the cacophony of melodrama out to sea.

'Do you believe in time travel?' Erin asked. 'Mr Devilskein says he has time traps in his flat. Do you think it is possible to go back and change the past?'

That made Aunt Kate's heart ache for the teenage girl she at first hadn't much wanted to take on – she was more of an adventurer than a mother-and-wife type and unlike her sister, Erin's mother, Kate hadn't ever wanted the responsibility of any child. But Kate had grown very fond of Erin. 'We should invite your friend for dinner one day, he sounds interesting.'

'Oh, I doubt he'd come. He's grumpy and antisocial.'

Outside the South Easter began to howl and rampage through the streets of the town. It scuppered the orange cones around the Long Street roadworks, buffeted signs and ripped posters off streetlights. Skateboarders were blown off-course, pedestrians struggled to walk and all were bombarded with flying refuse. Although Aunt Kate's flat was small and not as glamorous as the Dearloves' mansion, Erin felt quite safe and cosy there with Kate, away from the violent wind.

'What does he do for a living, your Mr Devilskein?' asked Aunt Kate.

'I don't think he does anything. He's old.'

'Probably retired then.'

But that made Erin wonder. Even if he was retired, he must have had a job at some stage, and she was curious to know what profession such an odd and monstrous man would have had. 'He doesn't look like an ordinary person: he hasn't got a right ear.'

Fleeing footsteps of the child upstairs, once more in trouble for breaking something, thumped along the passage of the apartment above.

Aunt Kate dished out more jasmine rice for them both. 'Well, I wonder what happened to him? Do you think he was born like that?'

The wind outside was growing increasingly tempestuous, and Erin was thinking about luck and how sometimes what seems unlucky is actually lucky. She thought how it was unlucky that her parents were eaten by a crocodile and that she had lost her home, but how, in a strange way, she felt surprisingly lucky to be living with Aunt Kate in her ugly apartment in Van Riebeek Heights. It was unlucky and lucky at the same time, kind of how the crazy wind seemed awful but was also a good thing. People called it the 'Cape Doctor' because it blew away all the pollution and left the air clean and fresh and good to breathe.

Ping! Ping! Ping! shrieked the Company Soulometer on Devilskein's kitchen table. But Devilskein was lying on the floor clutching his chest.

Ping!Ping!Ping!

Ping!

Ping!

Ping!

'Shut up!' roared Devilskein. 'Can't you see I'm busy?'

Standing over Devilskein, Calvados let out a small whimper.

'Don't fret, it'll pass,' said Devilskein, grinding his peg teeth in agony. In one hand he clutched a piece of lapis lazuli and in the other a dolphin-headed key. 'Change is afoot,' Devilskein groaned, and then he began murmuring an incantation in his mother tongue, Babylonian. 'I need that heart now, dammit. These pills are not working.'

Ping!Ping!Ping!

As Erin listened to the gale she became aware of another sound, something inside the wind. At first, she thought it was just swooshing through a drainpipe, but after some time she became convinced that the sound was coming from inside the building, not outside.

'Do you hear something?'

'Uh-uh, it's just the South Easter.'

'No. Listen, Aunt Kate, it's not that; it's a person. It's somebody in one of the corridors.'

At that exact moment a gust grabbed at the latches on their front door and flung it open. Both Erin and Aunt Kate jumped; air rushed in and sent papers, boxes, paintbrushes and glasses tumbling. Erin ran to the door to close it again. As she was fighting to push it shut, she heard the strange human-like howling again. Still battling to lock it, Aunt Kate came to help.

'You must hear that?' Erin said. 'Coming from the stairwell?'

Slam! Together they managed to close the door.

'Phew!' said Aunt Kate, recovering from the rampage, gathering up papers and righting glasses. 'It's insane, like a hurricane or something.'

'Or something.' said Erin. 'That sound wasn't just the South Easter. I'm going to see.'

Aunt Kate frowned, and started to tell Erin not to be crazy, but it was too late, Erin was gone.

She sprinted down the corridor in the direction of the wail, then followed it up the stairs, up, up, up. She continued, buffeted by the misanthropic wind and blinded by the darkness of the top floor. The noise was coming from Devilskein's apartment. Without thinking of the consequences, she pushed open the door and tracked the agonised howling to the kitchen.

The monstrous man was lying on the floor, clutching his chest.

Beside an extraordinary bunch of keys on the kitchen table was a contraption like nothing she had ever seen, but there was no time to look at it more closely.

Erin had once done a first aid course and in an instant she was kneeling beside Devilskein, pumping the balls of her hands into his chest, counting as she did. Then, regardless of the hideous scars where lips would have been, she put her mouth to his and gave him air. Next she went back to pumping his chest. She had no idea if she was doing it right, but she didn't stop. On and on and on, she repeated the process. As she worked, a transformation came over Devilskein – it was something more powerful than mere resuscitation. His first instinct was to kill her, but what would that help – he wanted both soulmates' hearts. And what's more, a most uncouth sense of gratitude stirred in his little-exercised conscience.

Still, he couldn't allow her to remember any of this incident, though he would surely remember and consider it for a long time. Before he opened his eyes, he tapped the gadget on his belt and it let out another burst of pernicious mist.

5

Surely You Heard That Demonic Howl?

The South Easter raged on the next day, Saturday, growing even more forceful. It became a near-apocalyptic gale. Newspapers featured front page images of the devastation: metal drums and corrugated iron sheets torn from building sites and hurled through the windows of shops and offices; a six-foot-tall Afrikaans teacher had been blown over and both her arms broken as a result.

'What do you people in small flats do on days like this?' Erin, feeling more grumpy than she had in a while, asked Aunt Kate. 'I can't even go running. You can't go surfing. It must be terrible in winter.'

'Well, the important thing is not to get on your flat-mate's nerves,' Kate said. 'Otherwise it just ends in arguments over petty things. I don't much mind the rain. I go swimming in the rain. The South Easter is a summer wind though, so winter is better. I guess games are a good idea. Or painting – this is excellent weather for staying in and working on my paintings.'

In spite of the windy hullabaloo, the extra-long truck with the jangling empties barrelled along on its daily trip through the street below, stopping and starting, collecting bottles; though some escaped and strays rolled, crashed and clattered with dangerous abandon.

The wind did not in the least bother Kelwyn. In his bedroom full of plants and glass tanks (the homes of his various non-human friends) he was watching his chameleon, Aleg, who was poised to catch breakfast.

'I think I'm in love, Aleg,' he told the chameleon, whose salmon-coloured tongue shot out, nabbing a fat horsefly, which had been going about its business on the rim of a used coffee mug. 'Good one!' Kelwyn encouraged the diminutive green friend who, some months before, he'd rescued out of the mouth of a Siamese cat. Unfortunately, the cat had already damaged one of Aleg's legs beyond repair and so Kelwyn's confidant now had to make do with three. 'It's that grumpy girl along the way,' Kelwyn said. 'I don't know why, but I just can't get her out of my head.'

The chameleon rolled its eyes around in opposing circles, more interested in food than foolish love: Jackpot! He'd spotted a hover of fruit flies on an overripe banana.

'Can you paint, Erin?' Aunt Kate asked.

Erin was in a mood to argue. 'What's the point of painting something when you can take a photograph? I mean your paintings are so real-looking, sometimes I can't tell if they're a painting or a photograph.'

Even though Erin had sounded quite grouchy, Aunt Kate took that as a compliment and smiled. 'Well, what's the point in baking scones when you can go out and buy them from Woolworths?'

'Maybe Woolworths is closed, or you don't have money to buy them?' Erin snapped back. The wind outside sounded like a banshee in the Scotland Highlands. It flipped a crate of bottles off the empties truck and hurled them into a lamppost. Glass shattered.

'And don't you quite enjoy baking scones?'

A 'To Let' poster, a hat and greasy fish-and-chip wrappers whipped past the window. 'It's something to do, I s'pose,' Erin said, and then hearing how crotchety her voice sounded she sat up and decided she didn't want to be that way. Half-reluctantly, she admitted, 'and it is quite fun – to make things, I mean.'

'Exactly.' Aunt Kate was a true creative spirit, but she wasn't much into espousing philosophies and that kind of thing. Actually, Kate was becoming sort-of famous, she was an up-and-coming artist, her work had been acclaimed by local art critics, and if she'd spent less time surfing and more time painting, she might have been a great success, even rich. But money didn't excite Kate much, not like the sea, not like catching a brilliant wave.

'If I had a paintbrush and paints, I could experiment,' said Erin, feeling almost interested; she had read all the books in the house and it was too windy to go out to the library or the Internet café (and she didn't have any money).

'Have you tried sketching before?'

Erin frowned. She couldn't actually remember; in her head, there were big holes where ordinary memories should have been. 'Nope,' she said.

'That's where you should begin then. It's best to start off with pencil and ink sketches.'

Thump, thump, thump. Erin looked up at the ceiling. 'Sounds like that kid is playing tennis in his mother's lounge again,' she said, feeling a kind of comfort that comes with knowing the habits of a place and its people.

Aunt Kate opened the cabinet that housed all her art supplies and took out a small black sketchbook and a couple of pens and pencils. 'Here you are and…' She crossed to the kitchenette and pulled a tin of olive oil from a cupboard. 'Start by drawing this tin. You can date your sketches and even make comments about what you sketched and why, and maybe what was difficult about it.'

A month before, Erin would have refused to involve herself in one of Aunt Kate's silly activities like sketching olive oil tins, but the time had come that Erin was beginning to like her aunt and this sketching thing seemed a pleasant challenge and – Erin closed her eyes on a fleeting memory of a woman (her mother, but she could no longer see that) drawing. Erin's heart constricted, and she almost started crying, but without knowing why. One bad memory led to another: suddenly she remembered that she had left the turquoise door ajar, and she became extremely worried that Mr Devilskein would be lurking outside to box her ears as soon as she left Kate's flat. She had already decided she couldn't go out running so there was nothing left to do but stay in and draw.

'Music always helps,' said Aunt Kate and she put on a CD. A song about a little ghost muffled sounds of wind and indoor tennis. They both set about sketching. Aunt Kate was doing preliminary sketches for a new oil painting of a still life: a crate of oranges.

At first, trying to sketch the tin caused Erin to scowl; she liked things to go her way and the pencil in her hand just wasn't doing what her head was imagining it should. She ripped the page out of the sketchbook and scrunched it up. 'Wretched tin. What's the point of sketching it anyway?'

Aunt Kate was too absorbed in her crate of oranges to notice Erin's grumbling. Erin sauntered over to see her aunt's sketch. It was terribly good and that made Erin frown even deeper. She stomped back to her perch and her sketchbook and tried a second time to capture the oil tin, but the pencil would not co-operate. In a rage, Erin pushed it away and folded her arms.

'I hate drawing,' she said.

Aunt Kate was preparing her canvas with burnt umber. 'It can be frustrating, but don't give up.'

'No. I'm not doing this stupid tin anymore. It's boring. Just a stupid rectangle with words printed on it.'

Unfazed, Aunt Kate looked up and her gaze landed on a bunch of keys. With her brush, she pointed them. 'Try those, then. Keys are a great thing to sketch.'

Keys!

Erin remembered the elaborate bunch of keys at Mr Devilskein's flat, and in particular the beautiful dolphin-headed key. Caught up in that thought, she went over to the octopus hook where Kate's house keys dangled from a ring with a silver rabbit fob. Then, only half thinking about what she was doing, Erin set about drawing them. Her pencil strokes were violent and agitated, but she didn't realise it, she was too absorbed with wondering what doors Devilskein's keys opened and just how many doors there were in his peculiar apartment. She knew that there were six doors in the vestibule, and also in the room where she first met Zhou the cricket. Did every door lead to six more doors? That would make for hundreds, even thousands of doors. Where were they all going? While Erin pondered all this, somehow a set of keys was appearing on the page. It was very good, much better than the olive oil can. When Erin stopped thinking about the doors and looked down at what she'd drawn, she was astonished.

'Wow,' she said, impressed with her own drawing. 'You're right, Aunt Kate; keys are a great thing to sketch.'

'Let me see.' Kate got up and went to look at Erin's

picture. She was mightily impressed too: the image was far from perfect, the perspective a bit wonky, but those keys had such energy, the lines had motion and power. It was almost unnerving.

The wind snatched at the hook of the kitchen window and flung it open. A flood of pungent mutton curry scent swirled in. Mrs Pabu from downstairs was clearly cooking lunch.

'I wasn't even thinking about what I was doing,' Erin said.

'That's the secret.' Kate pulled the window shut, but the scent of oil, ginger root, and turmeric lingered like a ghost in the kitchenette. 'Overthinking sucks. Pre-conceived logic interferes with plain truth and imagination.'

'So I mustn't think?'

'Well no, you can't help that, but it's about moderation. See how good those keys are you've done?' Again, Aunt Kate felt somewhat unnerved by the palpable agitation expressed in Erin's sketch.

Next Aunt Kate set out a bottle of wine and a glass. 'Try these now.'

It was easy. As soon as she started on the sketch, Erin's thoughts went back to keys and doors and she realised she hadn't seen what was inside the room with the turquoise door; she had turned the knob and opened, but that was when she'd been distracted by the keys on the side table. The cricket! The cricket who promised to teach her Chinese had gone inside and he had spoken of a garden, so perhaps he had gone there. The Chinese garden! He had said he would take her to a Chinese garden. Over and over, Erin visualised the vestibule, the six coloured doors and she imagined opening each one, and although she tried to imagine what the gardens or zoos would be like, all she could see were doors: six doors to every door. That made a maze of many hundreds of doors. As if in a dream, yes, as if only half-awake, she became mesmerised by the task of trying to count all those doors. The number seemed impossibly huge.

In her mind, she wandered from room to room, always finding another set of six doors, and in her thoughts she would run and fling open every door, and beyond every door again would be another room of six doors. At a certain point, although she was still sitting in Aunt Kate's flat sketching the bottle of wine, she felt like she was in a maze of doors and rooms, all leading off the vestibule in Devilskein's apartment. It was as if she was in two places, like she had two bodies: one Erin was sketching, the other Erin was running across rooms to other rooms and the unfolding of doors and rooms never ceased. It was like a different universe. It was bewildering and there could be no other girl in Van Riebeek Heights who ever spent a more extraordinary hour travelling in space, the space of imagination or mind. Or perhaps it was another kind of realm completely, a place beyond logic. Erin felt small in that rambling world of doors and she was certain she was the only person to have ever seen all those rooms, all of them empty, although something told her that there was more to them. There was more than empty space and doors, but she could not see it. Why not?

In that trance-like state, she became almost panicked, desperate to see what was really there, and still she was running, on and on, through rooms with six times six doors, every door leading to yet another room with six doors. It was madness, and at the same time it was thrilling, and she was going faster and faster and faster. Erin felt like she was flying. The doors and rooms were beginning to blur, they were there and yet not there, everything became one great rush of possibilities. It was wild and exhilarating. It was dizzying. Erin's heart was racing (and back in Aunt Kate's flat, her hand was moving swiftly over the page in a storm of shading, stroking, stippling, her drawing of two simple objects tumultuous and magnificent – not that she realised it yet). She was whizzing through time and space and starbursts and her face was cooled by a galactic breeze.

Suddenly she was aware of the sound of a cricket.

Zhou! Is that you? Where are you? What is this place?

The sound of his chirruping echoed all about her and the rush and gush of doors and stars and rooms and doors continued. Erin was breathless and she thought her head might explode. And then she heard that banshee wail, like she'd heard the night before. It wasn't the wind. It was fretful, it was a moan. It was coming nearer. Crying! Somebody was crying. She wanted to stop, she wanted to help, and in the blaze of passing doors, she reached out and grabbed hold of one doorknob, and as she did the hurricane of time stopped. She heard a bunch of keys crash onto the floor.

'*What* are you doing here?' It was Mr Devilskein. He took Erin by the ear and pulled her out of a room she didn't recognise. 'Didn't I warn you about this place? How did you get in here?'

Erin stammered. 'I don't know… I was thinking of the keys… I heard somebody crying.'

'You heard nothing. Nothing.' Mr Devilskein's eyes were red with fury. 'Leave now and never return; you have this last chance to escape.'

'Ouch, you're hurting me!' Erin suddenly hated Mr Devilskein. 'It's not my fault,' she cried.

He was pulling her by the ear and pushing her out of the place of doors. 'Be gone, wretch! I have enough to do without looking after a meddlesome brat. Do not return. This is fair warning.'

And then Erin felt she was falling off the roof of the Van Riebeek Heights, but it was too impossibly high to be true; it was above the clouds. 'There was somebody crying… you must have heard?' she shouted into the abyss below, but Mr Devilskein made no answer.

With a jolt, Erin found herself back in the reality of Aunt Kate's flat. She was uncertain what had happened to her. Her cheeks were wet with tears. She looked about: music was playing loudly and Aunt Kate was still working on the crate of oranges and nothing in the flat had changed. Even the smell of Mrs Pabu's curry remained. Erin looked down and was amazed at the sketch she had done of the wine bottle and the glass. 'I couldn't have drawn that,' she whispered. 'It's too good.' The sketch wasn't perfect, but it was brilliant, roaring with emotion. Erin covered her mouth with her hand. The wind was still blowing and – there it was! A crying sound, a moan of distress. Erin could hear it, but did not realise that the source was a being exponentially more treacherous than her Mr Devilskein.

6

The Bunch of Keys

A few mornings later, when Erin woke up, she was aware of a peculiar silence. There was the drip of the bathroom tap; the electric purr of the fridge, but the wind had stopped blowing. She climbed out of bed and ambled over to the window, but leftover sleepiness was quickly replaced with excitement.

The atmosphere in apartment 6616 Van Riebeek Heights was leaden with the absolute opposite emotion. Mr Devilskein had begrudgingly washed down his morning tablets with a tumbler of absinthe. In his hand he held a double-dolphin-headed key. Just holding it was a mistake and he knew it – his demon boy would feel the connection and the consequences could be dire. But the Companyman was in the midst of an existential crisis. 'I wonder why we exist?' he mumbled at the key. 'I should say I, not we, because maybe you know why you exist. Is it possible that I am suffering from depression?' Devilskein had been tending towards losing faith in the Company but, fearful of the consequences of being an unbeliever, he had passed through years of paranoid loyalty to the cause and the CEO, followed by anguished months of growing scepticism. After the unprecedented events of the previous night, he had come to believe that the CEO was not the be-all and end-all. There was something greater than the Company.

'But if I am not a Companyman, what then?' said Devilskein, miserably. 'If the Company rules are a sham, then everything I've lived by for two thousand years is also a sham and I have been deceiving myself. Everything is an illusion.'

'Freedom is the answer,' said Zhou, the cricket.

Devilskein downed another glass of absinthe. 'You'd like to think so,' he said, and pushed his chair back. 'But I have souls to pawn, deals to make…' Before leaving the kitchen, he surveyed the shoeboxes. 'And keys to lose,' he said, regretfully.

'You can choose again,' said Zhou. 'Freedom is the answer.'

'Aunt Kate! There are no plastic bags flying about any more,' Erin called. 'The sky is blue and the city is peaceful!'

The storm was over, and for the first time ever, Erin thought how lovely the city looked at dawn: the mountain at the top end of Long Street loomed over apartment blocks and was pristine green, the sea on the bottom of Lower Long Street was glittering darkly blue, and even the street itself looked welcoming. And there was the homeless man in skinny jeans and sheepskin slippers.

'Glorious,' said Aunt Kate with a smile. She was already in her wetsuit. 'I hear there are good waves, so I'm going to have an early surf. Do you want to come?'

'Nah, I'll go for a run. Shall we have tea before you go?'

'Ace idea.' Aunt Kate followed Erin to the kitchenette, where Erin's sketch of the wine bottle was propped up on the counter next to a *Time* magazine. She examined the sketch afresh and once again experienced a sensation of being unhinged by the intensity of the strokes. 'This is remarkable, Erin. You're talented.'

Erin shrugged. Water swished into the kettle; upstairs an ignored radio alarm beeped with mounting menace. She felt a bit of a fraud. Since she hadn't been totally 'present' while sketching, it seemed like she hadn't actually done the drawing. The blue light came on when she placed the kettle on its cradle. And she didn't think she'd be able to draw like that again. After she finished that picture, she was exhausted and fell asleep and the next day she was almost frightened to sketch anything again in case she found herself back in the place of endless doors.

Erin picked up the magazine and paged through it without reading much, save a small article on technologies that would soon be obsolete. In a flat along the passage, a woman with operatic aspirations was singing in the shower. And two doors down, Kelwyn's home was in chaos. His pet mole snake had escaped just after he had left for dawn patrol with Sipho, aka Rover 2, and his little sisters, Lilly and Sabine, were now standing on the kitchen table squealing their heads off.

'Beginner's luck,' Erin said to Aunt Kate.

'No, Erin, this is way more than just luck. You've got something special going on.' Aunt Kate wasn't sure herself how to describe what she saw.

'Where are you going to surf?' Erin poured boiling water over the teabags in their cups, squeezed the bags with the back of a teaspoon, till the tea was strong.

'Mouillie Point. Come if you like. You can swim.'

'Are you crazy?' She added milk and passed Kate a mug of tea. 'That sea water is freezing.'

'I'll lend you a wetsuit. I've got a half one, you'll fit into it, I'm sure.'

'I hate sand and slimy seaweed. And the sea makes my hair sticky.'

Aunt Kate laughed. 'Another time then.'

Immediately Erin regretted being so prissy. She didn't want Aunt Kate to think of her in that way. 'It's not that I don't like the idea of the sea,' Erin said. 'It's a good idea, and surfing looks really fun… except for the sharks.'

'Ah, poor sharks have such a bad reputation. You've got more chance of being in a car accident than getting bitten by a shark, and that doesn't ever stop anyone from driving or going in a car. You can't live your life afraid of sharks, Erin, otherwise you'll stay in a glass box and maybe you'll be safe, but the danger in that safety is that you miss out on all kinds of really cool stuff. Everything has its dangers.'

'Not everything.'

The warbling in the shower intensified alarmingly. The aria was from Gounod's opera, *Faust*.

'Yes, everything.' Ordinarily, Aunt Kate would have left it at that, but she realised that as a kind of 'mother' to Erin, she should probably make an effort to explain it more. 'You think about it.'

'Ok, then, one day I will go swimming with you. Actually, I'd like to learn to surf, if you'll teach me, but not today.'

'Deal,' said Aunt Kate. And though she didn't mention it, she knew that Kelwyn was also very keen to learn to surf and she decided she would teach the two of them together.

'I have the subject in view, Rover 2,' said Kelwyn into his walkie-talkie. 'Black, male, juvenile.' Kelwyn was in Loop Street. 'Red collar.'

'Sounds like you've found him, Rover 1,' said Sipho, who was covering the streets perpendicular to Loop and Long. 'Approach with caution.'

'Affirmative,' said Kelwyn, making his way towards the Labrador puppy that had gone AWOL from his owners' loft apartment three nights before. They had almost recovered the missing pup the previous day, but just at the moment of apprehension, the noon gun went off on Signal Hill and he bolted.

'All things have a positive and a negative,' Kate said. 'If you can't see the negative or the positive in something, then you're just not looking properly.'

'You mean like with sketching? Like the logical mind making you see something that isn't really there?'

'Or not seeing something that is there.'

In a flash, Erin was back in one of those rooms of six doors. 'Not seeing what's there,' she said softly, more to herself than to her aunt. 'Yes, I understand.' She cocked her head and gave Aunt Kate a searching look. 'But if you're blind to it, it's hard to see what's real, isn't it, maybe even impossible in some situations?'

Aunt Kate thought Erin had summed it up beautifully. It seemed to her that this matter of being blind to things really troubled her niece, and as she was a naturally affectionate person, she responded by giving Erin a hug and saying, 'Nothing's impossible.'

If Erin were still her old self, she would have pulled away from Aunt Kate, but Erin Dearlove had changed quite a bit since she had first arrived at Van Riebeek Heights. Instead of recoiling from Kate's warmth, she put her arms around her aunt and returned the hug. She felt safe. She didn't want to let go.

'Nothing's impossible?' Erin said, untangling herself. 'That could have two meanings.'

Aunt Kate ruffled Erin's hair. 'You're too clever for your age.'

'It says in this magazine that DVD players and car keys

will be obsolete within five years,' Erin said, indicating *Time*. 'People will use smartphone apps to unlock their cars.'

They finished drinking their tea, both thinking about a world without car keys.

Meanwhile, the kitchen tap dripped; the singing down the hall stopped; a muffled argument broke out upstairs over the matter of burnt toast.

Both Aunt Kate and Erin went out in high spirits.

It was still cool and early and the traffic hadn't started building up. Suddenly alone, after spending three days cooped up with Aunt Kate, Erin realised that instead of being glad of being all alone in the world again, she actually missed her aunt. She felt a pang of loneliness and then overwhelming fear. She decided she would sprint two lengths of Long Street. So she began running as fast as she could, so fast that her lungs hurt. In addition to looking out for lampposts and pedestrians, she had to keep her eyes on the uneven pavement, which was strewn with obstacles left over from the windstorm, and the skateboarder coming in her direction. There was no time to think at that speed; it was all physical. She pushed herself to run harder. Her muscles, not warmed up, ached a little at first, but she ignored them; she was a speed demon and nothing mattered in the world except for running. Nothing, at least, until she glimpsed a poodle ahead. She blinked.

'Calvados?'

She was still running, but because her attention was on the poodle, she wasn't keeping an eye on the ground in front of her. When the pavement dipped unexpectedly, she tripped and went flying forward.

When she looked up the first thing she saw was a sign advertising for waitresses needed at a café called Lola's. '*Please Enquire Inside*', read the sign.

'You should be careful where you go,' said Mr Devilskein, who had appeared, it seemed, out of thin air. He was holding out a hand to help her up.

Erin was spread-eagled on the pavement. Her left knee was hurting. It was cut and bleeding. She took his hand and winced because her hand was also badly grazed.

'What are you doing here?' she asked, suspicious. 'Ouch.' When she tried to walk, her knee hurt something awful.

'Same as you: now that the wind has stopped, I'm taking my morning exercise before the crowds.' He proffered his arm to give her support and added to that a jovial grin. 'As you can imagine, I try to avoid being seen. People don't respond too well to my… appearance.'

Calvados growled at a happy looking tourist, one who was out early in a safari hat, shorts, a tucked-in shirt and sandals with white socks, who had turned to stare.

Erin leaned on Mr Devilskein's arm because she had to, but she was reluctant to accept his help considering that the last time she'd seen him, he'd pulled her by the ear and thrown her off the building. And even though that had been a kind of daydream, Erin still felt that Mr Devilskein was not to be trusted.

The tourist looked away and scuttled off in the opposite direction.

'The air is good and fresh after the storm,' Mr Devilskein said as they made their way towards Van Riebeek Heights. The poodle trotted on ahead.

In a most uncharacteristic fashion, he was making polite conversation, so when Erin did not comment on the air, he said, 'Quite a spectacular storm, wasn't it?'

Still she was silent.

He remained upbeat, next asking, 'And what have you been up to these last three windy days?'

'I'm sure you can imagine.'

With eyebrows raised in mock surprise, Mr Devilskein said, 'I assure you, I wouldn't bother to ask if I could.' He smiled. 'Imagination is a tricky thing. Why, one can speculate endlessly with imagination and ultimately never arrive at the truth. It is always easier to ask.'

Erin felt thoroughly disturbed by him, but she decided that if he was toying with her, she would do the same in return. 'Sketching, I've been learning to draw. How about you? Any visitors?'

'As you well know, visitors are not welcome at my home. Sketching, eh? Any good?'

'Actually, yes.'

'What, pray tell, did you sketch, Miss Dearlove?'

They had arrived at the steel gate outside Van Riebeek Heights; there had been a week of municipal strikes and the refuse bins were overflowing and ponged of dirty nappies, fermented vegetables and maggot-riddled cat food. Calvados was already waiting. Mr Devilskein took a small bunch of keys from his pocket. The keys hung from a ring with a six of diamonds card. He shook the bunch with unnecessary ceremony before inserting the required key into the gate's lock. The security gate squealed as he pushed it open and held it for Erin to enter first.

'You were saying?' he turned to Erin, offering his arm again for the journey up the stairs. There was no lift at Van Riebeek Heights. A small dog peering between the first floor railings began yapping in fright. Irritation gurgled in Calvados's throat.

The cut on Erin's knee stung badly each time she bent it to take a step up. Every one was painful.

'I don't think I was saying anything.' Erin grimaced as they made their slow ascent. Tears stung her eyes.

'Now's the worst. It'll heal quickly,' said Mr Devilskein, almost kindly. 'I can carry you if you like.'

Erin stopped. Her leg was so sore, still she was reluctant. 'You're too old to carry me.'

The yapping terrier went berserk; usually serene, Calvados bared his fangs and the owner of the small dog pulled it away from the railings and back inside.

'My dear, if you knew how old I am, you'd say I'm too old to breathe, but I assure you my lungs are in excellent condition.' With that, Mr Devilskein swept her up as if she were a feather and then to prove his point, he ran up the stairs so fast that they were at Aunt Kate's door before Erin could protest.

He set her down. And she would have demanded some kind of explanation, but echoing down the corridor came the cheerful sound of a cricket.

'Do you think it is Zhou?' she asked, forgetting to be suspicious. 'Will he remember me?'

'Of course,' said Mr Devilskein indignantly – he had returned to his contrary-wise self. 'How could he forget? It is not often that he is chased into his home by an urchin girl breaking and entering.'

Erin blushed. 'Does he live in a Chinese garden?' The cricket landed on the railing outside Aunt Kate's flat.

'What?' Mr Devilskein grunted, becoming extremely surly. 'Whatever are you talking about, silly girl?'

'The one beyond the turquoise door? Is it the Chinese garden? What is it like? Oh, tell me Mr Devilskein, I'm longing to see that garden. Will you take me there?'

'You and that cricket are dangerous, ignorant, and full of idle dreams. You don't realise what calamity your meddling could cause.'

Mr Devilskein turned on his heel and he and his poodle

departed. The cricket stayed behind.

'The Chinese garden isn't just a dream, is it?' Erin asked the cricket. 'It's not just a fairy tale?'

It chirruped.

'That Mr Devilskein is hard to understand. One minute he's friendly and the next he's a grouch.' Erin shook her head, still confused about the strange man's behaviour. 'Still, even though he pulled me by the ear, which is really not a nice thing to do, I like him.' She held out her hand and allowed the cricket to hop up onto her palm. It was a pleasantly ticklish sensation. 'I like you, too,' she said, and realised that she also liked Aunt Kate and actually rather liked Van Riebeek Heights, which was surprising. One floor down a new-born baby screeched, in the grip of colicky wind.

'And do you like me?' It was Kelwyn, who was leading the recovered Labrador puppy back to his flat and had been astonished to find Erin bent over, staring at her palm and making strange chirping noises to a cricket. His heart did a flick flack; he was very happy to see Erin.

For the second time that hour, she reddened, but this time with anger. She couldn't think of anything to say.

'I'll take that as a yes.' Kelwyn beamed. He thought of inviting her for a soda and fortune cookie at the Joy Café, where he worked as the official part-time orchid-doctor. And he meant to say something like, *How about a Fanta?* But that didn't sound quite right, and then he was looking at the cricket and what came out was: 'So you found yourself a friend?'

Doubly infuriated, Erin said nothing. How could she explain the cricket, and in any case, why should she have to? She glared at Kelwyn.

'Glad to see you haven't changed, Grumpy Girl.' He meant it in a positive way – he liked creatures too, and he liked that she was talking to a cricket. After all, he talked to Aleg, his chameleon, more than any other living thing (besides his mother, maybe).

But Erin took it badly. She gave an exasperated roar, the skittish Labrador yelped, and Zhou the cricket hopped down Erin's arm, into her pocket, out of her pocket, and then flew off. 'See what you've done? Now he's gone! It's your fault. Leave me alone.' Erin turned away from Kelwyn and she hobbled towards her door.

'What happened to your leg?' Kelwyn asked.

'I tripped,' she said sharply, not wanting to be grumpy, wanting to be her new self, but finding Kelwyn so irksome that she couldn't help it. She felt in her pocket for her front door key, and realised there was something else in there as well.

'Whose are these?' She looked at the small bunch of rusty keys that she'd also found in her pocket. They hung from a ring bearing a card; the six of diamonds. 'Oh no,' she groaned. They were Mr Devilskein's keys. Why did she have them? For sure, he would think she had pinched them from his pocket. She could only imagine how enraged he would be.

'Wrong keys?' said Kelwyn, happy to seize the opportunity to invite her over. 'Hey, if you need somewhere to hang out until Kate comes back, you're welcome to come to my place or…' This was his moment, he was sorting through the right way of saying, *You could come and have a Coke and a fortune cookie at the Joy Café with me.*

'No!' Erin scowled at him. 'Just go away! Leave me alone. I don't like you and I don't need to come to your place.'

Despite the tone of her voice, the Labrador decided that she was calling him to jump up against her and lick her. He leapt at her, barrelling into her injured knee. She howled. 'Get that creature away from me!'

He gathered up the puppy. 'Okay, okay, Grumpy Girl. We'll leave you.' He began walking away. 'However, if you change your mind…' In his head, he carried on talking: *Come down to the Joy Café. I get free sodas there, and fortune cookies and - I'd love you to come…*

'I won't.' Erin didn't understand why she found it so difficult to be nice to Kelwyn. She didn't want to be grouchy, but once again, she found she couldn't help being mean to him. 'Not in a million years!'

'Okay,' said Kelwyn. 'I'm immortal, I'll wait two million and then expect you for Fanta and cookies.' He winced slightly. *Fanta? Cookies?* That sounded all wrong.

Erin closed her eyes and stifled another roar of exasperation. When she opened her eyes she saw the bunch of keys again. Perhaps the cricket had put them there? But how in heaven would that have been possible?

She was right to question it; Devilskein would certainly not have sanctioned it, and Zhou could not have managed it, and the appearance of the keys was the work of a distinctly unheavenly being.

7

The Cricket Leads the Way

Gulls and ravens circled in the sky above and far below engines revved, skateboard wheels whirred, empty bottles jangled in the collections truck, and a gas bakkie full of orange canisters rumbled by on Long Street, belching out black fumes as it went on its way. Even though Erin's knee had begun bleeding again, she stood transfixed by the keys in her hand. She twisted the six of diamonds around and around, thinking about the significance of keys; of how they kept precious things safe and unwanted people out; about jailers and bankers, boxes, trunks, cupboards, vaults and prisons, gates and doors. It was as if they were whispering to her; telling her a tale of possession, of terrible loss and triumphant gain. She didn't understand the meaning of the keys entirely, it was all very grown-up and serious, but she was sure that the bunch in her hand was no ordinary one.

The six of diamonds glinted.

What doors would these keys open?

In her vision of the place of doors, there had been so many rooms, so many doors and yet they appeared to protect and contain nothing. She had always entered those rooms at

Mr Devilskein's without keys, and so without authority or the right to enter. In their whisperings, these keys now let it be known that having the right key to the right room would change her perception of what was inside. Erin convinced herself that all she wanted was to see the Chinese garden. She longed for its space and greenery; she had grown up used to having a garden and although she missed nothing else of the mansion with the glass stairs, she did hanker for the expansive gardens (she used to sit in a particular gazebo near a pond and watch with fascination the antics of the Egyptian geese, guinea fowl and honking Hadedas).

If the Chinese garden existed and was beautiful, perhaps she would visit it every day. She could take her sketchbook, close the door behind her, and escape the jangle and fumes of the city and the irritation of neighbours like Kelwyn.

Mr Devilskein's keys continued their enticing whispers, and the promise of what was beyond all those thousands of doors stirred Erin's imagination. When she had lived at the extraordinary mansion, she had spent most of her time alone, away from the world and people. She had been spoiled and bored and not curious and not really interested in trying anything or meeting anybody; she just couldn't be bothered. In that life she had been grumpy and purposefully contrary. But at Van Riebeek Heights she had ventured out and become fit and full of energy and inspired by possibilities like sketching, surfing and the strange world of Mr Devilskein.

Only three floors up, there was a door that lead to a Chinese garden! What a splendid thought. Yet, even though the distance to such a paradise was short, the obstacles between her and the garden seemed great: namely, the unfathomable Mr Devilskein, who one moment was nice and the next was in a rage. She couldn't decide if she liked him or hated him; she didn't know if she could trust him or if he was genuinely dangerous, even a murderer, as Kelwyn had suggested. That seemed unlikely, though. Mr Devilskein could have murdered her already, if that was what he'd wanted to do. No, he might be impossible to understand and extremely moody, but Mr Devilskein was no murderer. That made Erin feel a little better. She slipped the bunch of keys back into her pocket and decided that she would keep them with her at all times, and when she felt the moment was right (perhaps if she spied Mr Devilskein and his poodle going out), she would attempt to find the key to fit the turquoise door, which she felt sure would take her into the Chinese garden.

Although she did not realise it, a couple of hours slipped by as she stood there, thinking about the keys.

Two doors away, Kelwyn was sitting inside staring at a plant thinking about Erin until the doorbell rang.

'That'll be your mum,' he said to the Labrador with the smart red collar, whom he and Sipho had 'apprehended' earlier that morning. He carried the fat puppy to the door. And when he opened it both the dog and its owner who wore elegant red shoes yelped with joy. The owner thanked Kelwyn and was about to leave with her treasure when Kelwyn asked, 'So is there no reward for finding him?'

'Reward?' She seemed taken aback, expecting the sweet boy to be nothing but sweet. Then she felt embarrassed that she had been so ungracious.'Reward. Of course, yes.' She fumbled with the clasp of her red handbag and then rifled through her store cards, credit cards, medical aid card, gym card, driver's licence and old receipts until she came across a hundred rand note. 'Here you are,' she held it out. 'Thank you very much.'

Kelwyn was delighted. 'Thank you, ma'am, I'm saving up to go to university one day. I plan to study botany.'

*

Soon after Erin had gone back into Aunt Kate's flat and cleaned her cuts and grazes and made herself a cup of tea, her aunt returned. Her green eyes were especially green because the salt of the sea had made the whites quite red, but Kate was full of cheer and stories and her cheeks were rosy.

'The waves were awesome today,' Kate said. And then she noticed Erin's knee. 'What happened to you this morning?'

'Nothing. I fell. Mr Devilskein carried me up the stairs. Kelwyn was an irritation as usual. But this tea is tasty and I like hearing about the waves.'

'You're a character, Erin Dearlove.' Aunt Kate gave her a lopsided smile. 'You sure your knee is okay?'

'Positive.'

'I thought Mr Devilskein was very old? How could he carry you?'

'I think he has super-human strength or something like that.'

Aunt Kate laughed.

The newborn with colic was still howling.

'Well, we should make Mr Devilskein some scones to say thank you. I'll take them up with you. I'd like to meet this super-human monster you talk about.'

'Ah,' Erin bit her lip. 'Scones are a great plan, but he's shy and I'm not sure if it would be a good idea for you to come too.'

'No problem.' Still fairly convinced the famous Mr Devilskein was an imaginary friend, Aunt Kate tossed her beach bag onto a chair, turned on the music and gratefully accepted Erin's offer of a cup of tea. 'Got to do some work on my painting; do you feel like sketching?'

Bang. Bang. Bang. Somewhere in another flat somebody was hammering nails into a wall.

The dangers involved with sketching made Erin nervous. What if she went into that trance again? 'Nah.'

'Why not? You're so good, Erin.' Aunt Kate peered at her over the rim of her mug. 'I mean seriously talented. In fact, I think when it comes to the time, you should consider taking art as a matric subject at school.'

'Maybe. Except I'm not going to school.'

'We have to find you a school. You'll probably have to go for some interviews. I hear that's how it's done now.'

'No. I don't want to go to school.'

'You have to.'

'Who says?'

'The law. School's not so bad. You can make friends.'

'I don't need friends; I've got you and Mr Devilskein and the cricket.'

'Cricket?'

'You'll think I'm mad, but I have a talking cricket who is my friend.'

'Here in this flat?' Aunt Kate wasn't sure if she should play along with this or not, but she was convinced that it was this capacity to imagine and create that also made Erin so talented with a pencil.

'Not exactly.'

'Oh, I nearly forgot!' Kate went to her beach bag. 'I got you a present.'

'A present? Why? It's not my birthday.'

'I had to stop by the art shop on my way back from the sea and…' she took out a small boxed set of Faber-Castell Pitt artist's pens with superfine nibs. 'These seemed perfect for you; like they had your name on them. I thought that if you do more sketching, you might like to add colour sometimes, and you'll get great detail with these.' She handed Erin the box. 'Awesome colours, don't you think?'

Erin opened the box and her face was a study of incredulity and wonder: the six colours of the inks were exactly the shades of the six doors in Mr Devilskein's entrance vestibule. 'Yes… they're beautiful, almost unreal.' Erin smiled and stood up to give Aunt Kate a hug, and as she did so the bunch of keys on the six of diamonds ring seemed to grow warm in her pocket. 'Thank you, Aunt Kate. This is the best present I've ever had.'

'My pleasure, love. You may find sketching frustrating at first, but you'll get the hang of it soon enough.'

By now, the keys were vibrating, like hot atoms. A picture had come into Erin's head and suddenly she was keen to try the beautiful pens, to do some drawing. She took out the sketchbook Aunt Kate had given her and sat back in a chair with her sore leg up. She closed her eyes to see the picture in her mind. There she was again inside Mr Devilskein's apartment, in that vestibule with the six doors: turquoise, olive green, carmine, charcoal, rose and sienna yellow (exactly as the names on the bottles of ink). The place was as it had been when she had visited Mr Devilskein, except for one thing: there was light instead of gloom and shadows. A blaze of white light streamed through the arched ceiling of the vestibule, illuminating the doors and room brilliantly. The details of the place became clear. Around each door the wood was carved and the patterns were different for each door. And the floor! The floor was decorated with mosaics in the colour of the doors and the pattern was made of starbursts and every star had six points.

'So lovely,' murmured Erin.

'What is?' asked Kate, looking up from her painting of a crate of oranges.

But Erin did not hear. She was too lost in the vision of the room and doors, which she had already begun to sketch. Her eyes were open and yet she was not seeing the world of Kate's flat, she was seeing the extraordinary details of the vestibule in apartment 6616.

'Wow, Erin!' Watching the sketch take shape, Aunt Kate was freshly astonished by her niece. She might have asked Erin what she was drawing – it looked wondrous – but she didn't want to disturb the child's focus. She smiled when she saw Erin adding a cricket to the drawing of what looked to be turning into an exquisite room. Erin's hand remained focused on capturing that cricket for a long while, until the creature was produced in very fine detail, so rich and well-crafted that it seemed almost real.

As far as Erin's mind was aware, the cricket had returned. Her lips did not move, but she was speaking to him.

'I had no idea you could draw like this,' said Zhou.

'It's new; I never drew anything until I met you and Mr Devilskein.'

'I kept a sketchbook, when I was human.'

'When was that?'

'Many hundreds of years ago. I was an envoy from the court of Emperor Khan, sent to study the Kingdom of Angkor. Strange and glorious times…'

'Zhou? Did you put those keys in my pocket, yesterday?'

'Not me. It takes more power than I've ever had to do such a thing.'

'But even so, will you take me to the Chinese garden today?'

The cricket chirruped and hopped away. Erin's vision returned to the world of Kate's flat. She set the sketchbook aside and stood up, wincing as she put weight on her bruised knee. 'I'll be right back,' she said to her aunt, but didn't wait for her to respond. Ignoring the pain, she ran out of the flat, up to the top floor, and along the corridor until she came to Devilskein's door. She made it there without detection, in spite of the insects that usually acted as Devilskein's watchful eyes; they were temporarily blinded by a power greater than their master.

Zhou was waiting. He disappeared under the door, but Erin was reluctant to open it and follow. What if Mr Devilskein was inside? How could she explain what she was doing there? As if there was some magic in the air, at that moment a powerful gust of wind swept down the corridor and it was soon obvious that Mr Devilskein had not bothered to lock his door once again because it blew wide open. Inside, the cricket was waiting at the turquoise door. Taking a deep breath Erin ran to that door and turned the knob, but it was locked. She took the keys from her pocket and began to try each of them; the third key fit the lock, but the lock was rusty and the key didn't turn at first. It had to open. She jiggled the key and the lock. Still no luck. Her heart was racing. This time she couldn't fail. It occurred to her that if she put some oil on the key, it may loosen the lock. Surely there must be oil in the kitchen – there was a kettle, a fridge and a great variety of jams and teas. Erin ran in, opened the cupboards one by one until she found a bottle of oil – not anything like cooking oil though, for there was none of that to be had, it was something with a foul smell named Sulfur of Tartar, but it was oil nonetheless. She poured a few drops on the key. She thought she could hear footsteps coming along the corridor and she froze, but then the sound of footsteps vanished.

She ran back to the turquoise door, inserted the oiled key and turned it. The lock clicked and the door opened a fraction, but it was enough to allow a scent of jasmine to escape. Erin took a deep breath and pushed the turquoise door right open. She gasped but didn't move because she could hear footsteps in the corridor again. Then, in great excitement and with her heart beating faster than when she was sprinting down Long Street, she stepped into the Chinese garden and closed the turquoise door behind her.

And as its hinges creaked to shut, Kelwyn decided to go down to an Internet café to Google murders in South Africa and see if he could find out more about what had happened to the Dearloves. He pocketed Salma, one of his pet mice, and took her along for the excursion.

He was barely a few metres away from Van Riebeek Heights when he saw a handsome caramel and white mastiff crossed with a pointer bolting through the traffic.

'Bailey!' he shouted. 'Bailey, stop!'

The dog was on a mission. His brain was wired to gallop and though he thoroughly loved the squishy, dog-hair covered sofa that his owners kept for his sleeping pleasure, he also loved to be wild and free.

Kelwyn raced after the mutt which he had rescued a dozen times in the last six months.

8
The Garden of the Humble Politician

From inside a small house with turquoise stained-glass windows, Erin could see a winding green waterway flanked by maple trees and bamboo thickets. Across the inlet stood a rockery and a garden pavilion on stilts with a pointed roof. Leading to and from the pavilion were pathways. Erin began to follow a path of rickety planks over the water. Violet-coloured dragonflies hovered overhead and fat yellow Koi shimmered in the water below. Soon she found herself in a hidden courtyard full of jasmine, white butterflies and bonsai trees in elaborate porcelain pots of vibrant blues and jades. A white spider was busy spinning a silver web. She left that courtyard and found a small lake surrounded by trees. So she followed a path around the lake to an inlet and she continued beyond the inlet to another courtyard, where the walls were laced with flowering creepers that exuded a luxurious perfume so dense it seemed the air was hazy; the sweet mist made the place strange and mysterious. It was like no other place Erin had seen, not even in pictures or on TV. Dozing in the bowers were lazy moths with purple, velvet wings with a span wider than Erin's hand.

'Zhou,' she whispered, entranced. 'Are you here?'

The languorous moths watched. Nothing but silence answered Erin. A murmuring breeze moved the heavy blossoms on the creeper.

Although the cricket had not answered, he too was watching Erin and at that moment, he felt a pang of guilt.

'I feel like I am the first person in the universe to visit this place,' she said to Zhou, who she believed must be there.

Absorbed and awed, she wandered on through courtyard after courtyard, each one different from the last. Some were dedicated to fruit trees, some to flowers, to orchids, to trees. She saw brilliant emerald scarab beetles, blue-spotted geckos and birds with scintillating tail plumes. And then she came to a section of the garden enclosed in turquoise lattice, all threaded with what once must have been a Chinese rambling rose, except the plant was dead, or near-dead, dormant perhaps, as if it were mid-winter in that part of the garden. Going through a pavilion into the courtyard, Erin saw only desolation: where there should have been a pond full of fish, there was cracked earth; where lush plants once grew, all had died. There was no colour, no scent, and apart from the tangled weeds that seemed to flourish, there was no sign of life anywhere. It was bleak, as if it were a cursed part of this paradise; it was gloomy, even though the sun was shining and sky above was blue. Sky! What place was this? How could Erin have gone through a door in Van Riebeek Heights and arrived here? Never mind, even this cursed corner of the Chinese garden was a splendid place; it was her place, away from the world.

She would come here every day, she decided. She would find out why this particular garden had died, she would pull out the weeds and make it beautiful again. In her old life, she had relied on gardeners to make her world beautiful, but in this world, she would be the creator, she would clear the brambles and nurse the wilting plants back to life. Zhou had followed her into the courtyard and now made his presence known: with trill of chirps he flew in a circle around Erin and landed on a delicate but decayed carved bench under a bower of dried-out climbing roses.

'Zhou! You are here! I am so happy. This is the most breathtaking place I have seen... well, apart from this dead section.'

'You are in the Courtyard of Sorrow and Confusion,' said the cricket. 'It is the flipside; all things have them.'

'I want to make it live again, like the rest of the garden. Do you think it is possible?'

'Nothing is impossible,' said Zhou, enigmatically.

'My Aunt Kate says that too.'

Erin examined the rose bower. She snapped off a twig and saw it was dry and dead. She reached further into the tangle of branches and tried to snap off another. This time the sound was less clean and the twig was unwilling to break. Erin yanked at it and eventually it peeled away from its branch, revealing a green, living inner core. 'See! It's not dead! It's not hopeless.' She looked about her. 'What went wrong here, Zhou?'

The cricket trilled. 'This entire garden was the domain of a wealthy politician who lived many centuries ago. One night he went gambling and was tricked by a wicked spirit and he lost his whole fortune, including the garden, in a card game. Out of grief for this loss, he died within a week, but before his death he spent a day and a night in this courtyard, weeping into this pool. The salt of his tears caused the pool to dry up, and eventually the plants that relied on that pool withered and turned brown and their leaves fell off and their flowers perished. Loss is the flipside of love.'

'That's a very sad story,' said Erin. 'I'll have to find a way to give these plants water again. Perhaps there is a watering can around here. Or maybe I'll bring one next time.'

'You plan to return?'

'Every day until the garden has flowers again.' She began to pull at the weeds; their spines were sharp and it stung when she was pricked, but that didn't deter Erin. Although she'd never got her hands dirty in a garden before, she was determined to clear those weeds. 'I should bring thick gloves next time, too.'

Zhou observed her as she worked away at tending the Courtyard of Sorrow and Confusion. It was hot and thirsty work, and soon Erin was parched, but she didn't stop. She wiped her brow and continued. Even though her knee was sore and her back was hurting from bending so much, Erin was actually enjoying the job. And she might have gone on for hours, had the cricket not alerted her to the imminent return of Mr Devilskein.

'He is on the ground floor. If you leave now, you will escape his notice.'

'Beautiful as it is, I have no right to be here, do I? Will he punish me?'

'Whoever knows what Mr Devilskein will do?' the cricket mused. 'There is no pattern to his nature, aside from chaos.'

'Very well. I'll go for now, but you promise to tell me when it's safe to return?'

'Yes, of course,' said Zhou. 'And I will show you the quickest way out of this part of garden. You have come so far, but I don't think you can remember how to get back to the turquoise door!'

Erin smiled. 'I hadn't even thought of that.'

The cricket trilled and circled and she followed him, running lightly beside the lakes and inlets and walkways of the Chinese garden. Soon she was at the turquoise door, then through it, and finally she was racing down the stairs and back to Aunt Kate's flat three floors down.

The day was nearly spent, the sun was setting, neon signs

quivered and buzzed on Long Street, where a chef at Mama Africa restaurant was marinating crocodile tail to make tender kebabs (a favourite among the tourists).

A few shops down from Mama Africa, Kelwyn had Bailey, the runaway dog, tethered by a bit of old string, sitting next to him, actually sitting on Kelwyn's feet. They were in an Internet café. Bailey's head was on Kelwyn's knee and he was sleeping sitting up. Kelwyn had procured some meat bits from his friendly 'boss' at the Joy Café for the dog whose owners had their phones off.

Bailey was snoring, but Kelwyn was reeling from what he had read about the Dearloves' last hours. Brutal as it was, the Dearlove attack hadn't even made the headlines. Kelwyn sighed and prodded Bailey. 'Let's get out of here, boy.'

'Aunt Kate, I'm famished,' said Erin, as she burst into the flat.

'Glad to hear it, you're just in time for *Katerina's Pasta Pomodoro*!'

'Wow, that sounds awesome. Who's Katerina?'

With a laugh, Aunt Kate said, 'I think that's the Italian for Kate.' She filled two bowls with spaghetti and tomato pasta sauce and grated cheese over both. When she put one in front of Erin, she noticed that her niece's hands were dirty, that her nails were caked with earth and her skin was marked with cuts. 'You'd better wash those hands of yours, Erin. You've been gone for ages. What on earth have you been doing?'

'Gardening at Mr Devilskein's place.'

'Really? Does he have a balcony?' Aunt Kate frowned, because as far as she knew that top floor was deserted. In living memory, the space had always been uninhabited, and there had never been a balcony with a garden. 'It must have been very recently renovated up there.' But she was perplexed, since she'd not heard of any such remodelling work. However, she could not deny that Erin's hands looked like those of somebody who had been gardening. Perhaps Mr Devilskein was more than imaginary?

Erin shrugged. 'Maybe. Anyway, it's not a balcony, it's a courtyard.'

'Wow! He must have great views of Table Mountain.'

'Not that I saw, but it's a very nice garden.'

'Has Kelwyn seen it?'

'No!' Erin looked up, horrified. 'Why would he? It has nothing to do with him.'

'Okay, okay… it's just that Kelwyn wants to be a garden designer. That's his big dream in life. If you'd ever gone into the Talmakies' place you would see how he has filled the lounge with orchids.'

'Orchids?'

'Yep, quite the green thumb, Kelwyn is.'

'He wants to be a gardener?' Erin sucked in a strand of spaghetti and chewed. 'That's quite cool, actually.'

Aunt Kate smiled. 'Finally!'

'What?'

'I was waiting for you to dis him. You know how you love to dis poor old Kelwyn.'

'I don't.'

'Oh, yes you do.'

Three storeys below, the venison chef at Mama Africa was perspiring and red-faced from the effort of tenderising Kudu steaks with a wooden mallet.

Up in the Talmakies' apartment Kelwyn's twin brothers were building a rocket out of Lego, his little sisters were watching *Madagascar* for the umpteenth time and their mother was on the couch reading. Kelwyn wasn't doing anything. Lying on the floor next to Bailey, he was just staring at the carpet fibres around the dog's floppy white-and-caramel spotted paws. He felt sick about what he had recently learned about the Dearloves. He stroked Bailey's silky, square head and sighed heavily.

His mother glanced up from her book. 'Why the big sigh and the deep frown?'

'No reason,' he said, looking beyond the TV to one of his pots of orchids; it was his pride, that orchid, which currently boasted a flourish of brilliant pink and yellow speckled flowers. *How can the world be so amazing and beautiful and yet contain such ugliness at the same time?* he wondered.

'What's the matter, my boy?' Mrs Talmakies knew her son better than he knew himself.

'Nothing,' he said, and he was being honest, because right there and then he decided that God couldn't exist, there could only be chaos ordered by nothing: because a kind and loving god would allow only orchids and chameleons, and not brutality, like the Dearlove murders.

'Can we adopt Bailey, Ma?'

'Absolutely not.' On this point she would not budge, the last thing they needed was a big dog with a habit of running away.

'But his owners are looking for a new home for him; they say they can't stand the stress of Bailey running off all the time. They had a baby recently and they say they can't take him for walks as regularly anymore.'

'So he's talking himself for walks.'

'Exactly. But I'd take him for a walk every day and...'

'No. We can't afford to feed a big dog, Kelwyn. Besides, it's cruel to keep him here with no garden.'

'I'll pay for his food. I've got money saved up.'

'No.'

This time Kelwyn knew his mother could not be swayed.

In Aunt Kate's flat, Erin pulled a face. 'If I "dis" him, Kelwyn deserves it. He's far too friendly. It's irksome.'

'Too friendly?' Aunt Kate frowned and smiled at the same time. She suspected Kelwyn had a crush on Erin because the boy was always asking about her. 'So if he was unfriendly, you'd be friendlier in return?'

Erin pulled a face. 'That would be stupid.' She finished her bowl of spaghetti in silence. The theme tune to a soap opera drifted around the corridors of Van Riebeek Heights, and most of the other nearby apartment blocks. Using the prong of a fork, Erin set about trying to remove the excess dirt from under her nails.

'Erin, stop it! You're being uncouth! There's a nail brush in the bathroom, so use that.'

'Uncouth?' Erin smiled, she liked the word. 'Okay, I'll stop being uncouth. I really need to get a pair of gardening gloves and a watering can.'

'Certainly looks like gloves would be in order. What's it all for though?'

'A project I'm working on.'

'Ahh. Sounds promising.' Aunt Kate decided not to push for too much information about 'the project' – she had a better idea. 'Ask Kelwyn, he'll be only too happy to lend them to you.'

Erin was reluctant; she didn't want anyone else coming up to her garden, especially not that silly boy. That world beyond those six doors was her secret, well, hers and Mr Devilskein's and the poodle's and the cricket's. After Aunt Kate had finished her spaghetti, Erin cleared the bowls and took them to the sink under Kate's oil painting of the sea and green avocados. Erin had become quite an ace at doing the dishes; the deal was if Kate cooked, Erin washed up, and if Erin cooked, Kate washed up. They wore yellow rubber gloves, which Aunt Kate said were essential to protect the soft skin of their hands. Usually, Kate did the cooking because Erin was only good at making scrambled eggs, omelettes and melted cheese toast (which sometimes got a bit burned).

'Maybe Kelwyn can help you and Mr Devilskein in that garden?'

'No!' That was exactly what Erin did not want. 'Kelwyn is not welcome in the garden.' Erin did want a watering can but she didn't have any money to buy one of her own. 'Aunt Kate, would you mind asking him if you could borrow his watering can? Please don't say it's me that needs it.'

'Why, Erin?'

'Just because. Will you help me or not?'

By now, the moon had risen over Long Street; the evening was peaceful, on TVs around the block lovers professed their love before an ad break, the Company Soulometer in Devilskein's kitchen cried out *Ping!Ping!Ping!* and Aunt Kate relented. 'Ok. I'll go tomorrow.'

'You're the best,' Erin said, and she would have said more, but then there was that noise again: the wailing in the stairwell. 'Do you hear that?'

'What? Oh, the wind is back.' Unperturbed, Aunt Kate picked up a surfing magazine, sat down on the sofa and curled her legs under her.

Erin listened more carefully. She gazed out of the kitchen window at the side street below. No plastic bags or newspapers were stirring in the gutters. 'It's not the wind. There is no wind.' To be double sure, Erin opened the front door and stood in the open-air passage. It was a perfectly still evening and there was somebody crying in the stairwell. Erin went back inside. 'Surely, you can hear that sobbing?'

'I'm sure it's the wind,' Aunt Kate said.

'No, it sounds like somebody crying.'

Glancing up from the *Surfer Times*, Aunt Kate said, 'If it's not the wind, then it's no business of ours, Erin. Whoever it is probably wants to be alone, and that's why they've gone to the stairwell.'

'So you can hear it!' Exhausted as she was from her afternoon of gardening, Erin went out to investigate. She ran up and down the stairs, from the ground floor to the top floor, but although she could hear the crying, she could not find its source; it seemed to be everywhere...

9

The Cricket and the Boy

True to her word, Aunt Kate procured for Erin a watering can and a pair of thick cotton gardening gloves, blue in parts but mostly blackened with potting soil. Untrue to her word, Kate did mention to Kelwyn that it was Erin who wanted these things.

'She's shy around boys,' Aunt Kate had said with a wink. 'She doesn't want you to know they are for her.'

Even though Erin had the equipment she needed, two full days went by before the cricket returned to alert Erin to Mr Devilskein's departure from the apartment on the top floor. When on that sweltering hot summer's day Zhou came chirruping into Aunt Kate's flat, Erin did not waste a moment. She grabbed the watering can and gloves and raced upstairs to the Chinese garden, or rather the Garden of the Humble Politician, as Zhou called it.

Her nerves about encountering Mr Devilskein were overshadowed by her excitement at returning to the magical realm. She had read stories about people who find secret and enchanted gardens, but those things only happened in fiction and in faraway places like England, never to girls in Cape Town. How lucky she was to have ended up at Van Riebeek Heights she thought, and then felt a twinge of guilt because she did not wish the ill that had befallen her parents – it couldn't have been nice being eaten by a crocodile. They had become such a distant memory, that mother and father in their designer mansion. They seemed like strangers, unreal, figments of a strange dream. And unlike them, Aunt Kate was so down to earth and affectionate. Even this curious realm beyond the turquoise door in apartment 6616 was more real than the mansion with the glass staircase had ever been.

'Take me back to the Courtyard of Sorrow and Confusion,' said Erin to Zhou. 'I want to water the plants there and bring them back to life. All that sorrow doesn't have to last.'

Zhou chirped and led her along the walkways beneath maples. The sweet scent of moonflowers filled Erin's nostrils and she sighed with joy. 'It is too beautiful here. And so cool.' In the city beyond and far below the turquoise door, Long Street was grimy and stifling hot; people were irritable and the hooting was more aggressive than usual. But Erin had escaped all that.

It was a slow process, carrying water from the lake outside to the Courtyard of Sorrow, but Erin made sure that every plant each got a whole can, some of them, the bigger ones, got two or even three.

As she worked the cricket watched, impressed by her dedication. They talked, but in English, as Erin said it was too difficult to weed, water, and learn Chinese all at the same time, even in an alternative realm. 'I'd like to learn one day, though,' she said, scooping the can through the cool green lake to fill it up. 'Perhaps when the garden is healthy again.' She lugged the filled can through the dry archway of rose branches. 'How come you are a cricket?'

'If I tell you, I will never have the opportunity to be a man again. Ask me other questions.'

'Oh.' She was sorry, and simultaneously more curious, but respected his request. 'Okay then, well… you said you were an envoy to a place called Angkor. What is that?' Gently, she poured the life-giving water into the soil around a potted topiary tree.

'Angkor was the centre of the universe,' said Zhou. 'Well, that was according to the barbarians, who called out this nonsense when a commander of our army of a thousand men acting in the name of the Son of Heaven, my Emperor, arrived at the Khmer king's palace to plant the Standard of the Tiger in the heart of that city.'

'Barbarians?' Erin was confused. 'Who were they?'

'At the time, we considered anyone who wasn't Chinese to be a barbarian. In this case, it was the Khmer people, those who dared to claim that Angkor is the universe! Of course, we thought them fools and doomed. We believed that China was the universe and that our Emperor was the Son of Heaven.'

'Everybody always wants to be the biggest, the best, the richest, and the most powerful,' Erin said, pulling dead flowers off a rose bush she had watered. 'My dad was like that.'

Sleek black crows circled overhead, eyeing the activity in the courtyard of sorrow.

'Alas, that is true. The Khmer king laughed at the power of our Emperor and the magnificence of our Chinese lands and he claimed that he was the devaraja, the God-king, and Angkor was paradise eternal. He said the magnificence of his city and his temples were beyond compare.'

'I bet your commander and his army were very angry when he said that.'

The cricket chirped. 'Oh yes, they thought the Khmers

had insulted the greatest civilization on earth, and to show their disgust the entire army spat in the direction of the five-towered temple of Angkor. And then they cursed it, saying that one day the great temple would be nothing but ruins.'

Erin was grimy with soil and perspiring with the effort of being a bearer of water to the plants of the courtyard, but even so, she paused upon hearing about the curse. 'How awful. I bet that Khmer king was furious, too.'

'Oh yes,' the cricket said. 'Our commander and every man in our army were executed and the golden tablet bearing the instructions of our Emperor, the Son of Heaven, to those wayward people was melted down and used to make bracelets for one of the Khmer king's favourite dancers. Imagine!'

'That must have made your Emperor very, very angry. Did it cause a war?'

'Angry he certainly was,' said the cricket. 'But it did not cause a war because the Emperor was cunning and did not wish to cause more unnecessary deaths among his soldiers. Instead, he decided we would find out more about those Khmers, learn their weaknesses and pretend to be friendly. He sent a diplomatic mission to Angkor, and that is how I found myself very relieved to be sailing from Ningbo in China on the second moon of the year 1296.'

'1296!' Erin spilled water she was so surprised. 'That can't be right? That's almost a thousand years ago.'

The cricket trilled. 'I told you I was old.'

'But that's impossible.'

'Remember what your Aunt Kate said. Nothing is impossible.'

Later on, sprinting back downstairs, with muddy clothes and the watering can, Erin bumped right into Mr Devilskein.

'Hello, Calvados,' she said cheerily, though she didn't

really feel cheerful, she felt like she'd missed catastrophe by a matter of minutes. Patting the poodle, she willed her cheeks not to blush and so give away her secret about the Chinese garden. 'And how are you today, Mr Devilskein?' She forced a bright smile.

The old monster gave her such a wily look that the hairs on her arms stood up. 'Why, Ms Dearlove, I never know where I'm going to see you next. You flit about just like that cricket.'

Erin giggled nervously. 'We're friends now, Zhou and I.'

'Don't think I haven't noticed. Always liked the girls that boy, I mean, cricket. You are welcome to come for tea this afternoon.'

'Oh, well…' for a moment Erin was speechless, and then she wasn't sure why she was so shocked at his invitation. 'Thank you. I don't think I will have time to make scones, though.'

'Never mind. Calvados and I have a surprise for you.'

Oh dear, thought Erin. A surprise sounded a bit ominous, but then again everything Mr Devilskein said had an ominous ring to it; it was just the way the man spoke. 'You shouldn't have.' Then Erin was cross. 'There is absolutely no need for a surprise.'

In truth, Mr Devilskein, in spite of his surly demeanour and unpredictable temperament, had decided he almost liked the scrawny, grouchy girl, who actually wasn't so scrawny anymore. And rather more importantly, he owed the child a debt of gratitude – this had been on his mind since the unfortunate failure of his heart pills to do their job properly – she had already saved him once, and ultimately, if things went to plan, she would, willingly or unwillingly, save him a second time with her glorious heart. Yes, scones and jam aside, he still wanted her heart. *Alas Ms Dearlove, this cannot end well for both of us.*

'Well, there is a surprise,' he said, curtly, and quite angrily too. 'So, it would be rude if you don't come at six o'clock. No earlier because I will be out from five to six. And no later because lateness is intolerable.' Feeling he'd been entirely too civil for one encounter with a small creature he ought not to be so friendly with in the first place, Mr Devilskein continued on his way up the stairs without a goodbye, pausing only to say over his shoulder, 'Remember, there will be tea, but do not expect any conversation. I can't abide chit-chat. I'm too old to bother with it.'

Erin breathed a great sigh of relief when Mr Devilskein was gone. Her armpits were newly wet with perspiration, and it wasn't on account of the heat or the gardening she had been doing in secret in a room off the vestibule in the monster's apartment.

The cricket chirruped and landed on her shoulder.

'If I go for tea,' she said, 'I'm sure he'll read my mind; he'll know and then…' A horrible thought occurred to her. 'What if he changes the locks, so that the keys don't fit? Or worse, what if knows I have the keys and when I am there, he takes them away?' She leaned against Aunt Kate's door wearily.

'Don't fret, child,' said Zhou. 'Your work in the Chinese garden will remain our secret.'

Erin nodded okay and then, out of exhaustion and relief, simply slid down the door and sat on the doormat, staring out at the line of blue sky visible over the corridor railings. A police siren wailed at the far end of the street.

'Back in the garden, you said you were relieved to be sailing away from Ningbo. Why?' She turned her head to look at the cricket who had settled on her knee.

He chirped. 'It was one week after my fifteenth birthday. My father, an ambitious and wealthy man, had just informed me he had selected my future wife and we would be married in the spring.'

'You were going to get married at fifteen?'

'Quite normal in those times.'

Erin was horrified. 'Was she nice, your wife-to-be?'

'Not really. Beautiful, yes, but nice, no. "Cheer up and let us drink to your future success. You should be pleased with our selection of wife," my father had said, bristling with satisfaction on the day. "She has exceedingly fine features, that woman. Her elegance will be a useful complement to your brilliant mind and my connections." My father was pleased with me for mastering so well the teachings of Confucius that I had been one of the four hundred thousand candidates in that year's prefectural examinations. Moreover, in the exam, I scored in the top one hundred. The result was that I was not only eligible for a seat in government, but I was also singled out to be groomed as a high official.'

'That sounds pretty impressive,' said Erin.

'Impressive perhaps, but not necessarily a recipe for happiness.'

As Zhou trilled and chirped, neither he nor Erin heard Kelwyn coming up the stairs. Kelwyn could hear Erin making conversation, but he couldn't see who she was speaking to. He slowed his pace and crept up the stairs, listening more closely to what she was saying.

'Why wasn't your fiancée nice? I mean, was she grumpy like me?'

'No, no!' The cricket chirped a laugh. 'She was pretty, like you. Wherever my fiancée went, men paused to look at her. Pretty as she may have been, and intelligent too, there was also a bitterness, a childish cruelty about her. Her family once owned thousands of hectares of rich land, but laziness of the sons, the extravagance of their mother, and a dose of poor fortune caused their wealth to be reduced to nearly nothing. I wanted to love her. There were moments when she was charming and tender, and I almost loved her then. But she was interested only in possessions, and if she could not have her way, she would narrow her eyes and become quite devoid of any gentleness. She seemed to hate men.'

Erin was pensive. 'I'm not pretty, Zhou, but I fear I am like your fiancée in other ways. I am never gentle and sometimes I am very cruel, to Kelwyn for example. I often say cruel things to him, just because – I don't even know why. He's sometimes too friendly, too happy. It gets on my nerves and I say unfriendly things. And actually he's not that bad. Or maybe he is: isn't it fake, always being so positive? There's no reason at all to be so constantly friendly and happy. It's dishonest.'

From his position on the stairs around the corner, Kelwyn considered this revelation with mixed feelings: some delight and some residue of sadness left over from what he had read about Erin's family. He peeked around into the corridor and was surprised to see Erin alone. Who was she talking to?

'Erin,' said the cricket, 'Your unfriendliness does not compare to my fiancée's. Even on the last day I saw her, at the engagement dinner, before I set sail for Angkor, she had demanded money from me, as well as a priceless jewel. I thought it was a joke, and anyway, I was not at that time in a position to give her those things. She had pouted and criticised me throughout the meal. "I don't understand your meanness. Maybe you are deluded, husband-to-be? It is not normal." I did not know what she was on about. There was no logic in her arguments and she went on repeating obsessively the details of this silly matter, for so long that I began to think she was not entirely sane. My appetite for the excellent soup evaporated. "Can you explain it to me?" With her chopsticks she picked pieces of pheasant out of my bowl. "This abnormal behaviour of yours, husband-to-be?" Finally, I was so infuriated that I stopped talking. I did not look at her or speak to her for the rest of the meal. After a few sips of tea, I rose and left the banquet in silence. Never to return. I did not survive the trip to Angkor… not as a fifteen-year-old in human form that is.'

'She must have been sad about that.'

'Perhaps. If there is one thing I tried to achieve, Erin, it was to remain on the best possible terms with all people. A bad relationship is like poison in the air and in the heart. My fiancée was not a wicked person – difficult, greedy, perhaps – but I was difficult too and I felt I had been less than gracious over the teahouse banquet. Before leaving on the journey to the Kingdom of Angkor in Cambodia, I left a gift with a message for her, apologising and expressing my sincere hope that she would be happy and comfortable while I was away. Truly, I wished only happiness for her.'

Erin and the cricket talked on about his departure for Angkor for another quarter of an hour and she asked the cricket many questions, for she was fascinated by his knowledge and experience of a time long past in a place so far away.

'Can you go back to Ningbo? Or to Cambodia?' Erin asked.

'Why would I want to do that?' It was the first time Erin had heard Zhou sounding irritated and she couldn't understand why.

'Why are you here? Why is Mr Devilskein here? What is that place with the six doors? It's not at all normal; it is not like any other apartment in Van Riebeek Heights.'

'Curiosity killed the cat.' Suddenly, the cricket was cross. 'Don't ask too many questions. That's enough chattering for the day.' The cricket sounded so annoyed, that Erin realised she had better shut up. 'I'm going,' said Zhou, not his usual genial self. With that he rose up and flew off.

Erin remained sitting on the doormat. She did not like Zhou

any less as a result of his crossness; being an easily irritated person herself, she didn't see anything wrong with crossness. It was normal, she thought, and it was abnormal to try and pretend to be happy all the time.

Kelwyn announced his arrival with some throat-clearing coughs. 'What are you doing on the mat there, Erin?' he asked, trying hard not to sound too friendly. 'Seems an odd place to sit.'

'What's it to you?' Erin said sharply, without a smile.

Kelwyn's natural inclination would have been to laugh at that snipe, and to reply in a friendly fashion with a joke, for like his ma he lived by the idea that 'sticks and stones break bones but words can't harm you'.

'Nothing at all,' he said, making a great effort to sound rude. He took his front door key out of his pocket, turned away from Erin, opened the door to his apartment and went inside without saying goodbye. Unlike Erin, Bailey the dog (who had still not been collected by his owners) was overjoyed to see Kelwyn; every bit of him was wagging hello.

It was most odd, thought Erin, how grumpy Kelwyn seemed to be that day. She was quite taken aback, so much so that she stood up and dusted off her jeans and resolved to find out the cause. It was disconcerting, not to be irritated by Kelwyn's friendliness, but rather to feel hurt by his unfriendliness. She convinced herself it was only because surliness wasn't what she expected from him.

In turn, Kelwyn was feeling shoddy – what he wanted most in the world was to give Erin a hug, to hold her for a long time and to keep her safe from any future unhappiness. Instead of hugging Erin he knelt down and put all his affection into nuzzling Bailey. But then his doorbell rang and there at the door was Erin with a smile instead of her usual scowl.

'Hello,' she said lightly, fighting the urge to be curt.

Her brightness threw Kelwyn off course, and he almost

grinned, but instead he pushed the happiness he felt at seeing her away because of what he had overheard her saying about his friendliness being irritating. He just stared at her blankly, and then, as inhospitably as he could, he mumbled, 'What do you want?'

Now she couldn't help laughing. 'Who are you?'

'I'm Kelwyn,' he said, and cocked his head and gave her a bored look. 'And you're Erin and I've got a dog to look after, so this conversation is over.' He made to close the door on her.

An incredulous and beautiful smile spread across her face and she put her hand out to stop the door closing. On the other side, Kelwyn's heart was racing, he couldn't believe his luck; he couldn't believe how contrary girls could be; he couldn't believe that being rude was more effective than being friendly.

'Hey, wait,' said Erin, feeling a little shy and awkward about this business of being nice to a boy. 'Ah, I just wanted to say thanks.'

'Okay, we'll you've said it.' Kelwyn pushed against the door so that it closed.

Erin stood there dumbfounded. She rang the bell again.

'Get a life,' said Kelwyn as he opened the door with a fantastically sour look on his face. A dog with a baleful stare and soft floppy ears appeared beside him.

For the first time Erin noticed how blue Kelwyn's eyes were, how they were flecked with green, and how long his lashes were. His hair had grown, it was curly and blond and very pleasing. Even the smell of kelp wasn't so bad. And that dog was undeniably cute. She smiled. 'I didn't finish. The watering can and the gardening gloves, they were for me and they've been very useful. So thank you.'

Kelwyn was bursting to ask what she was doing with them. He loved gardening and he would have liked to know what she was planting. Instead of commenting, he was silent, and stared at her, all the time thinking, *Do not smile Kelwyn, do NOT smile.*

It was very awkward for Erin: for the first time since the attack on her family she was really making an effort to be nice, to be polite and to make conversation, but it was proving to be hard work. Especially now that Kelwyn wasn't responding and she was obliged to come up with something else to say. How exhausting friendliness was. It was much easier to be grumpy. She racked her brain for something to say and came up with, 'Aunt Kate says you have a lovely potted garden on your balcony.'

Kelwyn nodded, but his expression was ungiving.

Erin's smile became almost desperate.

'I like your dog, is he new?'

He shook his head but didn't elaborate.

Why wasn't he talking? He was usually such a chatty soul and here she was making an effort and he had turned into a sullen blob. It had become a matter of pride and a challenge; she was determined that her attempt at niceness would not be such a disaster. There must be something she could say to draw Kelwyn out of his strange mood.

'Will you show me your pots?' Erin said, and then she totally forgot about discretion and said: 'I'd really like to see them. Maybe you can give me some tips? Aunt Kate says you're very good. I'm doing a big garden myself. It's really a challenge. Oh, but it's so beautiful there. I feel like I'm in another world...' She blushed. She had said too much. 'Silly me.'

This was all too interesting for Kelwyn to keep up his act. He was curious. 'I'll show you mine,' he said, opening the door properly and allowing her to enter, 'if you show me yours.'

Erin gulped and followed Kelwyn and the caramel dog with big paws into a small apartment identical to Aunt Kate's place, except it was like a greenhouse inside: full of lush potted plants, orchids, bonsai trees, and also full of children and cages of birds, mostly blue budgies and canaries, all very noisy. From the bedroom side, music was playing and there was lots of laughter.

The forest of greenery was too astonishing for Erin not to be impressed. 'Wow, did you do all of this?'

'Guilty.' Kelwyn couldn't help smiling. 'The balcony is even better. Come and see.' He led her out there and it was a glorious sight, so colourful and lovely and fresh that Erin looked at him and said, 'No wonder you're always laughing and friendly, your whole life with all these plants is beautiful. When you have this to come home to, I guess everything seems okay. It doesn't matter what mean things anyone says to you, you always have your plants.'

Kelwyn's smile spread across his face. 'Exactly. The plants are friends.'

Erin was so touched by the world Kelwyn had created she couldn't help herself from saying, 'I have found a most wonderful garden too. And I've noticed that since I first went there, I've felt much happier.'

'Where is this garden?'

Her cheeks coloured. Erin bit her lip and looked away from Kelwyn and stared fixedly at a pot full of magenta flowers. She didn't want to lie and she didn't want to tell the truth. In fact, the truth was that she wasn't sure where that garden was. Sure, she knew how to get into it, but she also knew that the garden wasn't where it seemed to be, that somehow it was a garden of a different space and time.

Kelwyn noticed the blush.

'Is it in Mr Devilskein's apartment?'

Her blush deepened. She turned to him, her eyes wide and worried. 'Can you keep a secret, if I tell you? It's going to sound mad, and also it could be dangerous. It probably is dangerous. In fact, I may die if they find out that I told you.'

She said the last sentence with real trepidation; she did not understand the realm of Mr Devilskein and the cricket Zhou, but she sensed that it was composed of equal measures of beauty and violence. There was a dark secret to that apartment with all its doors as well as the loveliness of the Chinese garden. Her gut told her it had what Zhou the cricket would call a 'flipside'.

Kelwyn was confounded by her apparent fear. He might have made light of it, but she seemed so genuinely anxious that he felt nervous of what he might hear. 'Sure, my little brothers, Max and Milos, are always telling me secrets. I'm great at keeping secrets. I'd be dead if I wasn't, they would've ganged up on me and killed me in my sleep by now, I know far too much.' As soon as he said that he regretted mentioning such violence, but Erin seemed oblivious.

They were close to a hanging orchid and standing side by side and without realising what she was doing, Erin took his hand and squeezed it as if imploring him to keep this secret especially safe. 'You're right,' she spoke quickly, in a whisper, keeping his hand tightly in hers all the time. 'It is in Mr Devilskein's apartment, and yet it is not, and he doesn't know that I know it is there and if he did, he might kill me. He has told me before he would kill me and although he was probably joking… well, he may not have been.' She broke out into a sweat. 'But it is the most exquisite place I have ever seen and it is not right that it should not be enjoyed! He keeps it behind a turquoise door and I stole the keys, or rather the cricket stole them and gave them to me.' Now there were tears in her eyes. 'There is part of the garden that has died of sorrow and that is what I have been tending – pulling out weeds, watering plants, cutting off the dead flowers.'

It was such a jumbled tale that Kelwyn wasn't sure what to make of it; it did sound crazy, but he liked having his hand held by the girl of his dreams, even if she had gone slightly mad. 'Sounds super cool…' he said.

'It is! It is most unbelievable and magical! Yes, that is what it is – a magical garden in another realm, but it appears to be in Mr Devilskein's apartment, although it cannot really exist there.'

'I'm not sure I understand.'

'Nor do I!' Her eyes had become wild and in spite of herself, she felt a compulsion to verify the garden's existence by sharing it. 'It's such a conundrum! There is no other word for it, and the only way to believe is to see it. I will have to take you there.' She remembered Mr Devilskein was going out at five o'clock. 'Meet me in the stairwell at five past five. Not a minute sooner or he will see us and be suspicious.'

10

The Cabinet of Albertus Devilskein

Erin headed back to Aunt Kate's apartment in a flustered state. She closed out the sound of sirens in the street below. Since her aunt was out, Erin let herself in, and with a head still whirring with thoughts, she picked up her sketchbook, which she had not touched since the last episode of visions it provoked. She chose a black pen and suddenly her mind was back in the Chinese garden, or rather, above the garden. She had a full bird's eye view. She felt she was flying and circling through the air, with the garden and its waterways, courtyards, and maple-lined paths stretched out below. Her hand moved the pen over the page as her thoughts hovered over the garden, processing the most intricate details of its design. One page was not enough. Without being conscious of it, she tore out the first completely filled sheet and started a second one. It was more like a decorative map than an illustration, embellished with details of peony beds and lily-filled lakes and courtyards of ancient bonsai trees. As she drew, she could hear a voice: the voice of the garden designer, explaining the Feng Shui of place. A third, a fourth, a fifth, a sixth... forty sheets were soon filled with the details of this garden and without knowing it, she had placed them on the floor, so that full blueprint of the Garden of the Humble Politician emerged.

There was a knock at Kelwyn's front door, and he hurried to open it, expecting Erin, but there was a woman with dark rings under her eyes and a baby in a pouch on her chest. 'You left a message on my phone about Bailey,' she said.

Kelwyn called for Bailey and he came to meet his human with moderate excitement. She patted him without too much vigour. 'Thank you,' she said to Kelwyn and because she was used to collecting her fugitive hound from Kelwyn, she knew about the reward. She gave him fifty rands this time. Kelwyn embraced the broad-necked dog and reluctantly waved goodbye.

Time vanished.

It was long after five, in fact, almost six o'clock when Aunt Kate arrived home to find Erin engrossed in drawing the magnificent garden.

At the same time as she was drawing, Kelwyn, who had given up waiting for her, was on his balcony with his bonsai clippers. Lovingly, he was trimming into shape an extraordinary metre-square labyrinth made of bonsai boxwoods. Sending Bailey back to his real home had left Kelwyn feeling lonesome; he was fond of the dog with a taste for adventure. Clipping the labyrinth always made Kelwyn feel better.

Instead of regaling Erin with the tribulations of the traffic in Long Street, which was blocked off by police officers on account of an 'incident', Aunt Kate gasped at the myriad of drawings on her lounge floor. She said something of it, but Erin, still entranced by the voice of the garden designer, did not hear. Gently, Aunt Kate shook her shoulder. 'Erin!'

With a start, Erin ceased drawing and looked up. 'Aunt Kate, I didn't hear you come in.'

'That's okay, you're busy. Very busy.' Aunt Kate kneeled down to look at the drawings more closely. 'I've never seen anything like this, Erin.'

Erin looked at her handiwork and was surprised. 'I have. It's a magic place.' And then she remembered the meeting with Kelwyn. 'Oh dear… what's the time?'

'Ten to six.'

'What! Oh no, I was supposed to meet Kelwyn almost an hour ago.' Erin threw down her sketchbook and ran out of the flat, leaving Aunt Kate doubly bewildered.

'If this is not genius, I don't know what is,' Aunt Kate said to herself as she studied the illustrations.

Minutes later, Erin was banging on Kelwyn's front door. With the bonsai clippers still in his hand, he opened the door, and this time his didn't smile as warmly as usual. In spite of the bonsai labyrinth, he was feeling quite hurt.

'I forgot!' said Erin. 'I'm so sorry. I lost track of time.'

Kelwyn nodded and gave up the bit of hurt that was holding back his smile. 'It's okay. You don't have to apologise.' But he wasn't going to let her get away without a bit of teasing. 'I knew you were making it up.'

'I'm not! It's real, I promise.'

'Yeah, yeah.'

Then she surprised even herself, by taking his hand again and pulling him out into the corridor. 'Come here and I'll show you.'

He allowed himself to be dragged along to Aunt Kate's flat, where the masterful puzzle of the garden was still laid out on the floor. 'There,' said Erin. 'That is what it looks like.'

Kelwyn couldn't hide his amazement. Silently, he studied the pieces of the artwork that were so exceptionally good.

At length, he asked. 'You did this?'

'I came in and found her drawing,' said Aunt Kate before

Erin could reply.

'It's enchanting,' said Kelwyn.

'I told you, it's a magic garden.' The kitchen clock showed a minute before six. 'I'll take you there one day, but now I must go. Mr Devilskein is expecting me for tea.'

He knew he was finally making progress with her and that at all costs he mustn't be too nice. 'Come off it, Erin,' he said, unexpectedly harshly, more so than he intended (and he felt bad immediately). 'You don't expect me to believe that.'

His sudden unfriendliness stung. And it was then that Erin realised she quite liked him, which caused a whole confusion of emotions.

'Fine,' she said. 'Believe what you like. I must go.'

'Damn,' thought Kelwyn. 'I blew it!'

And so Erin left Aunt Kate and Kelwyn gobsmacked in front of the drawings.

'She's one of a kind, our Erin,' Aunt Kate said. 'I'm glad to see the two of you are getting along better.'

'Not really.' Kelwyn shook his head. 'We were supposed to meet at five and she stood me up.'

Disappointed, Aunt Kate offered Kelwyn a cup of tea, but he declined. He needed time to think and decided to go for a walk. Dusk on Long Street was unusually melancholic that night; the sky was dark with sombre clouds; a tourist had been stabbed for his mobile phone in the afternoon. The atmosphere was gloomy. Kelwyn stared at the tips of his sneakers as he walked and, caught up in thoughts, not really paying attention to the world around him. But somewhere a kitten mewed, and the note of distress in the creature's voice broke through Kelwyn's despair. He looked up and around trying to place the source of the sound. There it was again. Behind to the right. He swung around and saw to his horror a white kitten in the middle of Long Street. Worse! Bearing down upon the little cat was a taxi, going fast, only metres away. Worse still! The frightened kitten had started running towards the taxi.

'Stop!' shouted Kelwyn. He ran into the road, waving his arms to attract the taxi-driver's attention. Seconds away, the driver finally noticed the boy and braked hard. The kitten froze, shocked by screeching wheels, and Kelwyn sprinted forward and scooped it up. He took the little creature over to the driver's window and held it up to show the driver and his passengers what they had saved by stopping. And instead of thanks, the poor terrified animal put up an almighty struggle trying to escape from Kelwyn's grip; he bit and clawed and hissed, but Kelwyn's hands were strong and eventually he managed to soothe the kitten. He tucked it into his jacket and headed for Joy Café, where he hoped to procure some free fish for his new friend.

'Come in, Rover 2,' he said into his near-vintage walkie-talkie.

'Yes, Rover 1,' crackled Sipho's voice on the other side.

'Rendezvous at Joy. New subject recently rescued.'

'Roger that, Rover 1. Give me five.'

Six floors up, Erin was sitting across from Mr Devilskein, watching him pour tea.

'Your silence is heavy today, Ms Dearlove. Why is that? Is your conscience troubling you, perhaps?' It was a case of the pot calling the kettle black, for Devilskein himself was troubled with conscience. He rather liked these teas with Erin and she had already saved his life, yet there was that small matter of her heart: he needed it. But it was a problem and a decision that could be deferred, at least until his Physician sent word that the time was right for the transplant. 'Terrible what happened on Long Street this afternoon,' he said, not particularly concerned by the 'incident', but wanting to refocus his thoughts.

'Are you making conversation?' she snapped. 'I thought you didn't do that sort of thing. I wouldn't have come if I thought there would be polite chit-chat. I have discovered once already today how ghastly it can be to make friendly conversation.'

'As you like it.' Mr Devilskein put a dash of milk into his tea and waited for it to cool before he took his first sip.

Thereafter they sat in stillness; the only sounds were the ticking of the clock, the sipping and swallowing of tea and the contented snore of Calvados, who was asleep under the kitchen table.

In a strange way, the quietude was calming and at length, when her tea was finished, Erin asked, 'What's the surprise?'

A smile crept onto Mr Devilskein's hideous face, and it would have been fearsome had there not been a twinkle in the monster's eyes. 'I have heard, or let me be honest, overheard, that you have an interest in the sea.'

Erin stared at inside of her cup, where a last drop of tea rolled away to reveal a delicate image of a lady's face. 'You mean surfing?'

'That involves the sea, doesn't it?' He frowned.

'I guess so.'

'Well,' he clapped his hands together, and produced from his palm a key. 'This is the key to the turquoise door and it will take you to your surprise.' He placed the key before her. It didn't look at all like the key Erin already possessed for that particular door. It was older and more brassy and ornate. She felt she was being tricked. She stared at the key without touching it.

'Oh for goodness and badness sake!' Mr Devilskein looked fierce. 'Finally, I give you permission and a key and all you do is sit there. Run along, child, and see what is beyond the door.'

Erin looked from the key to Mr Devilskein and then at Calvados, who had opened one eye and was watching with interest. 'Where is the cricket, Zhou?'

'You will not need the cricket for what is behind that door. Now go before I change my mind.'

Quite slowly and reluctantly, Erin left the kitchen where they had been having tea, passed through the shadows created by the towers of shoeboxes and up to the turquoise door. The lock had definitely been changed; it had a wider gape, fit for a fatter key than the one she owned. She inserted the key and gave it a turn. As she stepped across the threshold, she was sucked inwards into a cool, green, underwater realm. The door was no longer visible. *Ah! He has found me out and now he is murdering me: a deep-sea death.* At first she thought she would surely drown, because try as she might to surface from the salty world, no matter how far up she swam, there never was a brim or top or surface. It was water everywhere. Soon she realised she could see quite well in spite of the salty atmosphere and that she wasn't struggling to breathe. On the contrary, a stream of bubbles moved with her as she went, and when she touched her cheeks it felt like she had developed gills. How curious and how glorious! As she was beginning to enjoy being like a fish, from nowhere came the whooshing sound of water bodies and momentarily she was overwhelmed by thousands of translucent jellyfish, brilliant yellow arrow squids and indigo-blue flying squids, all with waving, feathery legs like those of dancers. If the sight of them had not been so beautiful and strange, Erin might have been frightened, especially since if they so chose, the jellyfish could have stung her to a painful demise. But the creatures were not interested in harming her, they were on their way to an important gathering and they were moving at a rapid pace. Soon they left Erin behind in the peace of the ocean and its corals of many hues.

It was dreamy and serene until the swishing of currents and kelp was outdone by a clatter of armour-coated claws and feelers. Coming up on Erin's left was a vast blue and orange battalion of lobsters, spider crabs, horseshoe crabs, and porcelain crabs. Erin yelped, for fear that they would trample her as they went their way, but she need not have worried, as they parted briefly to accommodate her presence.

'What is this place?' Erin asked nobody in particular, since there was nobody to ask, except the slither of ten thousand green and blue sea snakes that, like the crabs and the squids had appeared from nowhere, and were heading somewhere in a great hurry. Never having been a great fan of snakes, Erin froze in horror at the sight of all those beady eyes and lithe, patterned bodies. Again her trepidation was unnecessary; the creatures had no interest in the human who was not hurrying to the ball, like every other body in that watery realm.

If the snakes had not been terrible enough, next came whale sharks, those magnificent spotted giants of the sea, and all other kinds of shark, including scary-looking hammerheads. She felt sure they would devour her, but they too went on their way single-mindedly, without giving her even a cursory glance.

It seemed she was on some kind of highway and so she decided to swim off to the right, to get to a quieter part of the ocean. What she discovered next was a galaxy of shells: turret shells, auger shells and tibias. She gathered some in her hands to study their markings and colours; they gleamed and dazzled her.

But nothing was as astonishing as the herd of six-headed sea-dragons that went marching along the shelf below the rocks where Erin was examining the shells.

Again Erin asked, 'What is this place?' But the purple-and yellow-scaled sea-dragons, each with many sets of sharp teeth, made no reply.

After an uncertain amount of time, Erin heard her name. It seemed that Mr Devilskein was calling her back to the kitchen. It was hard to imagine that all these creatures existed in a room in Van Riebeek Heights and that beyond the turquoise door Mr Devilskein was sipping tea and Calvados was snoozing. Without being sure of any direction, Erin willed herself back to the door and at the same moment as she saw it, she was through it. Just like that, she was back in the vestibule, but to her surprise she wasn't dripping wet.

'Don't forget to lock the door this time,' called Mr Devilskein.

With eyes bewildered by the underwater paradise, Erin ran to the kitchen, panting from the oddness of breathing oxygen with lungs again. 'What is that place?'

'It is an ocean cabinet – a kind of zoo, if you like.'

'What are you?'

'Sit down and finish your tea, or it will get cold and that would be a waste; it is fine stuff from the palace of Xanadu in China. People have written poetry about that place.'

Erin sat, but could not think of drinking tea. 'You didn't answer my question.'

'I am not obliged to, little wench.'

'Don't call me that. Just tell me. What difference can my knowing possibly make?'

'You are a curious creature,' he said. 'And you have worked hard in the Chinese garden.'

'You knew?'

'I know everything that happens in my home.'

Erin gazed at Mr Devilskein. 'This is not a home. What is this place? What are you? What is your job title?'

'Untitled job.' He chuckled. 'I am a Lord of Imagination. I am immortal; I am a hunter, a killer, a broker, a trader, a safe keeper of creatures, plants, keys, and souls. I am Albertus Devilskein.' He held out his hand to shake Erin's. 'It has been an unexpected pleasure to meet you, Ms Dearlove. You are a remarkable child. In a thousand years, I have not met one with your abilities.' He was once more satisfied to see the pure silver shimmer of her soul.

'I don't know what you're talking about. What do you kill? What keys do you keep and whose souls? And why are you here at Van Riebeek Heights?'

'That last is easy to answer: nobody would expect to find me here and nobody has, until you arrived.' Suddenly exultant, Mr Devilskein said, 'There is a great deal of work to do and I could use some help, if you are willing and not lazy.'

'If you want, I'll come every day, no matter what. This is the best place in the world as far as I can tell.'

'Excellent.' Mr Devilskein stood up and began to pace up and down, muttering to himself about possibilities. 'You must never forget to lock the doors – that is important.'

'Will I be able to go back to the Chinese garden?'

'Time permitting.' Mr Devilskein chortled. 'You have no idea how many gardens there are here.'

'But I want to mend the Courtyard of Sorrow,' Erin stared into her teacup and slumped slightly. 'I want to make it grow and be healthy again.'

'If you can, so be it.'

Erin perked up. 'I like you, Mr Devilskein. There are only four people in the world that I like, and you are one of them.'

'Only four. And who are the other three?'

'Aunt Kate, the cricket and Kelwyn, even though he doesn't like me anymore.'

'What of Calvados? He will be hurt not to make the list.'

'Five then.' She smiled at the poodle. 'I do like you, Calvados, even though you smell of pepper.'

Mr Devilskein laughed. 'I thought I was a strange misanthropic being, but you, child, are even stranger.'

'Do you like me, Mr Devilskein?'

That made him laugh more and from his belly and his eyes glinted in the shadows. 'Indeed I do, Erin, and so do Calvados and the cricket.'

The clock in the vestibule struck eight.

'You should go now,' said Devilskein. 'Your aunt will be waiting to have dinner with you.'

Erin didn't want to leave; she wanted to start working straight away. She was worried that if she went, Mr Devilskein would change his mind, or worse, he would vanish completely and she would wake to find it had all been a dream, or that she was crazy like Kelwyn said she was.

'Run along, child. Be off! Don't try my patience.' He was back to his usual, sour self and Erin was glad, that was how she knew him. So she made for the front door and was at the point of leaving, when he called out to her, 'Whatever happens here, you must never tell another soul. Understand?'

She thought of Kelwyn, of what she had said about the Chinese garden, and decided not to confess anything because that was in the past anyway, and this was a new deal with Mr Devilskein. 'I will never say a word.' *And*, she thought, *I will never speak to Kelwyn again; it's too dangerous.*

'Never is longer than eternity,' said Mr Devilskein, in a cautionary tone.

'Never. Never. Never. I will never speak of this place or what we do.' And Erin meant that with all her heart, because more than anything, she didn't want to lose the wonder of what was behind the doors in apartment 6616. And yet, even as she said those words, somewhere in her mind, she sensed this perfect magic could not last. It was too good to be true.

11

Gardens and Ocean Cabinets

Still excited, Erin ran down the stairs two at a time, ignoring her complaining knee, which was still sore from when she had fallen. When she arrived back in Aunt Kate's flat her face was red and her hair was dishevelled. The kitchen smelled of lamb, sizzling mushrooms, and boiling rice.

'The chops are cooked.' Aunt Kate was frying the mushrooms in olive oil with fresh oregano from the potted herbs on their windowsill. 'I decided to start without you.'

'Sorry I'm so late,' Erin said. 'Mr Devilskein was very talkative tonight.'

'I thought you said he never speaks?' Aunt Kate turned off the stove and transferred the pot of brown rice to the sink where a sieve was waiting to catch the grains, which fell in a billow of salted steam.

As she watched, Erin wondered whether it was okay to mention anything at all that happened in apartment 6616. She decided that it would be fine to talk about the tea. 'Well, we were having a rare tea from a palace in China and that probably made him more chatty than usual.'

'A rare tea from a palace. Wow, that sounds grand.'

After shaking the red colander free of excess water, Kate dished up two servings of rice, added a chop to each and finished it off with mushrooms and Parmesan shavings.

'Yes, he's a bit of a sinophile,' said Erin.

Aunt Kate raised her eyebrows at the word – she was still often surprised by Erin's vocabulary. 'So it seems, what with that mysterious Chinese garden he has hidden behind the turquoise door.' As Aunt Kate placed a plate in front of Erin, her heart sank into her running shoes and she turned pale. Kelwyn! She should never have told him about the Chinese garden.

'No, There's no garden after all, I was making it up.'

In a mood to tease, Aunt Kate carried on. 'But of course there must be, you drew it and it is all spread out on our lounge floor. Kelwyn is positively entranced.'

'Kelwyn! What does he know? I was just joking with him.'

Aunt Kate grinned. 'I hear the two of you spent the afternoon admiring his plants.'

'We did not. I saw his balcony and that's all.'

'And you invited him on a date.' Aunt Kate tucked into her food.

'It was not a date. Nothing of the sort. Besides, I forgot to meet him.'

'So it was a date?'

Erin stared at her aunt and wondered why she was being so cruel.

'Okay, okay. I'm sorry, I'll stop,' said Kate, sensing the child's consternation. 'Eat your dinner. I won't mention Kelwyn again.'

Although supper smelled good, Erin had no appetite; she was worried that if Mr Devilskein knew she had drawn the garden and told Kelwyn about the six doors, and that Kelwyn had then told Aunt Kate, it would be the end of her friendship with Mr Devilskein and she would be fired from her job before she had even started. What would that job be, anyway? She cut and then speared some chop with her fork; she wondered on and never lifted the fork to her mouth.

'If the garden doesn't exist,' said Aunt Kate, watching Erin who was so deep in thought. 'Where'd you get the idea for that sketch? It's brilliant by the way.'

Erin didn't hear the question, she was thinking of keys. Mr Devilskein had been very vague. He had simply said during his mutterings, which were not aimed at her but at himself, that she would become a guardian of keys.

'Erin… Ehhhrin. Hellooo.' Aunt Kate waved a hand in front of Erin's nose. 'Are you ever going to put that piece of chop in your mouth?'

'Oh! Yes, of course.' Erin took a bite and then gathered a forkful of rice and mushrooms, as Aunt Kate continued to praise the quality of the sketches of the Chinese garden. Erin chewed and chewed and occasionally paused to sip water.

After the stabbing incident that afternoon, Long Street was slowly recovering – the police had departed and the eateries were once again filling up. Crocodile tail was being grilled on the stove at Mama Africa, much to the delight of the tourists. Kelwyn had returned home with his latest 'rescue' and both he and the white kitten were curled up on an armchair. When Leilene Talmakies got home she wasn't surprised to see yet another animal in the house, but she was amazed that both Kelwyn and the kitten were fast asleep, in spite of the cacophony of the twins' pre-bedtime mania.

The trauma of the day seemed to follow Kelwyn into his sleep.

He was swimming through icy black water dense with salt. The sky above was a dark void. The unending expanse around him was lifeless in every direction. Kelwyn shivered.

'Erin,' he called. 'I'm here. Erin, where are you?'

There was no reply.

She doesn't like it when I'm friendly, he thought, but he decided he couldn't pretend to be what he wasn't. 'Erin, I'm sorry I didn't believe you about Mr Devilskein. Or the garden.'

Still she did not reply.

'Girls are so difficult to understand,' he muttered. 'I'm apologising. At the very least you could acknowledge it.'

He swam a little further into the salty blackness and decided he should find a way out, and quickly. But then, he heard a strange cry coming from kilometres away. The ghastly sound came nearer and nearer, and when it was almost deafening, from the depths of nowhere leapt a pair of oil-black dolphins travelling at breakneck speed and pulling a vessel in which was seated a shadow; it was a boy, but all the existence had been sucked out of him, leaving him no more than an empty silhouette.

The eerie boy and his dolphins stopped short of tearing through Kelwyn.

'I know who you are,' said the shadowy figure.

'And who are you?' said Kelwyn.

'A friend of Erin's.'

Kelwyn doubted that very much.

The shadow held out a hand. 'You look cold, come and sit here with me.'

Almost against his will Kelwyn took the hand of ice and shadow. Sitting next to the boy Kelwyn felt even colder. His teeth chattered.

From nowhere the shadow boy produced a tiny cup of bitter Turkish coffee.

'Drink, it will warm you,' he commanded. Then the shadow boy smiled, but it was a smile of subtraction; it sapped joy rather than added comfort.

Even so, as soon as Kelwyn drank the coffee he felt warm. Next the boy offered him a leaden square. 'This is the finest chocolate in the universe,' he said.

And indeed, in spite of the weight of it almost bending Kelwyn's tongue, as it melted and trickled down the back of his throat the pleasure of its taste was ecstasy.

'Can I have another piece?' said Kelwyn, instantly addicted.

The supply was unlimited. As Kelwyn ate, the shadow asked questions about Erin, which Kelwyn answered without wondering why the boy wanted to know so much.

Finally, the shadow boy said, 'Clearly she is not interested in you and the best thing you can do for her is let her be alone, if that is what she wants; it is cruel to force your attentions on an unwilling heart.'

Kelwyn nodded.

And then he woke up. A wave of nausea swirled in his belly and he had to push the sleeping kitten aside and run to the bathroom. Over and over, he vomited torrents of clear and very salty water and then one tiny black worm.

'So does Mr Devilskein have books about gardens?' Aunt Kate asked Erin. 'Is that where you got the idea from?'

With a gulp, Erin swallowed a full mouth of brown rice and mushrooms and lied. 'Exactly. That's right. I saw a garden in a book.'

'Still, those sketches are very good. You should show your teacher, when you start school next week–'

'School? What do you mean?' Erin interrupted, newly flustered. She couldn't go to school – she had a job. Mr Devilskein was expecting her to work every day, she had promised.

'Don't be nervous, Erin,' said Aunt Kate. 'It won't be as bad as you think. We're really lucky to have found somewhere with a place for you, and you simply have to go to school. All children have to go to school until a certain age, it's the law. Nobody really wants to go. Especially not after a long…' Aunt Kate wasn't sure what the word was for a time taken off after one's family had been massacred, '…break. A very long break.'

'What if I refuse?'

'They'll send somebody to fetch you. Last week the school counsellor phoned, wanting to see you, so perhaps you can discuss it with her. I thought sooner rather than later, so I told her to come tomorrow morning.'

'*She's coming here?*'

Indeed, the counsellor, Ms Woolly, an attractive woman with bright eyes and a pert nose unspoilt by splayed teeth and a brace, and a Victorian style of dressing, arrived at nine-thirty the next morning. Around her neck she wore a chain with a locket and it caused Erin to speculate whose face she kept trapped inside that little gold sphere. She said she was very pleased to meet Erin and Aunt Kate and that she was very sorry to hear what had happened to Erin's family.

'I'm not,' said Erin. 'Coming here is the best thing that's ever happened to me.'

Ms Woolly took that as a sign of denial. 'Oh, poor child, I know how it feels to lose parents, both of mine passed on recently, too.'

Aunt Kate doubted that Ms Woolly had lost her parents in such an unspeakable way.

'I've almost forgotten them,' said Erin matter-of-factly, as they sat down to drink tea.

Denial or not, Ms Woolly was taken aback and gave a nervous laugh. 'It's part of the process, denial,' she said, as if she knew all the secrets of the universe.

'I'm not denying anything. I saw them both, dead in a

bloody pool on the shaggy white carpet in our mansion. It's just that I don't really care that they're gone.'

All the colour drained from Ms Woolly's plump cheeks. She spooned more sugar into her tea and stirred it briskly.

'That's not exactly true, Erin,' said Aunt Kate, concerned that if she gave the counsellor the wrong impression, the school, the only one with a space for Erin, would refuse to take her.

'Who do you keep trapped in your locket?' Erin eyed the orb at Ms Woolly's neck.

Ms Woolly cleared her throat and managed a kind of half-laugh. She fingered the locket. 'It is a picture of my parents on their wedding day.'

'How sweet,' said Erin. 'You obviously liked your parents.'

'And you did not like yours?'

'I hardly knew them. Anyway what does it matter? Aunt Kate is looking after me now and she's lovely. Of the five people in the world who I like, she is one of them.'

Ms Woolly frowned and then smiled and turned to Aunt Kate. 'Would you mind leaving us to talk for half an hour? I often find children feel more relaxed in one-on-one sessions.'

'If that's okay with you, Erin?' asked Aunt Kate.

'Sure. Ms Woolly isn't exactly a crocodile, is she?'

That caused the counsellor to chuckle nervously again. Erin noticed that her dark hair was streaked with strands of white. Her skin was youthful except around her eyes where there were lots of wrinkles.

'Okay then,' said Aunt Kate, standing. 'If you need me, Erin, I'll be at the Talmakies' place, it's Leilene's morning off.' And she said to the counsellor. 'Please phone me when you're done.'

When Aunt Kate closed the door behind her, Ms Woolly asked Erin, 'who are the five people you like?'

'Aunt Kate, Kelwyn, Mr Devilskein, the crick…' Erin stopped. Could she speak about the cricket without breaking her word to Mr Devilskein?

'Who?'

'A boy called Cricket. The fifth is a poodle. They all live here in Van Riebeek Heights.'

'I see. And does your Aunt take good care of you?'

'Yes. Better than my parents, even though she is poor and has no luck with men.' Erin looked at Ms Woolly's fingers and saw no rings. 'She's like you, I guess. You have no luck with men either, do you Ms Woolly?'

Ms Woolly rubbed her forehead and smiled with closed lips. 'You're too thin. Anorexia may seem glamorous because models look that way, but I assure you it isn't.'

'I'm much fatter than I was when I arrived. Isn't it rude to comment on a person's weight though? I mean how would you feel if I said you were too fat and that's probably why you have no luck with men?'

'As a matter of fact, I have fair enough luck with men,' said Ms Woolly, but her face looked unhappy and her eyes, though on Erin, were caught in some recent memory of a cheating lover. 'This is not about me, though. This is about you and your reasons for not wanting to go to school. What are you concerned about?'

'Nothing.'

'So then, why are you refusing to go?'

'I have a job.' The minute she'd said it, Erin knew it was a mistake.

'A job? You are too young for a job. Does your Aunt Kate make you go to this job?'

'No! Not at all, she knows nothing about it. It's not a job like that. I don't get paid, it's volunteer work really.'

'Oh yes? And where do you do this work?'

Erin felt trapped. '"Work" is probably the wrong word for it. It's playing. It's at Mr Devilskein's apartment.'

'He works from home?' Ms Woolly made a note on a lined page in a small black diary.

'Yes, ma'am.'

'And where is that exactly?'

Surely it could not harm to say where the place was, as long as she did not mention what went on behind the six doors. 'Top floor, apartment number 6616.'

Ms Woolly's mouth fell open. She automatically reached for her locket. '6616?' she asked in a worried voice. 'And he calls himself Devilskein?'

'His full name is Albertus Devilskein. You don't need to look so frightened, Ms Woolly. He's a bit of a grouch, but on the whole an extraordinary individual.'

'Is that so?' Ms Woolly clutched her locket and thought of her parents; her father had been a minister in the small town where she grew up. She had learned to read with the Bible as her first book. And in that book, three sixes in close proximity had a dark and terrible significance. 'I would like to meet this Mr Devilskein.' She stood up. 'Will you take me to him?'

A lump formed in Erin's throat. 'Now?' she said tremulously.

'It is office hours. If he works from home, he will be there. Yes. Now.'

What could Erin say?

'Don't look so horrified, Erin. I only wish to speak to the man. Surely he will not mind that.'

'He will. He's disfigured…'

Ms Woolly's eyes widened in fresh surprise.

'He avoids people in general, but otherwise he is a respectable individual. You cannot visit him. That would be unfair.'

'Ahh,' said Ms Woolly in a fashion that made it sound as if everything was suddenly clear. Indeed, she used her powers of deduction and arrived at the conclusion that this man obviously chose that number to make his flat off-putting to casual visitors and that he chose to avoid people because of his hideous appearance. 'Fine, well, come to school next week and we will continue to have these sessions every Thursday afternoon.'

'Why must I go to school?'

'It is essential.' Ms Woolly had a cunning thought. 'And if you do not come to school, I will be forced to pay Mr Devilskein a visit.'

Erin shook her head. 'You'll ruin everything. He'll leave and...' her voice quavered.

'There is no need to be so dramatic.' Ms Woolly gave her a broad and pleasant smile. 'Simply come to school, like every other child in Cape Town.'

'Will they teach me about the ancient Cambodian empire of Angkor?'

Ms Woolly was startled by her obscure request. 'Angkor! What makes you ask that?'

'I have a friend,' Erin faltered. 'Ah, my friend, Cricket, he has been telling me about it. He lived there for a while.'

'Do you enjoy History?' asked Ms Woolly. 'Studying things past?'

'If that is what they are,' said Erin. 'But as far as I can tell nothing is really past if you can walk through a door and find it all over ag–, I mean open a book. If you know about it, the past is not past, it's just in a different room, isn't it?'

'Nothing is past,' said Ms Woolly to herself, and she remembered something that had made her sad. She gazed at Erin for a long moment and then rubbed her eyes and stood up. 'It has been a pleasure to meet you, Erin Dearlove. I must go now.'

She telephoned Aunt Kate to advise her of her imminent

departure, and Aunt Kate, who had been having coffee with Kelwyn's mother (while Kelwyn was at school, like most other children on that day), came back home to thank the counsellor for her visit. She walked Ms Woolly down to the ground floor.

As they shook hands, Ms Woolly said, 'Now that I have spoken to Erin, I understand what you mean. She is a most unusual child, capable of advanced thinking for her age and, well, her relationship with your disfigured neighbour upstairs indicates great compassion. You don't need to worry, she's bright, and hopefully these past six months off school won't have too much of a negative effect on her overall school career. I would like to give Erin an IQ test; I suspect she is highly intelligent.'

Aunt Kate was pleased. And she was relieved to hear that she didn't need to worry about Erin's lack of schooling. She had so enjoyed getting to know her niece that she hadn't really made too much effort to organise the whole school thing – it was only when Kelwyn's mother had urged Kate to organise school for Erin that she'd begun to feel guilty at her laxness in that matter. And then she'd begun to worry that she'd caused Erin some serious damage by not sending her to school sooner.

'However,' said Ms Woolly, shouting over the roar of a speeding refuse van with four men in brown overalls hanging from its back end. 'From Monday she must attend school, otherwise I'm going to have to contact social services.'

Back in the apartment, Aunt Kate tried to be encouraging about school (even though she had hated it herself). 'You'll be able to have art lessons,' she said. 'That school has an excellent art department. It is one of the nicest things to do. And perhaps you can take an afternoon activity, like dance?'

'I have to be with Mr Devilskein in the afternoons,' Erin said woefully. 'I've promised him.'

'Now Erin,' Aunt Kate was unusually solemn. 'I know you're fond of Mr Devilskein, but you do need friends your own age. It's normal and healthy to socialise with other children and it can be fun.' Aunt Kate nearly said, surely you remember? Because Kate had often heard from her sister that Erin loved school and was a gregarious child with many friends. But Erin had refused contact with any of those friends offering their sympathies; she had deleted emails, refused phone calls and returned letters without opening them.

'So you say.' Erin didn't sound convinced. She thought only of the Chinese garden, which she wouldn't have time to go to if she had to go to school. When would there be an hour to tend the Courtyard of Sorrow, especially if she was the key guardian too, whatever that was? And she might have gone into a sulk, but something caught her eye. Zhou had landed on one of the sketches she'd done of the garden. She ran over to him and scooped him up in her hand. 'I will never abandon you,' she whispered, even though Aunt Kate was in the room and could hear.

Aunt Kate only smiled, thinking what an endearing imagination Erin had. Then she got to work on her still life of oranges in a crate, but as she painted she decided that as Erin's guardian she should at some stage go up and investigate this Mr Devilskein, even though Erin would probably be against the idea. She dipped her brush into a pot of linseed oil and then mixed it into a patch of cadmium orange; the kitchen clock ticked loudly; the baby with another bout of colic wailed in the distance; and two doors down a renegade worm munched the pristine leaves of one of Kelwyn's beloved plants, while Kelwyn, whose young heart was utterly entranced by the impossible Erin (so damaged, so aloof and so talented), decided he would give her all the space she needed and never bother her again. Still, when he closed his eyes he imagined kissing her, a proper French kiss. Only the beleaguered plant witnessed his blush.

12

I Am Julius Monk

With the cricket in one hand, Erin gathered up the sketches of the Chinese garden. 'I'll be back later,' she said to Aunt Kate.

'Take this,' Aunt Kate held out her mobile phone. 'Please phone me if you're going to be late.'

'Will do,' promised Erin as she left. Even though she had not been invited to start work at any particular time or day, Erin decided it would be that Friday because there were only three days left until Monday and the start of school.

She knocked on the door of apartment 6616. 'It's me, Erin Dearlove,' she shouted, pressing her cheek against the door.

'Go away, I'm busy,' called Mr Devilskein from within.

'But I am here to do the work you said I could do.'

After much grumbling and muttering, Mr Devilskein opened up. He was dressed just as smartly as yesterday, in fact, Erin thought, except for his cravats, he seemed to wear exactly the same type of outfit every day: a hat, a cane, fine leather shoes, a waistcoat, a jacket, an overcoat – all in the same shade of near-black. Today's three-piece suit was complemented by a cravat featuring diamond shapes. In one hand he had a handkerchief, in the other, a cigarette; his hairless brows were knitted over his hawk-like eyes and his beakish nose. Erin also realised that no matter if it was steaming hot outside, or windy and cold, the climate in Mr Devilskein's flat was always the same: cool and gloomy.

'Are you sure I said I had work for you?' he asked, gruffly.

'Were you sleeping? You sound a bit sleepy. I'm sorry if I woke you up.'

He curled his lips in disdain. 'Sleep? I have no time to sleep! What a preposterous idea.'

'I brought something to give you because I don't want anybody else to see it, after our deal and all.'

'We made a deal?'

'Yes! Are you losing your memory, old man?'

'How unwise,' he grunted and ushered her in with a wave of the hanky. 'I suppose I do know what you're talking about, but "deal" is not the right word for it. Be careful of deals, child. For the most part, deal-makers are an undesirable sort.'

'Well you made the deal, so that makes you an undesirable sort.'

'Exactly.'

Erin frowned.

'We should have a cup of tea,' he said, ambling through to the shadows to the kitchen. 'All this conversation is draining.'

'Do you ever turn any lights on?' She glanced right at the six doors: still there and still coloured as she remembered them.

'I am more a creature of the dark than of the light. Shadows are more becoming to my complexion.'

In the kitchen of shoebox towers, two cups and a full pot of freshly brewed tea were waiting on the table, almost as if he had indeed been expecting Erin, or at least somebody. He sat down to commence the tea ceremony.

'I'll lay this out on the floor, so you can see.' Without waiting for his consent, she began to arrange the sketches of the Chinese garden on the floor beside the table. He watched in silence and when Calvados came sauntering in he told the poodle to walk around the forming landscape. When it was all set out, Erin looked up at Mr Devilskein expectantly. He smoked his cigarette and said nothing.

'So, do you like it?' asked Erin, eventually.

'Does it make a difference? Do you consider yourself an artist?'

'No, but...'

'Good. Because you are no artist if you seek the approval of a viewer. There is nothing of true value that exists for the purpose of approval, such a vacuous and vain entity; approval is so contrary to the spirit of creation.'

'Blah, blah. I think you're quite rude. I'm giving you the sketches anyway, whether you think they are rubbish or not.'

'I certainly do not think they are rubbish. I told you before, you have a gift. Now drink your tea or it will get cold. And please stop talking, it makes my head ache.'

In silence then, they sat drinking tea and Mr Devilskein finished his cigarette and lit another. As he did, by sheer coincidence, winter approached the town. After a long while, Erin said, 'I have to start going to school on Monday. Still, I will come every afternoon to work, as guardian of keys.'

'School, pah! There is a small hell for some.' He smiled. 'You are sure to hate it.' He stood up and smoothed his waistcoat flat. A frown skimmed his forehead, for if anyone in the Company got wind of the fact that he had begun a project of sorting the keys, it would be the end of him. 'Well then, we'd better get on with the task, otherwise you won't know what to do when you come on Monday. I will not be here. So you will let yourself in.' He paused. 'You are good at that already, are you not?'

Erin blushed. 'Are you cross with me?'

'Crossness is a form of pettiness; I wouldn't waste my time with that. I am eternally furious.' He eyeballed her and in response she grinned and Mr Devilskein was pleased with his choice: as long as there were keys to sort, the grumpy girl and her soulmate could live, and he would cut back on pork crackling, butter and cigars and survive on the wretched pills until he could make another plan.

From the depths of nowhere, he produced a bunch of keys like Erin had never seen before. 'Behold the keys!'

'There must be five hundred there,' said Erin, touching one of the many ornate, angular and different sorts of keys on the bunch.

'It would be impossible to count them. They are keys related to the turquoise door, which is one you know well by now, and that is why I am making these keys your first charge. Do not ask questions of the keys, and if they talk to you, do not listen, for they lie. Your job will be to make a reckoning of every key, its door and what it keeps safe.'

A blue-spotted gecko scuttled across the wall over the kitchen sink.

Erin opened her mouth to ask something, but Mr Devilskein shushed her with a wave of his hanky.

'I will give you a book of accounting. Draw each key, find each lock, and note what its keepsake is, sketch that too; close and lock each door and return the key to the bunch. Never forget to lock each door.'

'Why? What will happen?'

'You will be responsible for any loss. Understand that everything behind these doors is priceless beyond all conception.' He closed his eyes, momentarily angry that for so many millennia his loyalty to the Company had led him to trick and betray so many exceptional souls.

'And you trust me with it all.'

'Out of necessity, I do, but remember to say nothing of this to any other breathing being.'

Mr Devilskein produced a giant, leather-bound antique tome, a thousand pages, all blank. 'Begin now. And work with utmost care.'

So Erin chose a key and sketched it; how fine a sketch it was! Quite exquisite in its rendering, and Mr Devilskein was pleased. Then came the task of finding the door beyond the turquoise door that would take the key. It was a dizzying task in powers of six. She discovered that every door on the way to the matching door would accept the key, but every door on the incorrect path would stay locked and there would be no revelation of the keepsake until the matching door had been located. As if in a single breath, a whole day passed by, during which Erin matched only a single key with its treasure: a walk-in safe containing several undiscovered plays by William Shakespeare. In a flash, she remembered how her father had read Shakespeare to her using different voices for the different parts. He'd had her in stitches with All's Well That Ends Well. Erin had to fight the urge to steal the plays in order to read them. She simply couldn't resist dipping into at least one. It was about a king and his family who were murdered by their courtiers and before she knew it two hours had slipped by and nothing had been drawn.

It was after ten o'clock when Erin arrived home and Aunt Kate almost shouted at her for the very first time. 'You promised you'd phone, Erin, I was worried.'

'Sorry.'

'I thought you were sulking about school.'

'No, nothing like that. I'm sorry, really. I was busy with Mr Devilskein.'

'Gardening?'

'No. Something more complicated.'

'What?'

'I can't say and I'm too tired to talk. I have to go to bed.'

For the first time Aunt Kate really felt like a mother – she had been so anxious about Erin. Without doubt, she would have to visit that Mr Devilskein.

While Kate sat drinking hot chocolate and worrying (like mothers do), Erin collapsed into bed and was soon sleeping. However, later that night she woke to a sound of a wuthering South Easter. 'How strange,' she murmured between dreams. 'There was no wind earlier.' Gradually, she became more alert. 'It is not wind,' she said, sitting upright. Erin got out of bed and followed the miserable sound, a soft wailing. By then Aunt Kate was also asleep and the flat was in darkness and all quiet, save the soft ticking of the kitchen clock, the hum of the fridge, and the drip-drip-drip of the bathroom tap. She tiptoed to their front door and let herself out. 'It's coming from above,' Erin whispered to herself and then she headed for the stairwell.

It was beyond late, and as the tourist season was over the bars and nightclubs of Long Street were closed. Only the strange crying could be heard. The stairwell was eerie and dank; the only light came from the lamps in the street below. Cockroaches watched from the gutters as Erin progressed slowly upwards until finally she was at the top floor. The sorry sound drifted along the corridor. 'It's coming from Mr Devilskein's apartment! Somebody is crying in there!' She stopped, uncertain whether or not to continue. 'Could it be Mr Devilskein?' It did not sound like his voice, it sounded younger. Erin decided to carry on, her bare feet silently padding along the dusty passage, leaving behind a trail of size-four footprints.

When she arrived at the door of 6616, she pressed her ear against it and listened. The crying was definitely coming from in there. Recalling that in spite of the gigantic bunches of keys

Mr Devilskein possessed, he had a habit of leaving this front door unlocked, she turned the handle. The door opened and she stole into the vestibule with her heart racing, uncertain of who or what she would find there. It was dark, there was no sign of Devilskein and so she had more time to look around than usual. It was a handsome room. In addition to the six startling doors, there was some very fine antique furniture and art, pieces and paintings from many countries and periods. Though Erin knew nothing about either, the eccentric lavishness of the place made it evident, even to her untrained eye, that Mr Devilskein must be very rich. But why, then, did he live at a place like Van Riebeek Heights?

As if sensing there was a new presence in the apartment, the crying became louder; it was coming from behind one of the six doors, the yellow door.

Erin blinked three times and pinched herself to check that she was actually where she thought she was and not dreaming, for suddenly the strangeness of it hit her. It all seemed like an elaborate dream or a vision: the place, the doors, the crying. She had found that ever since the death of her parents, her dreams had become so vivid that often she would pause inside a dream and ask herself if it was imagined or reality. One way she had of checking the validity of a dream was to find a high place and jump from it: invariably, in her dreams, before she could crash to the ground and death, she would flap her arms, which acted as wings and soon she would be flying.

She did not want to make a noise by jumping off a table right then, so she took the flesh of her thigh between her fingers and dug in her nails and it hurt; she concluded that she was not dreaming. She tried the handle of the yellow door. It opened. Knowing the rule of 'nothingness without the right key', she did not expect to see anything inside that room, but instead she was dumbfounded. There were candles everywhere. There was a bed, like in any ordinary bedroom, except this bed was anything but ordinary, the ceiling was impossibly high and all the way up the walls were lined with bookshelves bereft of books, and beyond the bed there was a screen, a chaise-longue and a writing desk.

Slumped over the latter, was a youth, with inky hands, crying. He had long honey-brown hair. He heard Erin entering and looked up. His face was angular and his eyes beautiful, but they were full of youthful rage, the eyes of boy who hated with good reason.

'What are you?' he said at last between his sobs and wails. 'A demon? A spirit? A dream?'

'None of those, I hope,' said Erin. 'And you?'

He frowned and rubbed his nose with the back of his hand and stared at her, as if she ought to vanish, but she did not. After several minutes, he said, 'I am Julius Monk, bastard son of the Devil.'

One vicious, unthinkable memory tore through Erin's mind: *her mother screaming hysterically, 'HAVE MERCY!' at the man who then shot her son execution style. 'DEVIL! YOU'RE NOT A MAN, YOU'RE THE DEVIL!'* But Erin forced the memory away with all her might – it must have been some bad movie she'd seen, she thought – and said 'Well, I am Erin Dearlove. I live downstairs with my Aunt Kate. And what do you mean by "the Devil"?'

'My father. I am cursed.'

'I don't believe in curses and there is no such thing as the Devil,' said Erin, although she was not sure why she said it. These thoughts seemed to come from a different Erin, maybe a dream of a previous her. 'I do not believe in good or evil, those are just convenient words used by people wanting to understand an unfathomable universe.'

The youth stopped crying. 'Come closer. Let me look

149

at you properly.' He struck a match and touched the flame to a candle beside the notebook he had been working in. The air smelled of sulphur and whale oil. Apart from the book and a quill there was a pack of playing cards on the desk. Tentatively, Erin drew closer. He put out a hand with long nails and touched her face. 'You feel like a living creature, not a dream. Often I dream so vividly, I think my dreams are real. Where did you come from?'

'I told you, downstairs. I also have that thing with dreams. Then I pinch myself and if it isn't sore, I know it is a dream. Shall I pinch you?' She did not wait for his consent; she just reached forward and took the flesh of his left check between her fingers and pinched it as hard as she could.

'Ouch!' He jerked away and rubbed his cheek with his elegant fingers, but he smiled too. 'What do you mean "downstairs"? What made you come here?'

'Crying. I thought it was the wind at first, but then I realised it was a person, and this is not the first time I have heard you. Why are you so sad?'

He laughed, but this was not a happy sound either, and it echoed around the empty bookshelves. 'You would be too if you were doomed to an eternity in the Haga.'

'The what?'

'This place, my home, if you will: it is called the Haga. What did you say your name was?'

'Erin Dearlove. Do you know about the yellow door and the keys?'

'What door?' He seemed briefly frightened. 'There can be no doors in this place! It is the Haga.'

'Of course there are, how do you think I got here? There –' Erin turned around to point at the yellow door, but it was no longer there. Her breath caught in her throat. 'It's gone. How could that happen?' She was mystified, and a little scared. The eternal whale oil candle sputtered.

'Because it never was there, except perhaps in my dreams. You must be a dream. I have no visitors, I cannot be permitted to talk or see or hear anything of the world beyond the Haga. Otherwise I may become a monster, a devil, like my father.' His eyes gleamed with duplicity.

'Oh, this apartment is crazy!' Erin said. 'All these rooms and locks and keys and secrets and treasures. You must be a kind of treasure if you are here. You must be precious to somebody.'

He was momentarily touched. 'Hard to imagine.'

'No. Mr Devilskein told me that all things behind these doors are priceless treasures. So what you are saying is wrong, or did Mr Devilskein just make that up? You're not a prisoner, are you?'

'Not exactly – I agreed to it. I stay in the Haga because the consequences of me being anywhere else are too horrible to conceive.'

'Nobody visits you, ever?'

'Who would want to?'

'Why would they not? What do you do here all day and all night?'

'I play six by six solitaire.'

Erin knew very little about card games, but the name solitaire caused her sudden uneasiness; she reached for her owl brooch, but of course it was not there. 'Where's your mother?'

An angry shadow darkened the youth's expression. 'She's dead. She died giving birth to me.'

'I'm sorry. My mother is dead too. Eaten by a crocodile. I don't miss her though. I have Aunt Kate and Mr Devilskein and the cricket.'

'Who is this Mr Devilskein you keep talking about?'

'Ah, he is…' Erin didn't know if she was permitted to talk about him or if that would be breaking the deal she'd made with Devilskein. 'Somebody I know. How long have you been here?'

'Always.'

'That's impossible. You must have been born somewhere with doors! Otherwise how did your poor mother get in and out of the place?'

He gave her a strange look with a half-smile. 'You're cunning. Are you sure you're not a demon?'

'Of course, I'm sure. I'm not a dream and I'm not a demon. I'm just a girl who lives downstairs at Van Riebeek Heights. Next week I'm starting school, which I'll probably loathe, and if I was a demon, I wouldn't have to go to school, would I?' She looked about her: up at the ceiling, which was high with wooden beams, and at the floor, which was tiled with black marble. 'I must say though, this place is like nothing I have ever seen before; it is very like a dream, and yet you insist it is real.'

'I'm glad you are not a demon and that you are real,' the youth said, 'but the consequences of your being here could be dire.'

Erin yawned. She needed to go back to bed. 'Should I leave then? Would you prefer that?'

'No, no! Please, stay. Sit. Tell me about this place you call "Downstairs".'

Even though she was exhausted, Erin was glad he didn't want her to go. She climbed up onto the end of the four-poster bed; it was high and her feet did not touch the ground. 'So,' she folded one leg under the other, getting more comfortable. 'What exactly do you want to know?'

'Everything.' Indeed, Julius Monk had not, as far as he could remember, seen beyond the Haga. He had a stream of questions, and Erin answered everything as best she could, even though some of her answers perplexed him. He sat with his chin resting in his hands and drank in all her stories of Van Riebeek Heights, Long Street, and life beyond the Haga. Some of the things she said amused him immensely and he laughed, this time with delight. When he asked about Mr Devilskein, she was evasive, not wanting to say much at all. She, in turn, learned that in the Haga, Julius Monk was never hungry or thirsty, even though he did not eat or drink.

'But how do you grow, then?'

He shook his head. 'I do not grow. I do not change. I do not age. I will eternally be the age I was when I arrived here.'

'That's impossible, if you're living.'

'I am fifteen forever.' He sounded matter-of-fact about it and did not find it strange at all; it was the reality he was accustomed to and he did not wish to dwell upon it. But he loved the sound of Erin's voice and her tales and he wanted to talk on and on. Eventually she curled up on the bed, still at the end though, but facing him. She told him of more wonders of the town and began to feel extremely drowsy, but though she closed her eyes, she carried on talking – and answering his questions. She was entranced by him, and without realising it, she told him all about her job as guardian of the keys. When she almost fell asleep mid-story, he said something that made her eyes spring open.

'I think I have met Mr Devilskein,' he said.

'How, suddenly after all this conversation, do you know him?' She was a bit cross, she thought he might be trying to trick her into saying things she shouldn't, but she couldn't remember saying anything she shouldn't have said.

'You were right when you said I must have been born elsewhere. Yes. I must have been, and you were right when you said I couldn't grow if I didn't eat or drink.'

Erin sat up. 'And you're fifteen.'

'Exactly.'

'So you must have spent some years elsewhere.'

Julius Monk, son of the Devil, nodded. 'There is a dream

I often have about a man who cared for me as a child. In fact, in my dream, that man is the one who catches me as I am born. In the dream I remember being born. He fed me, he protected me. He set a pair of dolphins the task of being my friends.'

'What did he look like?'

Standing, Julius Monk looked at himself in a mirror on the wall beside him. 'When I see my reflection, my skin is smooth, my features regular. But that man was something else to behold.'

'Disfigured? Monstrous?' Erin said.

'Until I saw you, I thought I must be the disfigured one, but now I look at you and you are lovely. And your skin is so soft and smooth. It makes me –'

Erin had gone quite red.

'I'm sorry, I didn't mean to embarrass you,' Julius Monk said. 'I was just trying to explain that, ah, the man was different from both of us and so perhaps you are right to say he is disfigured. I definitely remember that he has one ear missing.'

'That is the same Mr Devilskein.' Erin stared. It had never yet occurred to her that a boy might be anything but irksome like Kelwyn, but this Julius Monk make her feel strange, she felt like she wanted to be near him, even to kiss him, even though she had never kissed a boy.

'Do you think you will always be in this place?' she asked.

'No doubt. It is for the best.' He was indifferent, or at least playing at being indifferent.

'Why? Don't you want to live, to experience the world? To eat and drink and grow?'

The angry shadow returned to his face. 'I do not want to be here but I do not want to be out there. This is my limbo. When I think about it, I cry.'

'And that is what I heard: you crying. It's a heart-wrenching sound.'

'Let's not talk about it. Tell me about Mr Devilskein. I'm sure he is the one who once looked after me. It means I must have lost most of my memories of any life before here.'

'I cannot say more about him,' warned Erin in a low voice. 'I promised him.'

'Please, don't be cruel.' He had become quite wild-eyed. 'Do you understand this could be a breakthrough for me. I have no idea how long I have been in this limbo, frozen without even memories to keep me company. Tell me about him, please.'

Erin's heart constricted. If he pressed her further she might not be able to hold back. Something about him caused her to chatter like she had never done before; he was so engaging, he was hard to resist. She felt she wanted him to like her, but she knew she must be careful.

'I can't! I can't say any more. It will ruin everything.'

He was an expert manipulator; he had been born with a talent for it. He stared at her as if she was heartless and unreasonable. 'How? You are being so mean. Everything is already ruined for me, and you have the whole world to enjoy, the sky, the sea, the mountains, a long street full of curious people, neighbours, friends... You have all that and all I ask is for a little information, nothing grand, nothing extreme.' He came and stood at the bed next to her and took her hands. 'I crave to find my memories and you have the answers to my questions. I need to know about this Mr Devilskein. Please, Erin Dearlove, have mercy and tell me more.'

Closer up, his eyes were more beautiful. 'If I tell you,' she said, 'you must promise not tell anyone. It must be a secret.'

'Who could I tell? My whole existence is a secret.'

'Promise,' pleaded Erin. 'I shouldn't be saying anything at all...'

'Okay, I promise.'

So she began to explain about the vestibule and the six

doors and the multitude of doors leading from those doors.

'Perhaps, if you feel brave, you could come through the yellow door with me sometime, just to glimpse the world outside of the Haga. We could take a walk down Long Street.' She smiled. 'There are shops and cafés. We could have coffee or, no, a milkshake would be nicer.'

His smile was charming but wily and he went and sat next to her. 'I would like that very much,' he said, with a look of innocent wonder in his eyes, as if suddenly there was a possibility of something other than the Haga. 'It could not be for long, of course,' he said, quickly. 'I must return. You understand.'

She nodded, enthusiastic at the prospect of showing him Long Street. Never before had she thought of it as such a marvellous place, but compared to the Haga's eternal gloom it was full of life and excitement.

'Tell me more about Long Street.' He lay back and stared up at the drapery of the four-poster bed's canopy.

She regaled him with its scents and colours and sights. She told him about the South Easter and about running at sunrise. And she told him about her aunt and the cricket.

'I did not know insects could talk,' he said, but he was being forgetful, or perhaps deceitful.

'Zhou is not an ordinary cricket. Perhaps you can meet him too and hear about his experiences in the royal court of Angkor. If you stay in the Haga all the time, you will miss out on so much. If you are not a prisoner, then why come back?'

He sat up and took her quite gently by the shoulders. 'I know you do not understand, but trust me, I must return. However, one glimpse of the street can surely do no harm. I will come back and then I will never leave here again, and you must not return either.'

Erin looked down. The cut on her knee had already

begun to heal. 'You're right, I don't understand.'

She looked doubtful; perhaps she was having second thoughts about being there at all. To guarantee her return, to arouse her sympathy further, he decided he would allow her a glimpse of how painful it was to be inside his soul.

'I'm going to show you something.' He went to his desk and gathered up the book he had been writing in. He placed it on her lap. 'Open to any page and read.'

She did so and read and simultaneously as each word filtered through her brain she recoiled. They were unlike any words she had read before, so vivid, they seemed not to be words but rather images, and the images were of multiple horrors and the bloody ends of worlds. Almost immediately, she slammed the book shut. What she had seen was too much for her young and mortal mind to process. She had been tired before, but what she saw in those seconds exhausted her completely.

'I am glad you came here,' said Julius Monk. 'But you are tired now. Go back to your "Downstairs". And when the time is right, Erin Dearlove, please return, for I would like to see Long Street. Now you should go.'

She nodded and, still dazed, climbed off the bed. 'I don't know what that book is, and it doesn't matter to me anyway. I will come back, Julius.'

'And I will keep your secrets. Perhaps one day, I will teach you to play solitaire.'

'I'd like that,' she said over her shoulder as she walked away. At her first thought of the yellow door, it appeared and she was through it and Julius Monk was gone. Now there was only the gloomy vestibule. She crept out of apartment 6616 and back down the dusty corridor. The sky was already becoming light. The only evidence of her night-time visit was a double trail of size four footprints.

13

A Young Demon

On that Saturday, Long Street was made eerie by a mist so thick that neither the mountain on the right nor the sea on the left were visible; in fact, nothing beyond a metre of where one stood could be seen. The mist made everything quiet and cool, and everyone who was out walking there on that morning felt alone. This was as true for the beggar in skinny jeans and sheepskin slippers as it was for the woman in the floral skirt who near knocked over the poor man as she sped to work on her white Vespa. The mist had stolen all the energy from the street and the traffic moved as if in a dream. And on his balcony where the white kitten was curled up on bag of potting soil, Kelwyn gently spritzed the earth around a glorious magenta orchid he had named Erin.

When the doorbell rang, his mother directed Sipho, aka Rover 2, to the balcony.

'Got the flyers,' said Sipho, waving some photocopied pages at Kelwyn.

Found: White kitten, outside Zula Sound Bar. No name tag. Not chipped. If he's yours, please phone Kelwyn.

*

Two doors down, the orchid's namesake wanted to ask her aunt a question, but as Kate had just secured a buyer for her series of 'fruits in crates' paintings, the last one of which was very near completion, she was busy painting and listening to music through her headphones and clearly didn't want to be interrupted. Erin was perched on a barstool near the open window that usually had a side-view of a fragment of Lion's Head Mountain, but today there was nothing to see but glum, stifling mist. She was thinking about Julius Monk. Could he really be the son of the Devil? No, surely not. Erin didn't believe in the Devil. It was hard enough to believe there could be oceans and gardens beyond six doors in a fusty apartment on Long Street, and yet, there they were, so perhaps? No!

She heard a chirrup, and there was Zhou the cricket on the windowsill.

'What's up with you?' he asked. 'Why the frown? Why so deep in thought? Has something happened?'

'Yes.' Erin decided it was fine to speak to Zhou, since he knew everything about apartment 6616, and she trusted him not to tell Mr Devilskein. 'Last night, I heard crying coming from upstairs, from the top floor. At first I thought it was the South Easter, but it wasn't.'

'Impossible!' the cricket made a consternated trill. 'There was nobody crying on the top floor last night.'

She stared beyond the cricket, remembering Julius Monk's beautiful eyes. Then her attention and her gaze returned to Zhou. 'It was especially loud, so I followed the sound up the stairs, to the top floor. It was coming from Mr Devilskein's apartment. I went in and then through the yellow door. It was a boy called Julius Monk who was weeping. He was in a place he calls the Haga.'

The cricket's chirps became frenzied and he started flying round in tight circles. 'Oh, Erin! Oh Erin!' he chirruped in fright. 'You could not have! You should not have! What a bad habit I have taught you to go into Mr Devilskein's home without permission! I will be in trouble. All will be in danger. I said nothing! I said nothing. He will banish me. Oh! What is to become of me!'

'Don't be daft,' Erin said. 'Mr Devilskein need not know. Julius won't say anything to him. And I certainly won't. Nobody will banish you. And all we did was talk. Julius is terribly lonely. I know how it feels to be lonely. Julius was glad to have company.'

'He was? And he let you leave?' cried the cricket. 'Without a scratch? The young demon allowed you to go? He did not unleash his unfathomable wrath upon you? You have no idea what danger you were in, or what kind of creature that Julius Monk is. Neither your body nor your soul are safe in his presence. Oh, oh! Oh, you foolish girl, Erin!'

'You're so dramatic, Zhou, really,' she rolled her eyes. 'He's not a demon. He's just a lonely boy who's seen nothing of the outside world. There was no sign of unfathomable wrath.' She thought of the horrifying book he had been working on, but said nothing of it. 'I would have left sooner, but he wanted me to stay. I told him about the town, about Long Street and Van Riebeek Heights. He was delighted by it all and I've promised to go back.'

'What? Never, you cannot go back there. As it is you were lucky to leave. You are too young to know what evil is, to understand the peril you were in. There is no other living soul who has looked him in the eyes and lived to speak of it.'

'Don't be absurd! Julius has the most beautiful blue eyes flecked with green.'

'Beautiful? What? You mean you looked into those fearsome eyes?' The cricket was more agitated than Erin imagined any cricket could ever be.

'In fact, we gazed at each other.'

'Gazed at Julius Monk! Upon my word, what a tragedy. You are doomed, I am doomed. What will Mr Devilskein do when he finds out? He will squash me with his foot. For all these centuries, he has trusted me and now he will crush me for being a traitor.'

'Relax, Zhou. I don't understand why you're so worried – you had nothing to do with me meeting Julius. I did that myself. And neither Julius nor I will say anything to Mr Devilskein. So, Zhou, as long as you don't say anything,' said Erin, firmly, 'my visits to Julius will stay a secret.'

'Visits? Plural?' The cricket collapsed, his legs splayed out on the windowsill.

'Yes, Julius Monk has asked me to return when it is safe and I will, because I enjoyed his company, which is rare. I don't often enjoy the company of boys.'

'You like me though.'

'Well, you're not like most boys. So anyway, I'd like you to help us – to let me know when Mr Devilskein and Calvados are out, so that it is safe to visit. I don't want to visit when I'm working on accounting for the keys because that would be wrong.'

'"Wrong", you say? There is nothing right or good about any of this and if Mr Devilskein finds out I knew what was going on yet said nothing – I am doomed for sure!'

'Nobody is doomed.'

'You are doomed, Erin, if you return, perhaps you are already. Child, you have no concept of how vicious Julius Monk is, of what darkness is in his heart, and what power is his to wield.'

'Stop exaggerating. He likes me. He'll do me no harm.'

'You are putting your faith in the son of the Devil?' the cricket tut-tutted. 'Let me tell you how black with poison that creature's heart is.'

'Don't, if you are going to launch into another crazy exaggeration.'

The cricket ignored her. 'Take all the worst of men in history: the tyrants, the vile abusers, the destroyers of joy and innocence, distil them to a strong collective essence and multiply it by ten thousand and then you have only a fraction of the blackness in the heart of Julius Monk. Only a fraction!'

Erin rolled her eyes again. 'Zhou, I don't know what has got into you. Julius Monk was nothing but pleasant and curious. All these crazy things you're claiming of him, I just can't believe you, I'm sorry! He has been locked away his whole life in that doorless limbo called the Haga.'

During all this Aunt Kate was making excellent progress with her portrait of oranges. The cricket stared up at Erin and considered her for some moments. 'Perhaps you are in possession of some saintly magic? Otherwise, surely you would not be here today.'

'Magic is for fairy tales, Zhou. I have no magic, but I assure you that I do not believe in saints or demons. There is no good or evil, there just is the universe.'

'Ah, so wrong you are Erin.' The cricket was agitated and once again flying in circles. 'The world will end. You cannot go back to the Haga. I don't know how you managed to find a way inside in the first place.'

'I told you, I followed his crying and I walked through the yellow door – I didn't even have a key, but this time it didn't matter, there he was. In fact, he thought I was a demon.' Erin laughed.

'There is nothing to laugh about, unless you have a death wish.'

'Of course not. Please believe me, Zhou, all Julius Monk wanted was to talk.' She looked away, remembering the agreement to take him to Long Street. 'If he was so terrible, surely Mr Devilskein would not have saved him as a baby and cared for him all his life?'

'How do you know that?'

'He told me. At first, he couldn't remember anything other than his life in the Haga, but slowly, as we talked, things came back to him. He described Mr Devilskein exactly and he remembered him from his moment of birth.'

'A cursed moment! The beast is father of his own father.'

'Huh?'

'It is a riddle from a prophecy.'

'Whatever, but he did mention he was cursed, which I don't believe. Julius doesn't want to harm anybody. Frankly, it seems to me you're all confused about him. I believe he can be trusted and that he should be allowed to live and be free – it is his human right – but he says it is his choice to stay in the Haga. He says he is neither living nor dead, that the place is some kind of indeterminate realm, like a room between life and death.'

'That bit's true. Exactly true.'

'And that's why he cries so wretchedly. So what's the point? Why did Mr Devilskein save him as a baby only to leave him to languish on the edge of death, in a halfway house with no doors, no windows, and no views? Nothing but one dreadful book-in-progress, some kind of memoir of miseries. Anyone in such a place would go mad; it's amazing he is still gentle and sane.'

'Gentle?' The cricket flew up to sit on her hand. 'The problem, Erin, is that you trust him. I was once in love with a Cambodian girl whom I trusted fully, but she turned out to be cruel beyond my understanding. I would never have believed her capable of what she did, had I not seen it with my own eyes. Nobody on earth could have warned me.'

'What was her name?'

'Peafowl.'

Erin smiled. 'That's a funny name.'

'Perhaps here and now, but there and then, it was quite

ordinary. I thought she had saved me from a pit of despair. I thought the Kingdom of Angkor was a wonder of our square heaven. I can still hear the singing of all those birds even now: rising up to the Cambodian sky, as sweet as Peafowl. I can see us walking through a private jungle garden. We share a pomegranate – our lips and fingers are sticky from the juice. In this paradise, every plant looks new and breathtaking to me; the only familiar ones are pomegranate trees, the sugar cane, the river lotus, the cannonball tree, the banana palm, and the parsley shrub. I take out my knife and cut a length from a sugar cane plant for us to suck on. She strips it first, so deftly with nimble fingers that can arch back and bend into exquisite shapes...'

The cricket was silent for a while, then he said, 'She was fourteen and a dancer; she danced for the king. And she lived with her family in a garden with lychee and orange trees. Those plants of Cambodia were strange to me and there seemed to be more luscious scented flowers of many more species. Peafowl tried to teach me her language. In the heat of summer, we swam every day in a pool filled with aquatic blooms and leaves floating on the surface. Her Chinese was better than my Cambodian. We walked in that Cambodian jungle, and the flowers were astonishing, wild-looking and brazenly colourful, with butterflies to match. I thought my heart would explode with all the love I felt for Peafowl. How wrong I was.'

'I'm sorry it didn't work out,' said Erin. 'What happened?'

Suddenly Zhou did not feel up to reliving the memory. 'It is long past,' said the cricket. 'Very well. I will advise you of when it is safe to visit Julius Monk, but only because I know you will go anyway, and at least if I know you are there, I can...' He did not end his sentence, for as far as the cricket was concerned there was really no saving anyone from Julius Monk. With that he departed through the open window and into the cool mist that was finally lifting to reveal the Lion's Head Mountain.

It was several hours later when Zhou returned. 'If you must go back there, come quickly. Mr Devilskein and that dog will be out for an hour.'

Erin pulled on a denim jacket and then ran up the stairs, with Zhou following. As soon as she passed through the yellow door, she was back in that peculiar place called the Haga. Today the fireplace roared, illuminating the room far more than before. Erin could see the colours of the rugs – they were old, but silken-threaded and lovely. Julius sat on a rug staring at the flames, with his back to Erin, but he knew she'd arrived, and without looking round, he said, 'You came back! I didn't think you would.'

'I promised I would,' said Erin, irked that he had no faith in her. 'Didn't I?'

'Come and sit here at the fire.' He turned to her. 'I'm happy you're here. I've been thinking about you.'

She sat down next to him. 'I've been thinking about you too. I told the cricket I had met you.'

He scowled. 'Why did you have to do that? Are you a gossip?'

'No! And how rude of you to suggest such a thing.'

'Perhaps you're not what I thought. What did he say to you?'

Erin was silent.

'I'm waiting. We cannot be friends if you are going to be dishonest.'

'He was right. I shouldn't have come.' Erin made to stand up, but Julius caught her hand.

'What did that cricket tell you?' He gripped her hand firmly.

'Nothing that you hadn't already said yourself.' She pulled her hand free. 'You're not at all like you were last night. I made the effort to come here and you're being mean.' She shook her head. 'I'm going.'

'Wait.' Julius Monk's tone and expression softened. 'Please, stay.'

She gazed at him.

'What are you thinking?' he asked, batting his beautifully lashed eyelids.

'Three things.'

'That's very specific.' Julius Monk smiled. 'Please sit and tell me about them.'

Her heart was beating fast and Erin found that even though her head said 'leave', her heart could not resist him. She sat. 'Number one: I was thinking about Long Street and how I cherish it. I never thought I would, but I have grown fond of that place.'

'I want to know more about it, but tell me first, what are the other two?'

'I was thinking about Mr Devilskein.' She decided it would be okay to talk about her feelings towards him. Besides, talking to a cricket was one thing, but she hadn't been able to talk to a proper person about the old man she'd become quite attached to and whom she longed to spend more time with. She wished Devilskein would talk to her more, he seemed so wise and wonderful. 'He's pretty grumpy. I don't want to hurt Mr Devilskein, I don't want to disappoint him or let him down ever. I would rather die than hurt him or fail him. It worries me that by being here I am.'

'This is what the cricket told you, that you were hurting Mr Devilskein by being here?' His eyes clouded to a black beyond black, but Erin did not notice the transfiguration. *If I could get rid of Devilskein, and escape, the world would be mine.* He blinked and his eyes returned to their usual colour. A parasitic worm squirmed in the palm of his hand.

Erin didn't notice the worm, nor the shadows in his expression. She shook her head. 'No, not exactly. Anyway, the third thing is to do with the cricket. You see he was a boy about your age in Cambodia many centuries ago and he was in love with a girl and she turned out to be heartless.'

'In what way?'

'He didn't tell me. He only said she was capable of extreme cruelty and that he would never have believed it until the moment he saw it. Is that why you showed me the book?' She glanced across at Julius Monk's desk, where the book was open to a new page. 'Is it magic, that book? Some kind of dark magic?'

'No. Now, let us talk about Long Street.' He stretched lazily and stared at the wooden beams of the ceiling. 'You know so much of the world, Erin Dearlove. Tell me some more about it.'

So she described a coffee bar with a window that looked out across the road to a palm tree next to a yellow mosque. And then she had to explain what a mosque was and what the palm tree looked like and how coffee tasted with lots of sugar and milk and how tar smelled on a hot day after rain and how music sounded. She sang some pop songs to him and some parts of songs by bands that Aunt Kate listened to a lot. She told him about things she had seen and things she had heard from Aunt Kate, about fashion and perfumes and pizza and spaghetti and milkshakes and chocolate cake and nightclubs with dancing and the full moon over the mountain and the millions of stars in the sky.

'You have seen so much.' Julius Monk was indulging her; he turned over onto his side to stare at her, his head propped up on his hand. In the other hand, his little invertebrate envoy writhed with servile delight.

'Actually, I've never been to a nightclub, but Aunt Kate goes sometimes and she's so brilliant at describing things, you feel like you have been there after she has told you all about it.'

'I have never been anywhere,' he said languidly.

'But you will. We will go to Long Street.'

'No. Your cricket is right. I shouldn't leave here. And you shouldn't come back.'

Erin was startled. 'Of course I'll come back.'

'No. I would rather die than hurt you. You said that about Mr Devilskein and it is how I feel about you.' He sounded cross. 'So go. Don't come back.'

'You people in this apartment are so contrariwise! Anyway, I don't take orders from you.' Erin pinched her lips. 'And I never heard anything so stupid in all my life as the ridiculous things the cricket said. It's all rubbish. You'll go mad just staying in this room. You should go out and get some air and see things.'

Julius Monk rolled onto his back again. 'Just once in this existence, I would like to see stars. I would like to sit in a café on the street under the stars with you, drinking milkshake and eating pizza. After that I could stand this place for eternity.'

'Oh, eternity, that's so unnecessarily glum. Don't talk about it. Let's talk about Long Street and what else we can do there. You don't have to visit only once. We can go back often. It's just downstairs. I haven't told you yet about the Pan African Market – it's a fabulous place full of colour and curiosities. Oh, and according to my aunt there is a hotel with a rooftop cinema. Do you know about movies?'

Julius Monk shook his head. And so Erin told him all about film stars and comedies and tragedies – he seemed to enjoy the idea of those immensely – and sometimes she laughed about silly things she remembered from movies she and her aunt had seen, because Aunt Kate loved funny films more than any others.

Instead of a young arch-demon and a grumpy girl with a preternatural talent for drawing, not to mention a precious shimmering soul and a peculiar bunch of unholy keys, they were like a pair of totally ordinary teenagers just hanging out and having a good time together. But eventually Erin had to leave.

'I had a cool time,' she said.

'Oh,' he frowned. 'I'm sorry, next time I'll make sure the fire is much bigger.'

Erin giggled. 'No, you old Victorian. What I meant was that I enjoyed being here.'

'Promise to come back soon,' he said and he kissed her cheek, putting the worm into the pocket of her denim jacket as he did so.

Blush burned her skin. 'Tomorrow, I'll be back for sure.' But Erin did not return the next day. And nor did she realise that she had carried the beginning of Mr Devilskein's doom out of the Haga.

14

High School and Key Work

People called it 'town', from the days when it was just a town, and even though its area had expanded to include a population of millions, so that it was more of a city, the bit where Erin lived was still called town. The sky above it had been a grey sludge for a week and the rain almost tropical in quantity, unlike anything the city usually experienced in April. It rained on Erin's first Monday at school, which she told Aunt Kate was a bad omen. Aunt Kate had wanted to accompany Erin on the bus to school just for that first day, but Erin said it would be embarrassing; she was expecting the worst of the school.

In spite of the weird counsellor Ms Woolly, whose teeth splayed out like fingers on a hand but were being slowly pulled into shape by braces, the school wasn't all that bad. It was small and pretty.

One of the earlier classes on that first day was a double art lesson. After a short overview of the sketchbooks of some great artists, the students were given free range with pens, pencils and charcoal and their project was to create a sketchbook of their own. Erin spent her time drawing a section from the Chinese garden. The art teacher was thrilled with the results.

She said Erin could come and work in the art room at break times if she wanted to and Erin liked that idea because she hated the thought of sitting alone in the playground eating the hummus and bean sprout sandwich Aunt Kate had insisted she take. Thereafter, Erin went to the art room at every break and so she never had to speak to any of the girls in her class. They probably would have given her a viciously hard time over her unfriendliness, had it not been clear that she had a gift for drawing. One of the coolest girls in the class had informed her peers that Erin was obviously a genius like Van Gogh and that she should be left alone if that was what she wanted.

Although the difficult matter of socialising had been sort of solved in that way, the unfortunate matter of homework did not vanish quite so easily. Erin very quickly discovered this, and since she was behind in all of her subjects, she was given triple the normal amount. This she lugged home, heavy-hearted, every afternoon. Even with her book bag bulging, she still insisted on going to Mr Devilskein's apartment to do his key accounting.

'You are doing fine job,' he told her over tea, but she could hardly look at him because she feared that he would see her secret about Julius Monk. 'Even Calvados agrees you have been something of a blessing,' he raised an eyebrow. 'Using the term as loosely as possible. This is a place of uneasy treasures and yet you have proved loyal and diligent.' Mr Devilskein eyed her over the gold rim of his teacup.

She relished her conversations with Mr Devilskein, who was often in a foul mood ('You again,' he'd mutter, or some such thing. 'You're a real millstone, girl'. Then, he'd glower at her with resentment when they had tea.) But occasionally he was almost chatty, though she was cautious about what she said, not wanting to mistakenly say more than she should. Yet she had many questions she wanted answers for.

In the first place, had he really saved the baby whose mother died at birth? Was he the man Julius Monk claimed was present in that very early memory of that traumatic day? Would he really be enraged if he knew she had discovered this boy in the Haga? She thought that if he had saved the child, he must be somewhat fond of the boy, and if so, why should he be so angry if Julius Monk had made a friend? Perhaps she could confess to Mr Devilskein? She truly wanted to be honest with him and yet, deep in her heart, she had a sense of foreboding; there was always the possibility of disaster if he should find out. Then again, what if that was just a foolish fear all fired up by the cricket's paranoia – would it be so terrible to take Julius Monk to Long Street for a milkshake and a movie? It could not be good for the boy's peace of mind to be locked in that airless Haga writing that dreadful book; it would surely drive him to dangerous madness. Erin could not believe he had a dangerous bone in his body. He was moody, that was true, but so was she and so was Mr Devilskein. As far as she could tell, Julius Monk was no more a demon than she was; he was merely misunderstood, and she knew how that felt.

She thought of his beautiful eyes and how the cricket had made so much fuss over the fact that she had stared right into them. Julius Monk was definitely misunderstood, and what's more he made her heart flutter. He had told her she was pretty. Seldom had anyone ever called Erin pretty before, especially not a boy. Lately, she had noticed in the bathroom mirror that she was looking healthier from the occasional run that she still fitted in, not to mention the daily walk home from her school in Tamboerskloof, and probably also because she was happy living with Aunt Kate and working with Mr Devilskein. Aunt Kate had also encouraged her to get into the habit of washing her hair every second day, so it no longer hung limp and greasy as it had done when she'd been the skinny girl living in the mansion with the glass staircase.

'Pollution or not, the town air has clearly done you good,' Aunt Kate said to Erin one Wednesday afternoon in the corridor, and then she turned to Kelwyn, who had not spoken to Erin since the shadow boy in his dream had advised him to let her be alone if that is what she needed. 'Don't you agree Kelwyn? Erin's not so scrawny and her hair is glossy and her cheeks are rosy. She's positively glowing.' Aunt Kate thought it was because Erin had a crush on Kelwyn and she wanted to encourage the boy to do something about it.

Kelwyn's heart constricted, and without realising it his hand went to his trouser pocket where he perpetually kept a photocopy of the newspaper article about the Dearloves; there was so much he wanted to say to Erin, but the shadow boy with the black dolphins was probably right: Erin didn't need some boy chasing after her. He looked away from them and briefly contemplated the skyful of clouds that promised rain for the plants on his balcony. Then he smiled at Kate: 'You're looking very healthy too, Aunt Kate. Must be the food you're cooking. My ma says you're a great cook.'

'So is Erin.' Aunt Kate was determined to get him to compliment Erin. 'Have you ever tried her scones? She makes fantastic scones. Perhaps you'd like to come for tea and try some.'

'I don't much like scones,' Kelwyn lied. 'But thanks for the invitation. You're one of the kindest people at Van Riebeek Heights.'

'Well, I don't have time to make scones anyway,' Erin said. 'I've got too much homework, and my job with Mr Devilskein to do. It is very demanding extraordinary work.'

Both Kelwyn and Aunt Kate turned and gave Erin a

searching look, hankering to know more, but for different reasons both decided not to ask.

Even so, Kelwyn decided that he would investigate further. She didn't have sole rights to the top floor: if he wanted to go knocking on Devilskein's door, he could.

Meanwhile, Erin was thinking that if the town air had been good for her, then it really would be good for Julius Monk.

Over her cup of tea with Mr Devilskein that evening, she asked, 'Have you ever had children? You said you'd been alive for centuries.'

'No. I have always hated children,' he said crossly. 'Even when I was a child, I hated children. They are such manipulative little creatures. Always whispering, always staring and turning and pointing. They have no compassion for anything different. When on any unfortunate occasion I see a child, I growl or gnash my teeth, and it gives me great pleasure to see it burst into tears and run in fright. '

Erin considered his monstrous features. 'The children at Van Riebeek Heights think you're a murderer.'

'I don't care what they think.' He frowned. 'Perhaps they are right. Have you considered that possibility?'

'You're not so bad. You let me in that very first day, didn't you?'

'You're a unique soul, Ms Dearlove, and you do not yet know what that means. It can be good, but it can also be bad. Until you understand, you need to be careful. You must realise that in spite of its chaos, the universe is scrupulously fair, everything is balanced and there are rules: bad cannot win over good without fair warning or fair exchange. There will always be signs and messengers.' His smile was wistful.

But Erin wasn't concerned with warnings, she was preoccupied. 'Have you ever been in love?'

He grimaced. 'Love! Who could love me?'

'That is not what I asked. Have you ever loved anyone?'

Mr Devilskein sat back in his chair and studied Erin thoughtfully. 'I have, but it has not done any good. Love has dangerous consequences.'

'Like children?' she said, thinking of Julius Monk and being almost certain he must be Mr Devilskein's son.

He laughed heartily at that and she laughed too, but then he said sternly, 'Avoid love if you can, Erin.' Mr Devilskein sat up and pulled at his jacket collar to neaten it. 'Enough talk. To work now. I will accompany you today. Quality check.'

It was impossible for Erin to grasp fully the magnitude of what was behind the six doors in Mr Devilskein's vestibule. She knew this, yet didn't care because every day every door brought new adventures, new wonders. It was breathtaking and magical. She gathered her sketchbook and pens and followed Mr Devilskein, but was nervous when he selected a key which only fitted the lock to the yellow door. She turned the key with trepidation, expecting to see Julius Monk, but of course the key was not taking her to the Haga. There was no key for the Haga as it had no doors. It kept Julius in through will alone, but that will was not invincible. The yellow door opened to six more doors, the fifth of which welcomed the key in Erin's hand and opened on six more doors, the third of which again accepted the key and took Erin and Mr Devilskein to sixty-six other rooms and doors. Finally finding the correct lock, Erin turned the key and then there came a gust of warm savannah air and she and Mr Devilskein were plunged into an African night. The sky was red, scented with wild grasses, and grazing beneath leafless trees was a herd of impala with glittering eyes.

'Oh,' gasped Erin. 'They're too beautiful.' She sat on a fallen tree and began to sketch. Mr Devilskein watched, greatly pleased at her growing skill. One impala twitched its tail and looked up as if sensing a predator.

'What is this place, Mr Devilskein?' Erin asked.

From a distance, a stealthy leopard watched quietly. Mr Devilskein looked out and he knew the creature was there. 'One of the gazelles will die soon,' he said absently. He thought how curious it was to be able to cherish the beauty of a soul, or a creature, and yet be so able to feel nothing but fleeting chagrin for its violent demise.

'Hey, this is becoming a habit.'

'What?' He turned to her as if he had forgotten she was there.

'You're not answering my questions.'

He smiled. 'What are these places? Child, every room contains a pawned soul, or spirit, if you prefer that term; what you see before you is the physical manifestation of a soul.' He looked at her sadly. 'Foolish child, you cannot understand a thing beyond the confines of your small human mind.'

She ignored his insult; she was used to them by now. 'Pawned?' she frowned. 'Like at Cash Crusaders?' Erin had once gone with her aunt to buy a new toaster at Cash Crusaders; Aunt Kate bought quite a few things at the pawn shop as she said it was excellent value and often there were some good deals to be had.

'In some way.'

'So can a person who pawns their spirit buy it back?'

'If it is not too late. If time has not expired.'

'And what if it has?'

'Then the person is in a precarious position; such are the vagaries of life and death.'

The sketch was done.

'Let us move on.' Mr Devilskein clapped his hands. 'There are many keys and many rooms. This one bunch I've entrusted you with is a lifetime's work.'

Erin scrambled to her feet, trying to make sense of the

rooms being souls, but decided the grand implications didn't matter. Until she thought of her own soul, that is. 'Is my soul a garden, too?'

'I cannot answer that.' Mr Devilskein turned and walked back in the direction they had come. As they approached a tree, it became a door and the instant it did, Erin and Mr Devilskein were through it. 'Don't forget to lock it,' he said. 'These are precious commodities, remember. And we are the guardians of these souls.' A sigh of regret escaped from his lips.

'Do you know what your soul is like, Mr Devilskein?' Erin asked while they were passing, swift as light, back through sixty-six and more doors. Suddenly they came to an abrupt halt. He looked at her, his eyes filled with emotion. 'What makes you think I have a soul?'

'Doesn't everybody who exists have a soul?'

He shook his head. 'No, child. When a soul is pawned, it is halfway to lost.' *If the Company has its way, it is entirely lost.*

A chill breeze swept through the room. Erin shivered.

'Don't try to understand. You never will.' They continued until they were back in the vestibule.

Mr Devilskein was choosing another key when Erin said, 'If your soul was pawned, then I can find it for you.'

He shook his head but said nothing. He handed her a key.

'What does it look like, your soul? You know, don't you? You must know?'

He shook his head.

'Just give me a clue,' said Erin. 'I will find the key, I will find the door.'

'There is no door. There are no windows.'

'Like the –' Erin bit her tongue. She had almost said *like the Haga.*

'What?' Mr Devilskein narrowed his eyes. 'Like what?'

'A prison.'

'No. Nothing like a prison. They always have doors. Enough chit-chat.' He pointed to the crimson door. Erin thought of the midnight crying that had led her up the stairs, along the corridor and through the yellow door without a key into the Haga and how Julius Monk had insisted the place had no doors even though she had entered through one. Erin thought of something her Aunt Kate had once told her and she paused before she unlocked the crimson door with the new key. 'You know, nothing is impossible,' she said to Mr Devilskein. She wanted very much to tell Mr Devilskein about the boy with the beautiful eyes she had found. They had begun passing through dozens of other doors, on and on, the doors multiplying exponentially until, in a gust of dank air, they had arrived in a marble and brick courtyard with ornately carved stone arches and columns that overlooked a waterway where there were gondolas and buildings with many windows. The blue sky overhead was patterned with small clouds. Laundry fluttered from wrought-iron balconies. Chandeliers glittered in windows. The water lapped at the buildings and left an undulating line of black scum and shimmering moisture.

'It stinks here,' said Erin, covering her nose as she began to sketch.

'But it is not without its charms,' said Mr Devilskein.

At that moment, the sun grew stronger and the grim stones were transformed from grey to pale pink. A pair of double gates opened across the waterway to allow in a gondola bearing a man with a crown upon his head.

Erin watched and her breath caught as the gates swung wider, revealing stairs to a grassy garden with pots of roses and where there was music and laughter and the sound of glasses. As the sun became brighter, the green of the grass became all the more startling.

'It is like a field of emeralds.'

'Indeed,' said Mr Devilskein. 'Soon you will not even notice the stench of the polluted water.'

Already it no longer bothered Erin; she was so entranced by the scene. She thought that was how Julius Monk would feel when he was out of his doorless prison and strolling down Long Street.

'What are you thinking, Ms Dearlove?'

Erin looked up with a start. 'About something nice.'

'I see that. You are smiling.' And he was smiling too.

She blushed and thought quickly. 'My Aunt Kate is an artist. She would love to see this.'

That erased Mr Devilskein's smile. 'She can never see this.'

'I know. I know. I just thought perhaps I could take one of those roses…'

'Never!' His voice boomed along the waterway. 'You must not tamper with these rooms; you must NEVER take anything from here to the outside world. The consequences. I thought you understood that at least? Yours is a unique will, a pure conscience, and by giving you the keys to these rooms, I have entrusted you with a rare authority, a rare power. These doors do not open for just anyone who stumbles upon a key; they open because I – me, Albertus Devilskein – I have given you the freedom of the Indeterminate Vault; never abuse your gift of access.'

Erin stammered. 'I'm so, so sorry. It was a stupid idea, but that was all, just a fancy. I do understand. I would never do anything like that.' But she still did not understand what harm it could do if she took just a rose, nor if Julius Monk took a walk in Long Street. What could it possibly harm? Yet clearly Mr Devilskein felt it would have dreadful consequences, for he was trembling with anger. He snatched the sketchbook from her. 'We must go. This is enough for today.'

'I'm so sorry, Mr Devilskein, forgive my silly thoughts,'

Erin pleaded all the way back through the manifold doors. He gradually calmed down and by the time they were back in the vestibule he had regained his composure and was no longer shaking.

Very serious now, he gave her back the sketchbook and place his hands on her shoulders. 'This place is a secret, Erin; remember you promised to keep it so.'

'Yes, Mr Devilskein. I swear I will never do anything to harm you or this place.'

'Good, child,' he said wearily as he ambled away towards the kitchen where Calvados was waiting. 'Now go home, Erin Dearlove.'

And the black worm which Erin had unwittingly carried out of the security of the Haga into Devilskein's vestibule, where it had unlimited access to all realms, was making its way slowly to the ear of the Company CEO. For it had secrets to tell.

15

Stubborn Ms Dearlove

Despite her promise, between school, which was more okay than Erin had imagined it would be, homework and her extraordinary accounting job in apartment 6616, Erin simply had had no time to return to Julius Monk. The conflicted cricket, Zhou, who claimed he wanted her to have nothing to do with the demon boy, had returned several times to advise her that Mr Devilskein was out for an hour and she would be safe visiting the Haga behind the yellow door.

More than a week passed and still she had not returned to Julius Monk. She was doing her algebra homework when Zhou flew in, chirping and fraught with concern. 'If you do not go today Erin, you must never go back there.' Zhou knew the neutralising power of the Haga had been breached. He realised no matter what he advised to the contrary she would go back at some stage, but he feared that the demon boy would lash out and damage her irreparably, if she toyed with him any longer.

On Long Street the home-bound traffic was already jammed up, filling the air with fumes and the irascible sounds of road rage.

'I can't go today. I have a maths test in the morning and

now I have to study before Mr Devilskein is back and I go up there to do my job and weed the Chinese garden, so I cannot go there twice in one day at the moment.' Erin rather liked her dark-haired mathematics teacher because he wasn't like any of the other teachers at the all-girls school in Tamboerskloof. He was a man for one thing, and he had a tattoo, and whenever she saw him he was reading a book or listening to music. He even liked some of the same music as Aunt Kate. Somewhere in her head full of thoughts and souls, Erin was plotting to introduce them. They'd be a perfect match, she decided.

But Zhou the cricket was in a flap. 'You really don't know what kind of beast you are dealing with.' He tut-tutted. 'You promised you would return the next day and that was ten days ago. Julius Monk will already be enraged, believe me.'

Erin was tired of Zhou's histrionics about Julius Monk; she did not believe for one moment that Julius would be so unreasonable, and he certainly would not harm her. 'Well then, I'll just confess to Mr Devilskein and I feel sure that he will let me visit.'

If it was possible for a cricket to scream with fright, then that was how Zhou reacted. 'Confess! If you do that we will all be done for! Me and you and probably everybody in this building.'

'Don't be absurd.' Erin shook her head and returned to the algebra problem at hand. 'Zhou, I don't know what makes you think all these terrible things, but really you should just chill out. Enjoy this bit of winter sun.' The problem she was working on was an advanced one, a special task set for her because it turned out Erin was extremely good at maths.

Zhou settled some and as he watched her working he related a tale, more for himself than for her, since she, at first, was consumed with letters and numbers.

'You never know, Erin, what a person is capable of,' Zhou sighed. 'My love, Peafowl – I wanted to break my engagement to the woman in China and marry her. It would have destroyed my family, but so strong was my love – I would have done anything. I would have died for Peafowl, so sweet she seemed. But I was wrong.'

Erin was half-listening. Now she glanced up at Zhou.

'On the day I sought to propose, I went to her home. Members of her family held high offices in the walled city of Angkor, and because of their rank the family house was a large and impressive complex with gardens and verandas. The family temple and the main hall were covered in turquoise tiles, a precious stone that was highly prized and auspicious. All the outlying buildings were neatly thatched and of charming design. I went armed with poems and other gifts of fruit and porcelain and, of course, a ring to offer Peafowl; my hands were damp with the evening heat and anticipation. As noble as that family was, I was sure Peafowl and her family would not reject my proposal – after all, I was an Imperial Envoy from China!'

Erin had put down her pencil and was listening with rapt attention. 'It sounds so beautiful, that kingdom.'

'Oh, it was,' said the cricket. 'Powerful and magnificent and today it is nothing but ruins. That is what comes from carelessness, Erin.' He eyed her. 'They thought they were invincible, but nobody is invincible.'

'Yes, yes, but what happened with Peafowl? Did you propose?'

'No. My evening of love and proposals was thwarted by a thief. I arrived at Peafowl's home only to discover an angry gathering around a young man about my age who'd been caught red-handed stealing money from the household. There was great muttering and discussion, and some mention of imprisonment or torture, but finally the family resorted to a curious procedure. Peafowl told me it was a common way of dealing with crime in Cambodia, where nothing existed in the nature of a 'complete inquest'. The thief, although caught with a bag of money, claimed it was planted among his things and so denied the charge of stealing. Next I saw a kettle filled with oil. Then, to my horror, I realised it was being brought to the boil. Surely this cannot be? I thought. The house with its turquoise tiled roof was too elegant, sophisticated and serene to be witness to such an ugly spectacle. The oil was bubbling and smoking now. I could not believe they would actually –'

The cricket paused and twitched his feelers. Erin was wide-eyed. On the far side of Long Street police sirens wailed.

'Go on,' said Erin.

'The suspected man was forced to plunge his hand into the boiling oil. "This is horrifying", I said to Peafowl. She, though, was watching avidly and said that the supernatural strength of the god of her country would keep the suspect's skin and bones safe from harm if he was telling the truth, but if he was guilty, his hand would be burned to shreds.'

Erin gasped.

'The wails of agony that came from that wretched thief wiped out all thoughts of love. And then, as if nothing was happening, Peafowl picked up a lychee from the gifts I had brought her. With her nail, she slit the skin and popped the white berry into her mouth, sucking and able to look at the horrifying scene without any compassion or any of the revulsion I felt at seeing – and smelling! – the flesh cooked from this man's bones. She was not a bit moved by his suffering. Erin, his screams were like the end of the world, like the agonised cry of the end of a dream. It was barbaric! Yet Peafowl just took another lychee!'

Erin exhaled. 'So she was not as sweet a soul as you thought.' The swarm of sirens in Long Street had become louder.

'Exactly my point, Erin. If anybody had told me that the seemingly gentle, kind, loving, pretty girl I wanted to marry possessed such a strange and hard heart, I would never have believed them. So I understand why you do not believe me when I tell you Julius Monk's wrath is apocalyptic. There is a reason he is in the Haga. Do not be fooled by his appearance.'

At first Erin pinched her lips together, irritated that the cricket's whole story was aimed at justifying his paranoia about Julius Monk.

'I'm only telling you this because I like you, Erin,' he said.

'It's a totally different situation.' She looked down fixedly at the complicated equation written in her book in pencil. The question after it demanded a theorem be proved.

'Different people, in a different time, yes,' said the cricket. 'But there are similarities; mainly you have no idea of the culture that informs Julius Monk's ways. He is a demon and you are a girl. What is fine and normal to him is not going to be fine to you.'

She wanted Zhou to be wrong in his assessment of Julius Monk (how ridiculous to suggest the boy was a demon), and yet deep in her heart she knew the truth. Zhou's story of Peafowl was disturbing. It dislodged a brick from her mental wall of denial. Absently, she began the theorem's proof, but quickly arrived at an uneasy impasse – her approach was faulty.

'Very well,' said Erin. 'I will give Julius a quick visit now to prove you are wrong and to explain to him about my homework and all that.' She frowned. 'Not that I should have to explain anything to anyone. My time is my time.'

So upstairs they went. Erin passed through the yellow door and as if some will rather than any key now connected them, Erin was immediately inside the doorless, windowless Haga. Julius Monk was at his desk, his back was to her. This time the fire was unlit and the room was icy cold and unwelcoming.

'Why didn't you come when you promised?' He did not turn.

'I've been busy, working with Mr Devilskein and doing school stuff. Not to mention looking after the Garden of the Humble Politician – I've brought it back to life! You should see the flowers, but boy, gardening is hard work.'

Julius Monk's brow creased. His eyes had become a colder shade of sapphire. He condescended to look over his shoulder at her. 'Gardening! You belong to me. I will not let you leave again.' There was no trace of friendliness in his tone.

She was shocked, then furious. 'Rubbish. Who do you think you are?' Suddenly fear gripped her, but enraged further that he had unnerved her, she brushed it aside. She could be just as sour and stubborn as anybody else, and since she did not believe him capable of harm, she didn't care what foolish threats he made. 'You know nothing of the world; you're ignorant and selfish and no wonder you're lonely if you think for one moment that anybody can be possessed.'

'Yes, they can. You are mine.'

'No, Julius. I am a free agent, a free spirit.'

Three floors down Kelwyn knocked on Aunt Kate's door.

'Hello sweetie,' she said, always glad to see him. 'Oh, so cute!' She reached out to tickle the soft fur between the white kitten's ears.

'Yes, but nobody's phoned to claim him and my mother is insisting I take him to the SPCA, where they'll put her down if nobody adopts him. I don't know what to do.'

'Poor Kitty.' Kate held out her hands to take the kitten, but it didn't want to leave the warmth of Kelwyn's jacket.

'Would you like a kitten?'

Aunt Kate's expression showed she was torn. Yes, the kitten was cute, but animals were a responsibility and she already had more responsibilities than she had bargained for. 'I'll think about it.' It occurred to her that housing Kelwyn's kitten might give him good reason to visit Erin more. 'May I ask you a question?'

'Sure.'

'I've noticed you've been a bit unfriendly to Erin lately. Why?'

He thought about the dream and the shadow boy and said, 'I think she needs space. She's been through so much. I don't want to be suffocating – I want to give her what she needs and if that means avoiding her, then that's what I'll do.' Still holding the kitten in one hand, with the other hand he fished out the small but shocking article he had kept about the Dearloves from his jeans pocket. 'I found this.'

Aunt Kate read it. *A chilling message written on a piece of cardboard saying: 'We have killed them. We are coming back.' was found on the gate of the farm, Solitaire, where three people were brutally killed on Thursday. The victims of the murders were Dale Dearlove, 40, his wife Ruth, 36, and their 16-year-old son Joe. The Dearloves were murdered on their 18th wedding anniversary.*

The details of the attack were gruesome beyond words. At the request of the police, the media said nothing of the surviving child, Erin. After reading with trepidation – she tended to avoided such articles – Aunt Kate said, 'You're wrong, Kelwyn. What she needs is a real friend. Don't avoid her. She needs people who care about her more than anything.' She scrunched the article into a ball. 'She has a dark history, but it's over. Her future can be happy, full of sublime experiences; there is so much wonderment out there. I'm going to throw this away.'

As Kate dropped Erin's tragic past into the dustbin, Erin herself was defiant in the face of the demon boy. 'Possession is an illusion. I will do as I please, when I please, and I don't have to visit you if I don't want to. My Aunt Kate is always telling me how possessive men can be, how they think girls can't exist without them. Well I'll tell you something, I don't need you in my life. You're the one who needs me.'

'I will chain you up and keep you prisoner.' He stood up, and to Erin he seemed strangely taller.

'How charming,' said Erin fiercely. 'You really know how to win friends and influence people, don't you? You could write a book. Oh, ha, I forgot, you are writing one. You think you frighten me, with your depraved words and threats? Well, I've got news for you: I've seen it all.' She jabbed his shoulder with her index finger. 'And you don't frighten me. What good would it do you to have me chained up? Huh? Do you think I'll bother to talk to you? Do you think I'll like you? I won't. I will shut my mouth and you'll never ever hear about Long Street again. All you'll have is an enemy. Even in chains, I'll be a free spirit. So there!' She poked his other shoulder, even harder this time.

They glared at each other.

'You're so selfish and empty,' said Julius Monk, who was acerbic yet astonished by her courage.

'Me? What about you?' she spat.

He changed his approach. 'You know I am all alone here, that I have been here alone forever, and that you promised to come back and instead you've been playing...'

'Playing? I have been working, thank you very much. All you have to think about is yourself; you're probably the most self-absorbed person on the planet.'

'I am not.'

'Yes, you are. Who else do you ever think about except yourself and how miserable you are? Who else do you ever spare a thought for?'

'You. I think of you. I am not a selfish person.' He turned away and a large, disingenuous tear rolled down his cheek. In a self-pitying voice he said, 'It seems to me that what had promised to be some light and relief in an eternity of misery has vanished. I have no choice about being here in this limbo. You know that and yet you are so careless. So thoughtless, so selfish and unkind.'

'There is always choice.' Erin was unsympathetic. 'You are here because you want to be.'

'No,' he cried, indignant. 'You just don't understand. Even after I showed you the book, you still don't understand. You're cruel.' Now there were more tears his eyes.

'And you're pathetic. Look at you, crying again. Instead of making your life better, making an effort, all you do is cry, cry, cry.'

'Get out!' he bellowed. 'Get out and never return!'

'Fine.' As she turned to leave, she said, 'And to think I was going to suggest a trip to Long Street this weekend. It would have been such fun. We could have had pizza with pineapple and ham, and chocolate milkshakes and – and now you've ruined it all.'

By force of her unique will she once again conjured up a temporary yellow door, marched through it, and was immediately back in the vestibule.

Zhou was waiting. 'You're back!' He was delighted, for he had genuinely thought he might never see Erin again and he had become fond of the girl who was one among only a very few other people he'd ever encountered with the gift to communicate with crickets and cursed souls.

'What are you so happy about?' She stomped out of the apartment. 'Julius Monk is selfish, rude and stupid, like every other boy I know. I'm never going back.'

'Good. That's the best news I've had for several centuries.' The cricket followed Erin down the stairs. 'It's the right decision.'

'Leave me alone, Zhou,' said Erin. 'I want to be alone.'

He flew off, trilling happily.

At the same time Kelwyn was walking down Erin's corridor, very relieved to be rid of the article. Feeling more cheerful than he had for a while, he beamed when he saw Erin coming towards him.

'Hello!' he said, almost at the point of embracing her in a happy bear hug. 'You and your aunt may be fostering my white kitten – well, it's not officially mine, yet, but I'm working on my mother.'

'Leave me alone, Kelwyn,' said Erin, just as she had to Zhou.

This time, Kelwyn was bursting with affection determined to win her over. 'I just want to say if you ever need a friend I'm here for you – any time.'

'I want to be alone. Why doesn't anyone understand!'

Back at home, Erin gathered up her algebra book and went to her room, not feeling at all as excited about matching up Aunt Kate and the mathematics teacher as she had earlier. She was cross with Zhou and cross with Kelwyn for being so friendly again and cross with Julius Monk for turning out to be such a stupid boy. What was he thinking? Chain her up? Did he think he could scare her into being his friend? How silly of him, how petulant and ugly.

She had really been looking forward to going to Long Street with him. Somehow she'd imagined it could become a regular Saturday adventure – she didn't work at Mr Devilskein's on a Saturday and she didn't have to go to school. But now that would never happen and Julius could just stay in his horrible cold room with no doors and no windows and no fresh air and nothing but one dreadful book. She was in a filthy mood, unlike any mood she had been in for a very long time.

She almost forgot that she was due back at Mr Devilskein's apartment very shortly to commence work; luckily her alarm clock was set as a permanent reminder.

Mr Devilskein and Calvados were waiting with a pot of tea and a fresh stack of pancakes, whipped cream and honey, which Mr Devilskein said was from a mountain meadow in ancient Persia.

'That honey is a thousand years old,' he said.

Though she'd thought she'd never do so again after her horrible visit with Julius, Erin laughed. 'Well, it's very tasty for such old honey.'

'Ah, and I have a gift for you.' Devilskein was frighteningly cheerful.

'Why?' She thought of the last time they had spoken and how she had disappointed him by wanting to take a rose for her Aunt Kate from the pawned soul that was a courtyard in Venice.

'You have been working hard. And I have not been as encouraging as I should.' With a flourish he produced a wooden box. It was beautifully carved, but quite dirty with oil paint. 'I thought, as an artist, it would appeal to you.'

She opened the box. Inside were brushes, again dirty with paint. There was also a quill pen and a pot of half-used ink. Touching it made her think of her ink pens and she was filled with an intense urge to be sketching in the Chinese Garden. There was a small hand-bound notebook too. Only a few pages were written on. The handwriting was elaborate and difficult to read.

'What language is this?'

'Italian.'

'Oh.' Erin frowned because although she could not read all the words, there was a name she recognised: Leonardo da Vinci. 'What does it say?'

Mr Devilskein pointed to some words before the famous name. '*Some minor machinations and musings on creativity and the soul, by Leonardo da Vinci.*'

Erin ran her fingers across the page of parchment and India ink. 'Where did you get it?'

'It was in Leonardo's bedroom.'

'But I thought we weren't allowed to take things.'

'It was a gift.'

'Leonardo da Vinci pawned his soul?'

Mr Devilskein nodded. 'But thanks to your work in sorting the keys, he has it back. He is freed from the limbo of the soulless, and as he ascended to the higher realm, he left me with this gift as thanks for taking such good care of his precious spirit.'

Erin's jaw had dropped. *I helped Leonardo da Vinci?* She wanted to say it was impossible, but she had seen the gardens and rooms, and with Mr Devilskein really nothing was impossible. She was so awed and moved by the priceless box that she got up and gave Mr Devilskein a hug, which flummoxed him, surprised her, and made Calvados bark in consternation.

'Hush, dog,' said Mr Devilskein. 'It is all fine, the child is not trying to kill me.'

Still suspicious, Calvados (who could smell a trace of black worm on her) settled back down, stretched his paws out in front of him, placed his head on them and eyed Erin as though she were not to be trusted.

'This is an awesome present, Mr Devilskein. I don't know how to thank you. You're an angel,' she said. Then an idea came to her. She took from her pocket a small but beautifully crafted silver owl and held it out to him. 'This is the most precious thing I own and I want you to have it because you have made my life worth living.' Even through the gloom she could detect a hint of redness on his monstrous cheeks.

Devilskein closed his fingers around the delicate owl, and although objects do not have souls, their atoms do retain memories: he could feel the rush of a mother's fear and love and the sadness of a child. 'I will treasure this,' he said, pinning the brooch to his jacket. 'Thank you.'

She felt so fortunate to exist in the enchanted world and wanted to show somebody the astonishing gift. Immediately, she thought of Julius Monk, for although she had said she would never visit him again, her mood was completely different after tea and pancakes with Mr Devilskein. Now she felt fortunate and generous and sorry for Julius Monk, all alone in that bleak room. Perhaps she had been mean to promise she would see him whenever she could, only to leave him wondering for days what had happened to her simply because she was busy. Perhaps she had been unfair and unfriendly.

16

The Wrath of Julius Monk

It had been an endless day of extreme highs and disconcerting lows and after the wonderful gift he'd given her, Erin had worked extra hard that evening, cataloguing and accounting for the wild and strange plethora of souls Mr Devilskein kept behind all those doors in apartment 6616. And then she'd spent an hour weeding in the Chinese Garden, so when she finally arrived home, just after nine o'clock, she could hardly keep her eyes open. She murmured something about her handsome mathematics teacher to Aunt Kate.

'Handsome men can't be trusted,' said Aunt Kate, gently directing Erin towards bed. 'Except for Kelwyn,' she added hastily. 'He's one in a million: handsome and trustworthy.' But she didn't push the point too much. 'Take off your jeans and in you get.' She pulled back the covers and pulled off Erin's shoes and socks. 'I'll bring you dinner.'

A couple of minutes later Aunt Kate returned with a spinach frittata, a bowl of jelly and custard and a glass of berry juice on a tray with a sky-blue cloth. Aunt Kate was proud of the way Erin had taken to school. The guidance counsellor with the splayed teeth, Ms Woolly, had telephoned that afternoon to say that Erin's teachers were very impressed with her. Even though Erin did not realise it, she was an extremely intelligent girl with an aptitude, reported Ms Woolly, in every subject. The school was honoured to have her as a new student. This tickled Aunt Kate, since she'd been a disaster at school; she'd skived off maths lessons with her best friend to smoke Camels and eat tooth-curlingly sweet condensed milk at the far end of the school field.

After Erin had eaten and thanked Aunt Kate and mentioned the mathematics teacher again she snuggled into her pillow and drifted off. Somewhere between wakefulness and a dream she murmured, 'I will return to the Haga tomorrow if possible and apologise to Julius Monk.'

'The Haga? Where is the Haga?' asked Aunt Kate.

But Erin was in the land of Nod and she slept soundly until just after midnight, when she was jolted awake by the most terrible howling. At first she thought it was police sirens, but she soon she realised it was the sound of wailing and crying and shouting.

'Julius Monk?' she said to the darkness. 'How dreadful he sounds, how miserable. He'll wake the whole building.'

As the storm of grief intensified, Erin wondered why her Aunt Kate did not seem to have been roused by the sounds; they were unbearable. Erin wandered out of her room and peeked into Aunt Kate's room, but she was sleeping peacefully.

'It is no wonder Zhou thinks Julius Monk is a wretched boy; this noise is fearsome and ugly.' She stood in the shadows and covered her ears, trying to block out the sounds, but they just got louder. 'It is almost deafening.' She looked in at Aunt Kate again, but she had not stirred and looked to be in a beautiful slumber. Erin unlocked the front door and wandered out into the corridor, expecting to see at least some lights on. There were none. It seemed that everyone else at Van Riebeek

Heights was deaf to Julius Monk's demonic tantrum. Erin's head was beginning to ache with the sound. 'I have to stop this or he will drive me mad.' Suddenly, she felt angry. 'How dare he get inside my head like this!'

At that moment, Zhou appeared, trilling anxiously. 'Julius Monk is in a world-ending rage,' Zhou said. 'It is fortunate that Mr Devilskein is out, otherwise he would know your secret, our secret. Go to the Haga, Erin. Perhaps you can calm him down. You seem to have a gift for that.'

'Why should I?' she said fiercely. 'He told me never to return and now he's deafening me with his stupid wailing. Impossible boy. He has absolutely no manners, and he knows I have school tomorrow.'

The cricket stopped his nervous trilling and considered Erin. He had expected her to be shaking with terror and hiding under her bed, but she was doing nothing of the sort. No, she was furious, and it seemed to Zhou that it was precisely this feistiness that the demon boy liked. 'You're quite right,' he said. 'Go to Julius Monk and give him a piece of your mind, before we all go deaf and Mr Devilskein returns home.'

'Who is "we all"? Nobody else here seems to hear anything.'

'No. That is true. For the most part they are not tuned to the machinations of cursed souls. Lucky for them, but you and I and every other soul in the safe behind the six doors of apartment 6616 are. I tell you, Erin, the sound will soon begin to burn the thoughts from our heads and the hearts from our chests. If you do not do something, it is quite possible we will both spontaneously combust.'

Erin was incredulous. She began to laugh. 'Really, Zhou, you have an absurd but fabulous imagination.' She still could not take him seriously, and with mock sternness she charged up the stairs and into Mr Devilskein's apartment and through the yellow door. The Haga was in a state of disarray. Playing cards were scattered all over the floor.

'Oh stop it, Julius! Stop crying and performing, this instant! You're driving us all barmy. Some of us need to go to school tomorrow and some of us have an algebra test. Stop being such a drama queen and pull yourself together.'

Erin was so angry, so hot with rage, she didn't notice the biting cold in the room. It was close to freezing. Being reprimanded was an entirely new experience for Julius Monk. He swung around in shock at the bold intrusion in the shape of a young girl in an old blue t-shirt, big knickers printed with scotty dogs and a pair of oversized slippers. His face had lost all its beauty; his eyes were red, his lips contorted, wet with froth and spittle and his skin was grey and clammy. Any other soul might have fainted at the horrible spectacle of him, but Erin was in a foul mood and did not give a fig about his appearance. Julius Monk took a cavernous breath in and was about to let out another almighty wail, but Erin stunned him into silence.

'Don't you dare!' She ran up to him, shouting at the top of her voice and she shook him. 'Shut up! Shut that stupid mouth of yours. You're so weak! So pathetic. Be a man.'

He exhaled and all the fury went out of him, but tears were streaming from his eyes. 'I can't.'

'Yes, you can,' shouted Erin, her brows knitted.

'I am cursed. I am a demon. I am evil.'

'Oh piffle,' Erin clicked her tongue in irritation. 'I've told you before there is no such thing as evil. It is pure invention, a useful myth, a result of fear, a result of people needing to control other people, seeking the comfort of power, a way of making sense and order out of –'

'What is really an exquisitely simple, amoral chaos,' Julius Monk completed her thought. 'How do you know? You're only a girl.'

It had not occurred to Erin why she thought all these

things. She had never once had an existential conversation with any philosophical type. Yet it just seemed to be a certainty to her, like she needed oxygen to breathe. How did she know this? She didn't, she had never thought it consciously before; it was more an instinct. Without thinking too, she had taken the handkerchief out of Julius Monk's jacket pocket and was wiping the sweat and the tears from his face. At length, she said, 'It simply is. If you ever say you are evil again, I will laugh at you.'

'But I can do terrible things,' he said, meekly (and with cunning).

'That proves nothing. So can the weather. So can the sun. So can shooting stars.'

Perhaps Erin's instincts were childish, and spoken out of crossness and certainly not any kind of serious academic analysis. Still, they had an extraordinary effect on Julius Monk, the cursed boy, the son of the Devil. He had lived all his days imprisoned by the terror of his own demonic powers. He had dared not question all that before. His every moment was punctuated with darkness and knowledge that he was a destroyer of the worst kind. Now, here was this girl in a blue T-shirt and perhaps what she was saying contained some truth? Or maybe not.

'How can you be certain?'

'No, that is not a question worth asking,' said Erin lightly. 'The only certainty is uncertainty.'

Julius Monk sighed and all his interest in debating the matter went out of him. It was a pointless discussion and creating a storm of rage had exhausted him. Indeed, had it not been for the impenetrable walls of the Haga, the magnitude of his fury would have taken the city by its foundations and shaken it to a heap of rubble. But his wrath had subsided. He sensed her need to be the one to 'save' him from himself and, playing along, he edged close enough to her to enable his head to droop strategically onto her shoulder.

'You poor thing.' Erin led him to his bed and pulled back the sheets and instructed him to lie down. Doing as her Aunt Kate had done for her earlier, she took off his shoes. The room warmed considerably and the beauty returned to Julius Monk's face. His voice became gentle. He took Erin's hand.

'You are a brave girl. Fearless.' He smiled. 'Thank you for coming back.' It occurred to him briefly that perhaps he should chain her up to keep her, lest she did not return again, but he remembered what she had said about being a free spirit. Besides, he most definitely wanted to see Long Street and could only get there by invitation. 'If you are still willing, I would like to have a milkshake with you, and a pizza.'

In spite of herself, Erin's young heart fluttered. Julius Monk was an astonishingly handsome boy – better than any movie star – and certainly far more handsome than Kelwyn, no matter what Aunt Kate said. She pulled the blanket up over the impossibly beautiful demon and yawned, and suddenly remembered her algebra test.

'I must get some sleep,' she said, and then, without thinking murmured, 'You're lovely.' She kissed his lips. She blushed and smiled. 'I'm glad you are feeling well again. I have a test in the morning.'

'I will miss you. This place is so lifeless without you.'

'Now don't you get sad again.' She wagged a finger at him. 'I'll not have it.'

He smiled. 'Will you sing me a song before you go? The one that you sang before? The one your Aunt Kate likes.'

'Okay, but really, then I have to go.' She sat on the edge of the bed because she too was exhausted and sang a song about violence in Ireland. Julius Monk closed his eyes and drank in the sweet softness of her voice. He did not have it in him to sleep, for demons do not sleep, but when the song was over he kept his eyes closed, and so Erin could leave. In her oversized slippers she tiptoed away, unaware that to his powerful ears even dust stirring was noisy, even a shadow was loud.

And she was equally unaware that Kelwyn in his bed was tossing and turning, unable to sleep, plotting to visit Devilskein on the one hand, and trying to think of the perfect place to invite her for a first date on the other. In the end he decided on Kirstenbosch, the national botanical gardens. He would invite her for a picnic on the patch of lawn beneath Matthew's Rockery: a wonder realm of aloes, paperbark thorn trees, bewitching Nabooms, whisper flowers and a plethora of succulents in all shapes and sizes that made for a weird and magical landscape in every shade of green.

17

End of Days

Erin could barely open her eyes the next morning. She'd only got back to sleep at around four and when the alarm clock went off at half-past six, she was so deeply asleep, she didn't hear it.

Eventually, Aunt Kate came in with a cup of tea and a plate of extra-crunchy toast spread with butter and honey.

'I'm going to get all spoiled again,' said Erin drowsily, her eyes only half open, 'if you keep bringing me food in bed.'

'Too true!' Aunt Kate stroked Erin's hair off her face affectionately. 'No, no, we can't have that. I won't do it again, but you may as well eat this toast otherwise it'll be wasted.' She could see Erin was exhausted and thought it was simply due to the changes of the last couple of weeks: getting adjusted to school and, she hoped, the effort of making new friends. 'I could phone the school and tell them you'll be in late today.'

Erin shook her head. 'I have a maths test, first thing.'

'You're a good girl, Erin. Well, I'm going for an early surf, will you be okay? I've left money for the bus on the kitchen table; it's too late to walk.'

'Thanks,' said Erin, smiling, her mouth full of toast. She gave Aunt Kate a hug. 'Hope the surf is good.'

When Aunt Kate had left, Zhou showed himself. 'Mr Devilskein has not returned. We were lucky you could quell that demon's wrath last night, if we were found out, it would be the end of days for us.'

'He's not a demon.' Erin continued crunching on the toast and merely shook her head in exasperation. When at last her mouth was empty, she added, 'Zhou, you're very superstitious for a cricket.' She had an idea and with it in mind she jumped out of bed. 'If Mr Devilskein is still out, I will visit Julius quickly before I go to school.'

She was wearing her school uniform when she appeared in the Haga and for a moment Julius Monk was disappointed. The uniform was not flattering and she had looked much nicer in her T-shirt and funny knickers. He was at his desk again, writing in that ominous book.

'You have dark circles under your eyes,' he said. 'I'm sorry, that is my fault.'

Erin went and sat on the desk, swinging her legs back and forth casually, unaware of the gravity of the book beside her. Spread out across the top of the table was a row of cards, all red hearts and diamonds. 'I've got school now, so I can't stay long, but I'll be back soon. And then we can talk about Long Street.'

Julius Monk's face brightened and his blue eyes became bluer. 'I dreamed of Long Street last night.' He had not slept – her never slept – but a waker's dream is still a dream. 'I dreamed I was walking past the giant palm tree you told me about, next to the mosque and I heard your voice. I turned and there you were at that café across the road. You looked so beautiful. You waved and called me over. We ordered milkshakes.' Julius Monk sounded convincing, as though he was really and thoroughly infatuated with the brave girl. 'I will think about you and

Long Street while you are gone, Erin Dearlove. Good luck with your test.'

Feeling cheerful, Erin bade him goodbye and hurried off to school, where she aced her algebra test and managed to tell her mathematics teacher how wonderful and single her Aunt Kate was. She even gave him Aunt Kate's mobile number. 'It's just in case you ever need to speak to her about my progress at mathematics,' she'd said, as she'd handed it over. 'Or maybe if you feel like coming and having lasagna a la Katerina with us one evening. My Aunt Kate is a brilliant feminist, but she also makes a fabulous meaty lasagna and she calls it lasagna a la Katerina because that's Italian for Kate. Come whenever you like. Actually, tomorrow is Friday night. Come then.'

Erin's mathematics teacher had wiggled his lips and stifled a laugh. He glanced at his shoes and then back at Erin. 'I'm sure that lasagna a la Katerina is delicious Erin, but I can't just arrive without an invitation.' In fact, the mathematics teacher rather liked the idea of lasagna, and thought Erin a cute kid, so based on that and all the things Erin had managed to tell him about her aunt in the last week, he suspected she was probably pretty nice too. And he didn't have plans for Friday night, either.

'Well, I'm inviting you,' said Erin. 'Come at seven.'

He rubbed his chin and glanced at his black Doc Martens again. 'I'm not sure.'

Erin frowned. 'You're not married, are you?'

'Oh, no, no, alas, nothing like that.' He tugged at the earring in his left earlobe and tried not to laugh.

'Do you have a girlfriend?'

'Not any more.' In fact, he'd recently recovered from a heartbreaking engagement to a fairly mean and capricious but impossibly sexy Spanish woman who'd promised undying love to him before emptying his bank account and vanishing off to Argentina.

'Good. Then you're coming to dinner. I'll tell my aunt. We'll be expecting you.'

'I really don't–'

Erin didn't wait for him to refuse. 'Got to dash. See you at seven tomorrow night.'

A few hours later, after pruning, watering and weeding in the Garden of the Humble Politician, Erin was sitting at the Kitchen table of Mr Devilskein, who had only just returned from one of his mysterious excursions. Erin thought it better not to ask where he went when he disappeared. He was developing a habit of bringing her gifts. What he found irresistible was the freshness of her delight in all things: he had not felt much reason to find existence thrilling for an extremely long time, but seeing things through her eyes reminded him of just how much there was to be delighted with. Much to the disgust of Calvados, Mr Devilskein had returned from their most recent jaunt with a pair of small giraffes. They were not stuffed, porcelain or mechanical, no, they were real, living, breathing, leaf-nibbling creatures.

Erin squealed with delight when she first saw them on the far side of the kitchen.

'They're twins,' said Mr Devilskein. 'I came upon them this morning in a zoological garden. Of course, I must take them back,' he spoke gruffly, 'but I thought you would like to see them.' He frowned, as if saying something very solemn.

The giraffes flicked their ears about and one leaned in to test a biscuit on the platter Mr Devilskein had put out. Calvados did not approve and gave a disdainful bark.

'May I touch them?' Erin asked, walking closer.

'Of course, why else would I bring them?' Mr Devilskein said in his usual cantankerous tone.

Erin stood between the twin giraffes and ran her hand

down their long necks simultaneously. Then she ran her hand in the opposite direction and pulled a face at the roughness. She stroked their ears and fingered their furry hornlets. They were unfazed by her attentions and simply blinked their long-lashed eyes and continued enjoying the oatmeal biscuits. Erin put her cheek against one giraffe's cheek and closed her eyes and listened to the sound of the creature chewing. 'How wonderful the world is,' she said, still with her eyes closed. 'How fortunate I am to know you, Mr Devilskein.' The joy she felt was scarcely bearable. She thought of Julius Monk locked away in his miserable room and, more than ever, she wanted to share some of the delights of living with the unfortunate boy.

'What are you thinking, Erin?' asked Mr Devilskein, also biting into an oatmeal cookie. Since he had tossed one in the direction of Calvados (to be fair), both he and the poodle and the giraffe were all chewing at the same time. The kitchen was filled with a soft symphony of different types of crunching.

Erin opened her eyes. She could not tell Mr Devilskein what she had been thinking, but she didn't want to lie to him. She was quite convinced that he could see through lies. 'Nothing of importance,' she said. 'Except, well, how sad it is that some people live in the world but fail to see any of its wonders.' She shook her head. She thought of the Haga. 'Like they are in prisons of unhappiness, and yet, if they could only choose to, they would be free.'

'You are an idealist, child.' Mr Devilskein's brow creased very deeply. 'Be careful.' Fleetingly he thought of Chamberlain before the outbreak of the Second World War and he almost mentioned it to her, but since she was so young, he realised the analogy of a fair idealist duped by a human demon (in the form of Hitler), would be lost on her. And then he did something he had not done in some centuries: he thought fondly of Miranda. The notion of her he banished swiftly.

'Careful of what?' Erin wondered if he'd seen into her thoughts and already knew about Julius Monk. Perhaps that wouldn't be a bad thing – she was so hankering to save the young charmer. She believed it was possible. She ran her hands down the giraffes' necks once more.

'Dangers abound in the cracks between what is and what appears to be,' said Mr Devilskein. 'Promise me you will be careful, child.' The image of Miranda returned and his shoulders sagged. She had seemed so lovely. He looked at his hands, taking in the scars of time and the lines of age.

Sensing his melancholy, Erin felt bad and as the sun set over Long Street, she promised faithfully that she would be very careful.

Erin was leaving apartment 6166 when Kelwyn picked up the telephone and dialled Aunt Kate's apartment, hoping that this time Erin would be in – he had already tried a few times that evening.

'I'm so sorry, Kelwyn,' Aunt Kate said. 'She's still not back, but I promise that as soon as she returns I'll get her to phone you.'

Just as Kate put down the phone Erin walked in.

'Erin, please phone Kelwyn,' Aunt Kate all but implored.

'Kelwyn?' Erin frowned. She was intrigued, but all she felt like was soaking in warm water. 'I will after my bath, I promise.'

But again she broke her promise – not intentionally though, she was over-tired and simply forgot.

Kelwyn decided to do a recce up to Devilskein's apartment. He knocked on the door. Nobody answered. He knocked again. Still no answer. The cricket Zhou was watching though: he knew all about Kelwyn, Erin's soulmate.

Deflated, Kelwyn returned home. He'd try again later.

When all the stars were out and the midnight clock had struck its twelve, Zhou returned to Erin's room and informed her that Mr Devilskein and Calvados were out and that it would be safe to visit Julius Monk. 'I'm only telling you this,' said the cricket, 'because I know if I don't tell you, you will go anyway, and if you are not careful, you will be caught and that will be calamitous for us all.'

Erin rolled her eyes, and this time put on a dressing gown over her T-shirt before she crept upstairs to visit Julius Monk.

'You smell funny,' he said, without turning, knowing she was in the room. He placed a six of diamonds at the end of row of cards on his desk.

'That's a nice way to say hello.' She bent her chin forward and sniffed her gown and then her T-shirt. She was still wearing the one she'd had on at Mr Devilskein's and it did indeed have a very particular smell.

'Giraffes,' she said. 'I met a couple of baby giraffes today. We had tea.'

And then the idea of having tea and oatmeal biscuits suddenly struck her has funny and she began to laugh. Her laughter was infectious and soon the young demon was laughing too. It was such a novel emotion for him that the sound of his laughter travelled in the same way as the sound of his grief had travelled, all the way down the corridor, down the stairs, and down Long Street. Only those rare few who could hear the machinations of cursed souls could hear it, but for them it was loud as the thundering waters of Victoria Falls. And in the very distant realm where he was brokering for the soul of a geneticist, even Mr Devilskein could hear it very faintly. He frowned in that far-off place. 'What strangeness is upon us?' he remarked to his faithful poodle, but neither of them had an answer. And then the laughter stopped because there was a lot for Erin to talk about and she wanted Julius to teach her the card game.

'I'll teach you another time,' Julius promised, 'but tell me more about the world out there tonight.'

They lay on the carpet beside the fire and, staring at the ceiling, she told Julius Monk about her mathematics test and he wanted to know about mathematics. She told him what her handsome algebra teacher had told his class, that mathematics was the secret language of the universe, a beautiful magical thing, mostly misunderstood and badly taught.

'But it is not a language like most others,' she said. 'It has numbers instead of words.' Then she told Julius about how she had invited the maths teacher who wore an earring to dinner to meet her Aunt Kate. And Julius wanted to know about earrings.

'When we go to Long Street, you will see plenty of them. In fact,' Erin beamed, 'perhaps we can both get our ears pierced? It might be a bit sore though.'

'What do you mean?'

'They stick a needle into your earlobe, I think, to make the hole, so maybe that will hurt?'

'What is "hurt"?'

Erin sat up and studied his face and his strange blue eyes. 'Pain.'

He shook his head. 'I don't know about it.'

'But…' she considered the matter, trying not to be too bothered by this; she thought of the violent images in the book he was writing, 'you know about sadness, you cry don't you?'

He seemed confused, like somebody who had emotions but was not aware of having them.

'Remember when I pinched you,' said Erin. 'It was sore wasn't it? That's pain.' She pinched him again as a reminder. He yelped and she was pleased. 'See. You're just like everybody else. So if we go and have our ears pierced, it will be like somebody pinching you, except maybe worse.'

'I see,' said Julius Monk, but he did not see exactly because while his physical self could feel the pinch physically, he had no emotional response attached to the fact that his body was hurt.

Erin sensed that he had not understood and she was perplexed.

'It's probably because you've been locked up here for so long,' she said. 'You don't ever get hurt so you're not familiar with pain. In the world outside this room, there are all kinds of hazards, big and small, and they can cause pain, some of it mild and some of it very strong. Like if I step on a something sharp, it will hurt my foot.'

'So when we go to Long Street, we can have a milkshake and a pizza and I can experience this pain?'

Erin frowned and smiled at the same time. 'People don't usually want to experience pain, Julius. Milkshakes are good, and pizza too, unless it's soggy from too many mushrooms, then it can be a sort of pain. People prefer pleasure. They're opposites.'

'But how do they know it, without the pain? If I had not been alone before, I would not understand how precious it is to be with you, Erin Dearlove.'

'That's the nicest thing anybody has ever said to me.' And Erin was so freshly smitten and thrilled to hear those words that she forgot about the strange problem of Julius Monk not understanding pain. But of course, fire doesn't understand the damage and the pain it causes, otherwise it would not burn a thing, and night would be dark and rooms would be cold, candles could not flicker and stars could not glitter.

'Tomorrow, after the dinner with the mathematics teacher,' said Erin, excited, taking Julius Monk's hands in hers, 'if Mr Devilskein is out, then I will come to fetch you and we will visit Long Street. It's lively on a Friday night.' She had never actually been to any of the bars, but she had seen the lights and heard the music.

'Sounds splendid,' said Julius Monk and he squeezed her hands. And she wanted to kiss his lips again, but she didn't. Thinking of it made her blush, though. It made the heart in Julius Monk's chest flutter too, and that sent a tremor through the walls of the Haga, since the boy's soul was one with that desolate place; its walls and mortar were the outer layer of his mind. As if there had been a minor earthquake, a hairline crack broke the plaster around the yellow door in the vestibule of 6616.

Kelwyn's pyjamas were a royal blue flannel printed with red-outlined acid-yellow sharks. They were a fancy fashion brand from London, but his mum had found them for him at a car-boot sale near Deer Park. And they had only a tiny hole, which she fixed up smartly. In socks and a T-shirt and his shark pyjamas, Kelwyn made his way up to the top floor with the help of a flashlight. He made it to Devilskein's door and pressed his ear to the door. There was silence. He stood there wondering what to do next. Wondering what on earth possessed him to go up there in the middle of the night when he could be tucked up in bed. Some kind of dream had prompted him, but he couldn't remember any of it. His bed beckoned, so he turned the flashlight and padded back along the forbidding corridor. Cockroaches observed him as he went.

18

Dangerous Times

Mr Devilskein, though far afield, far arealm, in another time, could feel the disturbance in the corridor. The insect eyes that watched for him showed him the retreat of the boy in the shark pyjamas. A few months before, Devilskein might have leapt at the opportunity to ensnare Erin's twin soul, but now he was a changed monster. Or was he? The Physician had only minutes before left a message on his Company Soulometer: if the 'donor' heart was ready, the transplant must take place before the next sunrise.

Why is that boy there? And why at this hour? Why now? Devilskein asked himself, trying to ignore the pain in his chest.

He could not ascertain the nature of it exactly, but as soon as he and Calvados returned home he saw the effects of the near-quake that had rattled the walls of the Haga. He whistled to call Zhou, for like Erin Dearlove, many centuries before that young envoy had been an apprentice accountant in the unusual brokerage scheme Mr Devilskein was responsible for managing.

Anxious, the cricket appeared within seconds. They spoke rapidly in Mandarin. Mr Devilskein studied the cracks over the yellow door. He sniffed the supernatural bricks and his powers of detection were such that in the scent of their dust he could determine a trail to the origin.

'The Haga? A storm and then a quake!' said Devilskein rather angrily, causing stabbing pains in his ailing heart. 'What is it with that demon? What is he plotting?' He ignored his wretched heart and ran his fingers along the cracks and sniffed again; there was an unexpected smell of giraffe. And then unbidden the face of Miranda came to him again. Mr Devilskein shook his head and dismissed the beautiful, brilliant woman who had tricked him into fathering her son. With her in his head, the scent of the giraffe lost all significance. 'Why did you not alert me to this problem?'

If crickets could blush with shame, Zhou would have, but still he did not mention Erin's visits to the Haga.

'If his wrath gets out of control,' Mr Devilskein said, 'I am not sure that even the Haga will be able to hold him.'

'Well, sir,' said Zhou. 'I think you will be surprised. Your son Julius Monk is not the hideous demon boy he usually is. Ah, he has calmed, immeasurably. How it has happened, I cannot say. It is a mystery to me, a conundrum.' Zhou did not feel he was lying, for the strange effect Erin Dearlove had on Julius Monk was indeed a mystery to him. The small girl had somehow bewitched the demon boy and perhaps by some miracle her goodness had transformed him.

Zhou should have known better, however.

'It is beyond my understanding how the wrath he stirred up turned into something like…' Zhou paused, searching for an appropriate word. 'Happiness.'

'Impossible. Julius Monk is incapable of any such sweet emotion. There is no happiness in the Haga. Nevertheless, I will visit him and investigate the matter.'

When Mr Devilskein did walk through the yellow door

into the Haga, something he had not done for hundreds of years, he was rather astonished to find the air of the place was cleared of gloom, that instead of darkness, dankness and wretched cold, the fire blazed, the candles were lit, and the place glowed with warmth and contentment. To his utter amazement, there on the rug beside the fire lay Julius Monk surrounded by a circle of cards, staring up the ceiling and humming a sweet song.

Mr Devilskein went over to the *Book of Dooms* and was startled to see that the words of the last entry conjured up some kind of garden full of tall flowers.

'They're called agapanthus,' said Julius Monk. 'They're beautiful, are they not?' He sat up, smiling. He had known a certain visitor was on his way and he had a nasty surprise brewing for him.

'It has been a long time, Julius,' said Mr Devilskein a trifle nervously. He was not usually so anxious, but there was something very wrong in the Haga and it unsettled the broker immensely. 'You were unwell, last night?'

'Oh,' Julius Monk waved his hand. 'That was nothing. It is over; I am entirely rejuvenated. I feel so very different. I feel light.'

'You feel?' Mr Devilskein sat at the desk and regarded Julius Monk curiously. 'What do you mean you 'feel'?'

'Interesting, yes?' said Julius Monk. 'I have discovered I can feel things, sort of.' He realised it probably wasn't quite the kind of feeling that mortals experienced, but still it was something. 'I mean a feeling like I want fresh air.'

Mr Devilskein raised his brows, concerned. Could the neutralising power of the Haga be failing? Might the demon boy rediscover his particular capacity for violent emotions? No! 'Julius, it is impossible for you to feel anything. You *must* not feel anything.' Miranda Monk darkened his thoughts again and Devilskein closed his eyes momentarily. She had been an impossible beauty and unbelievably cunning; she had claimed to be an astrophysicist – indeed, her knowledge of the field was dazzling; her smile and her universal insights were breathtaking; and she had disguised her demonic nature until she was pregnant. Only then had she revealed her true profession and her fearsome job title.

She had wanted a baby as part of a greater plan, but a woman in her position naturally had no time to change nappies and play coochie-coo with a creature that didn't sleep. Instead Albertus Devilskein was granted a long stay of paternity leave. As a baby Julius was adorable; his father was besotted. And although he knew there would be a shadow side to the boy, he had thought he would be able to raise him like an ordinary human (for everyone has some wickedness in them). Albertus tried, but the depth and ferocity of Julius's evil took even him by surprise. At that early stage the child himself was conflicted about his nature. He begged his father to help him. Devilskein should have put him out of his misery, he should have killed his son for the sake of the world and for that of his son, but he could not do it. Behind Miranda's back he sought a last resort, something even she could not undo: conjured up by a Moorish sorceress, the Haga was the only solution.

Julius smiled as if he knew his father's thoughts. 'Fresh air will make me better. I feel more alive. I want to see the world.'

'You cannot leave here without invitation. You know the consequences, and you agreed to this,' said Mr Devilskein, solemnly. When he had first brought Julius Monk to the Haga, the child had been in a shrieking rage and had pleaded to be kept away from the world which he had so harmed (most recently at Hiroshima), calling for the safety of an airless, windowless, doorless place in which to keep his immortally cursed soul.

'And now I have changed my mind.'

'Well, I'm sorry, boy, but the dark charm is fixed: you

cannot exit without an invitation.'

'But I can have visitors and air. I am changed.'

Mr Devilskein swallowed and was alarmed. On the one hand, it tormented him that the boy was cursed to exist in the Haga, on the other hand, it was without doubt for the best. And yet even in spite of his dubious dealings of the past, Mr Devilskein – unlike the Company CEO, Miranda – had always been a scrupulously fair trader, apart from the purposeful losing of keys, which he did because he was following her orders, and which he was now in the process of rectifying.

'That is most unusual, you understand? What kind of visitors would want to come here?'

'Brave ones.' Julius Monk chuckled.

That startled Mr Devilskein. In all his time, he had not seen such a transformation in a soul. Could it be real, all this? Or was this simply cunning subterfuge? Could the demon be trusted? Dare he hope?

'I agreed to this, remember?' said Julius Monk, as if he had read Mr Devilskein's thoughts. Julius Monk's eyes twinkled and he summoned from his belly the breath of the Devil, then he exhaled, sending a sweet mist into the air, one so intoxicating that even the indomitable Mr Devilskein could not but be entranced.

'That is unforgettable.' Mr Devilskein slumped, his shoulders hunched and he wrung his hands. 'Well, well. This is unprecedented. It could be very dangerous, remember…' He shook his head, feeling slightly woozy, but put that down to his heart, which was due to be replaced that very evening, if he could bring himself to come up with a donor heart. It should have been an easy decision. *All these children!*

He thought of Erin and Kelwyn. He did not want harm to come to them, but he did not want to die. Was she really so important? Surely, he, Devilskein the Company man, was by

far the more important life to spare. He had to make a choice...
but that was another matter; Julius was an exponentially greater
problem by far. He did not want to harm his boy either, but he
especially did not want Julius to harm the world.

'All that is past history,' said Julius. 'I am different now.
When I remember, I cry, I am miserable, I feel in limbo and
lifeless. It makes me angry and then the *Book of Dooms* is my
only escape, but it doesn't have to be that way.'

'Feel?' Mr Devilskein shook his head, still unable to
comprehend that the demon could feel anything and yet, due
to feeling so lightheaded, he was finding it difficult to formulate
any clear-minded thoughts of opposing the boy. 'Feeling' was
not the way for a demon. He sat down at his son's desk. 'How
have you come to change so?' *Have I changed too? So completely
that I would give up my life when there is perfectly good heart
available to me?* Devilskein touched the owl brooch Erin had
given him.

Julius Monk blinked his blue eyes and also thought of Erin
Dearlove, but he did not say her name. 'Possibilities. I have been
awakened to the possibility of possibilities. I have realised that I
can choose again. That perhaps I do not have to be here.'

Mr Devilskein put his head in his hands. 'This is certainly
a new state of affairs.' He could not deny this transformation
in Julius seemed to be for the better, even though the change,
as change is sometimes wont to be, was terrifying. Was there
any possibility the boy could be allowed to receive visitors?
He could never leave, that would be asking for calamity, but
a visitor might be a possibility. He frowned, some part of him
shouted against such a disastrous line of action. And anyway,
who on earth would be brave or foolish enough to visit this
fearsome boy? Mr Devilskein looked up at Julius Monk and
thought of Erin Dearlove, but he too kept her name to himself.
She was one of the bravest souls he had discovered in all his

wanderings; she was true and natural, an ancient soul yet still a childlike idealist, and though the world had recently tried to ruin her early on with brazen violence, she had risen above all that. She still had no concept of her talents and gifts. Her gifts went far beyond merely being an exceptionally green-fingered gardener (even Devilskein was impressed at how her secret Chinese Garden was thriving). If there was anybody who could visit Julius Monk and survive, it would be Erin Dearlove, but what if the demon tricked her into letting him out of the Haga and into the real world?

'All this warrants consideration, Julius. I am impressed with your transformation. Still, change involves risks and sacrifices.'

Julius Monk nodded. 'But if I don't try, if I don't take the risk, I will never know.'

'We will speak of this again.' Mr Devilskein got to his feet pausing to recover from a spell of dizziness. 'I must leave now.'

With that, and with much to think about, Mr Devilskein departed. When he returned to his flat through the yellow door, Calvados was waiting. He ruffled the poodle's curly ears affectionately and murmured, 'These are dangerous times, my friend.'

'We must be cautious, Sir,' said the poodle who spoke with a Polish – not a French – accent.

An alarm sounded on Devilskein's belt. His expression crumpled: this was not the ordinary wail, it was the death knell for a Company man. His hand went to his breast, not to examine his shocked heartbeat, but to grasp the small silver owl brooch that he wore on his lapel, the gift from Erin.

And then the sky fell in. Literally, but in appallingly exquisite silence.

The heavens over apartment 6616 ruptured, great stabbing chunks of universe showered down, dagger-like, around the Company man and his dog until they were encircled in a cage of broken time and radioactive splinters.

Oblivious to Mr Devilskein's tribulations, Erin spent Friday in a cloud of blissful infatuation, while Aunt Kate and the mathematics teacher independently stressed about the unorthodox dinner engagement that Erin had insisted on, and Kelwyn wondered how long he should leave it before phoning yet again; he didn't want to come across as totally uncool before she had even agreed the date thing.

'Please can I keep the kitten, Ma?' he implored on behalf of the tiny creature, who didn't take up much space and didn't deserve an eternal sleep delivered by the slim, silver bite of a vet's needle. He told his mother so.

She wanted to cry. She liked cats, but she just couldn't afford another mouth, even a small one, to feed. 'Why can't Sipho keep him?'

'His father is allergic to pet hairs.'

'How convenient.'

'Kate and Erin are quite keen to take him, but they're still deciding. Please give him a chance.'

'Okay, you can keep him until you find another home, but that does not mean forever.'

Relief swept over Kelwyn. He took the kitten to his bedroom and lay on the bed, kitten on his chest, so that he and the tiny creature were nose to nose.

After making lasagna at Erin's insistence – she had promised the mathematics teacher they would have it – Aunt Kate went for a sunset surf near the lighthouse.

'He's coming at seven,' Erin said, with a frown. 'Don't be late home, okay? You have to put on make-up and stuff.'

Aunt Kate replied with a rueful smile, rather enjoying

Erin's motherly tone and happy her niece was finally coming out of her shell. She was actually surprised to find she was nervous. After a series of unfortunate relationships, she had taken a long hiatus from the dating scene and this dinner with the mathematics teacher, although not officially a date, was beginning to feel more and more like one. Especially since Erin had gone through the closet and selected a slinky black dress and a pair of high heels for Aunt Kate to wear. That was when she began to realise that Erin had more in mind than simply a social meeting with one of her new teachers.

Needless to say, Aunt Kate, in typical Aunt Kate fashion, lost track of time while she was surfing and only arrived back at half-past seven. The maths teacher, whose name was Greg, had been there for half an hour minus a good few minutes for fashionable lateness, during which time Erin had shown him all the stack of paintings in Aunt Kate's upcoming exhibition and opened a bottle of wine for him. Greg had also realised that his new star mathematics pupil was playing matchmaker, and since he too had foresworn any relationships after his disastrous engagement to Penelope the heartbreaker, he was also very nervous. As a result, by the time Aunt Kate returned, he had drunk three-quarters of the bottle of wine, his cheeks were glowing and he was in a very jovial mood.

Bringing with her a waft of sea air, Aunt Kate appeared through door with sandy feet, hot pants, a holy t-shirt – it featured the face of the Madonna, compliments of a nearby Mexican restaurant – and her wetsuit and board under her arm.

'She's been surfing,' said Erin, giving her aunt a glare. 'She always forgets the time.'

'Surfing! That accounts for the wonderful scent of sea,' cried Greg, who had drunk too much wine on an empty stomach.

Aunt Kate's hair was wet and tousled and her cheeks were pink.

'It was beautiful,' she said, still breathless from running up the stairs with her surfboard. 'The sunset… every sunset is the most beautiful one. Spring is coming.'

'Spring!' He sounded elated, though in truth Spring was quite far off. His heart was racing, and he really had no idea why. 'We should open the windows and let it in.'

That made Aunt Kate laugh, but she opened the windows wide and the sounds of Long Street – and some of its pollution – poured in.

'Not quite sea air,' she said. Still, Greg joined her at the window. 'It's a great view of the mountain, though. And if you lean out and turn you can actually see the sea… at a stretch.'

They both did exactly that and it caused them to laugh again because it was a very long stretch to see anything remotely like sea from that window and even though Erin thought they were being a bit silly, she was pleased.

'I've always wanted to learn to surf,' said Greg. 'I like snorkelling. Have you ever been to Windmill Beach?'

'Yeah,' said Kate, with a big smile. 'It's great. Snorkelling is the best. But you should learn to surf if you've always wanted to. It'll take a bit of time to get the hang of it, but it's such an amazing feeling. Being part of the ocean that goes on forever and ever…'

They were standing side by side, still at the window, and quite close to each other. Aunt Kate was surprised at how easy it was to talk to the maths teacher whose name she had forgotten. Erin had told her his surname, but they hadn't actually introduced themselves by first names. The teacher was also feeling unusually gregarious as a result of all the wine and he too was amazed at how easy it was to talk to Erin's aunt. And she was so lovely!

'The thing about surfing,' said Aunt Kate, 'is that all the rest of the world ceases and only you and the sea and its waves exist. You have a few seconds of really joining the incredible force that is the ocean. It sweeps you along, but you also have to master it, not that it can ever be mastered, it can't. It's a demon in some ways, and if you ever forget that you're in trouble. It's wild, it's not your friend, it's not human, it doesn't care about your fate really, but for those few seconds you join it, you feel all that power, millions of years and gallons of water, you're closer to all that than it is possible to imagine. It's the ultimate rush. It's better than any drug ... and believe me I've tried most of them.'

Spring may have been coming, but storm clouds had gathered low over Long Street, and cold wind gusted through the windows they had opened so wide. Aunt Kate closed her eyes and enjoyed the swirling air and briefly felt as if she was back on her surfboard. As if he knew what she was imagining, Greg closed his eyes too, and tried to picture himself on a wave, but as he didn't quite have the blond hair of a Norse god or Tarzan's physique, he changed the reverie to one in which he was swimming and Kate was surfing and only his head showed above the water. The important thing was that he felt really happy.

'Aren't you two getting cold?' asked Erin, who was finding it chilly.

'Not at all,' said Aunt Kate. 'The air is glorious.'

'Glorious,' agreed Greg.

'I'll put the lasagna in the oven to heat up,' said Erin, and went off to do so, grinning from ear to ear. She turned off the bright fluorescent lights between the kitchen and the rest of the open-plan room and lit a candle on the tiny dining table that had four chairs around it, although it was really not much more than a two-seater. Then the telephone started ringing. It was shrill and spoiling the romantic mood Erin was trying to establish. Erin answered impatiently.

'Hi Erin, it's Kelwyn here.'

She remembered that she was supposed to have phoned him. 'Oh no, Kelwyn, I'm so sorry I forgot to phone back, but I can't talk now. I'm right in the middle of something. Something important. I'm sorry, I'll phone tomorrow, I promise, but I have to go now. Bye.'

She put the phone down.

Kelwyn stared at his receiver. 'At least she said she'd phone back.' He smiled.

Erin put on Aunt Kate's favourite CD and Greg mentioned that he liked it too, so they moved on from talking about waves to talking about music. Soon, thirty minutes was up and the lasagna was hot, so Erin put out plates and dished up for everybody. 'Dinner is served,' she said. And as if in a dream, Aunt Kate and Greg moved from the window to the table, talking all the while and having almost polished off another bottle of wine. The topic had turned to Greg's dogs. He was a great lover of big dogs.

'Oh, my neighbour Kelwyn would love you, he's always rescuing dogs and cats,' said Aunt Kate. 'When I was a child I had a black Great Dane called Soot.'

Greg sat up, his eyes shining with wonder and delight at the unexpected pleasure of finding someone he could talk to so easily. Usually, he was awkward around beautiful women he fancied. That's how Penelope, the Argentine heartbreaker, had managed to con him with such swiftness. But she was history. Greg and Aunt Kate were mutually overwhelmed by the revelation that they both had a secret dream of doing a motorbike trip across Zimbabwe one day, when politics and budgets allowed it. They talked and ate with ravenous ecstasy, so complete that Kate failed to notice that Erin was only picking at her share. Very soon the dish of lasagna and a crusty loaf of bread were all gone, at which point Erin excused herself and went to get a jacket.

Erin had never worn make-up before, but before leaving she dipped her finger in Aunt Kate's pot of peachy lip gloss in the bathroom and rubbed some on her lips. She rummaged through an old toiletry bag and was intrigued to find things she very rarely saw Aunt Kate using. For the fun of it, she brushed blue mascara on her lashes and dabbed a spot of blush on each of her cheeks. She didn't know it, but the impending stroll down Long Street with Julius Monk was going to be her first and last 'date' ever.

19

Long Street Nightlife

At just before nine, Erin ran up the stairs two at a time, but as she reached apartment 6616, she heard the cricket chirruping in consternation.

'Don't go back,' said Zhou. 'Mr Devilskein is in trouble and you must hide. If they find you–'

'You're just saying that because you don't want to me to be friends with Julius,' said Erin petulantly. Nothing was going to ruin her big night out on Long Street. She reached out her hand to push open the door.

'Stop!' cried Zhou. 'You must never go in there again. They will be watching.'

'Who? Who are 'they'?' she asked, not interested in the answer.

How could Zhou explain? He said nothing.

'See, you're just being a drama-monger again.' Erin turned back to the door.

'You'll see when you go in,' said Zhou.

She pushed and the door swung open. But a power far greater than Zhou had blinded her to the chaos within Devilskein's vestibule. In her mind, nothing appeared out of the ordinary.

'I knew you were making it up,' she said over her shoulder as she unlocked the yellow door.

At that point Zhou fled.

In the Haga, Julius Monk was daydreaming about Long Street. He had become fixated with the idea and the mystery of it. He had built it up in his mind and written an ode and a sonnet and an epic poem dedicated to it. When he showed them to Erin, she was concerned he might be disappointed.

'It's only a street made of tar,' she said, but then regretted being such a killjoy. 'But it does have its charms.' Those words made her think of Mr Devilskein and the courtyard garden in Venice. She ignored a pang of guilt; there was nothing really wrong with taking Julius out for an evening stroll.

'Perhaps you should change your coat,' she said, looking at the demon's stylish velvet tailcoat.

'But I don't have another one.'

Her brow creased. 'You mean you wear the same clothes every day? I thought you were one of those people who has like seven of everything so they never look different.'

'No. I have a single set of clothes. What is the point of having more?'

'Seriously?'

'But what's wrong with that?'

'Well, for one thing...' She walked right up to him and smelled him, but there was no scent to detect, certainly no bad odour. 'Very strange.' She smiled. 'I don't suppose it matters too much. People on Long Street wear all kinds of fashions. They'll just think you a little eccentric.' She looked around the Haga. 'Something has changed here,' she said, but was unable to pinpoint the exact nature of the change.

'Changed for the better,' said Julius Monk, full of energy and anticipation.

'It could hardly have changed for the worse,' Erin said. 'I don't think it gets much worse than this place.'

'You have changed too,' said Julius Monk. 'Your eyelashes are blue and your lips are shiny.'

Erin's cheeks flushed crimson. 'It's called make-up. Women wear it when they are going out.'

'Why?'

'Dunno.' She shrugged.

'You look pretty,' he said. 'But you always look pretty.'

'I brought money,' she said, turning away from the compliment. 'We'll need it for milkshakes.'

'I told Mr Devilskein,' said Julius Monk.

'What!' Erin's jaw dropped. 'You told him about me, but you promised!'

'No, no, calm down, I didn't tell him about you. I just said I thought I'd like to go out some time.'

Erin breathed a sigh of relief; she had been all set to pummel him for revealing their secret. 'And what did he say to that?'

'He was evasive, but that's okay, change is always difficult for old men.'

'Yes.' Erin pushed aside the nagging concern about how Mr Devilskein would react and what he would do if he found out she had tampered with one of the rooms in his safe; this room possibly being the most sacred of all.

'No need to frown so.' Julius Monk smoothed away the creases on her forehead. 'What beautiful eyes you've got, Erin Dearlove. What are you thinking?'

She was imagining the worst. What would the worst possible consequence be if Mr Devilskein found out? According to the cricket, it would be doom, it would mean the end of days. But what was that exactly? She was sure Zhou was being melodramatic as always.

On the point of falling asleep, Kelwyn was startled by an unfamiliar voice.

'Oh, I'm a bad, bad, bad cricket,' it moaned.

Kelwyn looked around. 'Hello? Who's there?'

'There has never been such a good-for-nothing cricket in the history of crickets.'

'Hello?' Kelwyn sat up and switched on his bedside light.

'It's all my fault.'

'Where are you?' asked Kelwyn, getting up to open his cupboard, expecting one of the neighbour's kids to be hiding inside. There wasn't a soul to be seen. He was stymied.

'I'm here,' sniffed the cricket. And Zhou scuttled up Kelwyn's pyjamas, down his arm and into his palm. 'You should crush me.'

'I must be having one of those weird dreams again.' Kelwyn couldn't believe what he was seeing.

'No. That would be a nightmare,' said the cricket.

'Who are you? Or rather, what are you?'

'I should think it's very obvious that I'm a cricket. A terrible, terrible cricket. My name is Zhou. Crush me, please.'

Kelwyn sat down on his bed, careful not to close his hand, for certainly he didn't wish to crush the talking cricket who called himself Zhou.

'Please, please kill me and put me out of my misery.'

The white kitten was most intrigued by the insect and batted a paw in the direction of Kelwyn's hand. He lifted his hand out of its reach.

'Or feed me to the cat; I deserve it.'

'Absolutely not. Why would I do that? I can't believe I'm talking to a cricket. I must be dreaming.'

'Believe me, this is no dream. And I wouldn't be talking to you, but I don't know who else to go to. Erin is blinded by the demon boy, and Mr Devilskein…' Zhou broke down into sobs.

'You know this Devilskein person?' Kelwyn had decided that since this must be a dream, he would participate fully. 'I've been hoping to meet him. Will you take me to see him?'

'Know him? Know him? Know him?' Zhou did a dramatic dance whilst sorting through the absurdness of Kelwyn's question. 'Of course, I do. Take you? I will. Yes, yes, yes! Let us go. Now! Immediately. Hurry!' Kelwyn began to follow Zhou, but the white kitten let out a plaintive mew, not wanting to be abandoned, so Kelwyn scooped him up, held him close and zipped up his jacket so that the affection-hungry feline was safely contained in the warmth between his jacket and his chest.

'I'm wondering what flavour milkshake to order,' Erin said with a blink. 'Chocolate is excellent, but sometimes I prefer the simplicity of vanilla and very occasionally, if I'm feeling festive, then berry is the best option.'

Julius Monk embraced her. 'We are going to have a monumental time!'

She swallowed hard. For a fleeting moment she thought she'd made a big mistake. 'Julius, do you think that perhaps we should speak to Mr Devilskein, and come clean about going to Long Street?'

'I can't wait for his permission.' Julius Monk stepped back, still holding Erin's shoulders. 'That could take centuries!'

Something about that struck Erin as funny. She laughed.

'Well, then we must go. We must go now.' She drove all doubt from her mind, took his hand and led him to the gap between the Haga bookshelves – inside the Haga it seemed to be no more than stonework, but she knew the yellow door was on the other side. She did not know how it could be that merely by willing it she was able to take herself back through the door, which, looking from inside the Haga, apparently was not there. But it had been so the first time she had visited Julius, and every other time too, and she was confident it would be no different now. And so, holding his hand tight, she focused on going back through the door and before they knew it, they were standing in the gloom of the vestibule of apartment 6616. All was quiet, as before a storm. And although Erin saw nothing out of place, Julius Monk took in the wreckage and sighed with great satisfaction.

To Erin, Julius seemed to be frozen with shock at how easy it had been to step out of his prison. She drew him out of the apartment and into the twinkling night. In the corridor he paused in shock again, lifted his head and took in a deep breath of the world's air. It had been decades since he had last done that. The air was heartbreakingly sweet – wild grasses on the mountain, salt of the sea, life, perfume, baking bread. His eyes were big and bluer than ever. He and Erin made their way down the stairs. Julius kept lifting his head and breathing the deeply scented air that was laced with street sounds and music. He was listening in awe to the multitude of sounds. The Haga had possessed only the sound of fire and, when Erin came, the sound of her voice.

'It is so exquisitely noisy,' he said. 'And all those perfumes, what are they?'

'What perfumes?' Erin, a step ahead and still pulling him along, made a quick olfactory assessment: the first smell that hit her was that of chicken biryani and basmati rice cooking in the Lallas' apartment on the fourth floor of Van Riebeek Heights and then the aroma of sousboontjie breedie and apple cake baking in the Talmakies' apartment. 'Oh, you mean the food,' she said. 'It's spices and herbs and all types of food. People are having dinner.' For some reason, which she could not explain, she was whispering.

So he asked in a whisper too, 'What types? What are the different types, other than milkshakes and pizza?'

'Oh,' she gasped. 'So many wonderful, wonderful foods.' she began to describe some of her favourites, but then to her horror there was Kelwyn Talmakkies walking upstairs wearing his tracksuit jacket over his shark pyjamas. And for a reason Erin didn't at all understand, she felt guilty, like a wife flirting with a man other than her husband, and that made her terribly irritated.

'Ignore him,' she instructed Julius. 'He isn't real.'

And so as they neared Kelwyn, Erin looked at her feet while Julius continued the discussion about food. 'I want to try them all,' he said, very satisfied that she was not in the least interested in Kelwyn and had deemed him unreal.

'You can,' she said. 'But we must take it slowly. Let's stick to milkshake and pizza for tonight.'

'Hello,' said Kelwyn. Zhou had instructed him not to mention the fact that he had a talking cricket in his pocket.

But Erin went by without a word, like a sleepwalker.

'Hello!' Kelwyn called after her, to no avail. 'Erin?'

He was left unnerved – even though he knew he must be dreaming – and there was something else: jealousy. *Who was that boy she was holding hands with? What on earth was he wearing? Maybe the phone call wasn't progress after all?* The thought that Erin might have a boyfriend caused Kelwyn's heart to twist in his chest and his ardour for her grew all the stronger. He couldn't explain to himself why he felt such love for a girl who hardly ever spoke to him. He felt like he had met her in other lives and loved her for all time. And then felt foolish for being so stupidly romantic.

He longed for the impossible.

Erin felt jittery with excitement. Julius was so different, so cool, so handsome. Being with him was thrilling. Anything could happen.

Kelwyn knocked on Mr Devilskein's door. The white

kitten squirmed against his chest.

'There is nobody there,' said Zhou. 'Go in.'

Upon entering, for some moments Kelwyn was speechless.

Erin and Julius were at the metal grille gate at the ground floor of Van Riebeek Heights. She slipped her key into the lock.

'Are you ready?' she asked.

There was a lovely breathless silence and the key turned and the lock clicked and the heavy security gate fell open just a chink.

'This is it.' She pushed the gate wider, making space for them to pass through. And then they were out.

The night was chaos, the sky a surreal blue-tinged black. Fluorescent rods dazzled in shop windows, tail-lights glowed red, street lamps burned a warm yellow, silver cars shimmered and growled by. On the opposite side of the street, the balcony of a restaurant was festooned with a cascade of fairy lights. Bars, music, laughing crowds. People speaking Portuguese, German and French passed by. The pavement shone with arbitrary pools of dirty water. Waste bins reeked of decomposing food. Julius Monk's unearthly blue eyes drank it all in. Holding his hand, Erin pulled him through a series of orange tables outside a café where a woman smiled at him and commented on his jacket. A club called Joe's promised cheap drinks, a Mediterranean restaurant offered angel fish and salads. A sign asked *You Got Problems?* and in response it added: *Dr N.A. Ndos qualified lemon and herbalist have the treatments: Makes your wife stop complaining; To make your boss like you…* Crossing the road, Julius Monk stopped in the middle to take in the sights and lights of both sides and they were nearly run over by a black Jeep, jinking between other slower cars and studded around the edges and mudguards with fake diamonds. Its owner had painstakingly beautified – or defaced, depending on the beholder – it by pressing the glinting crystals along every one of its rims and flanks. The same owner swore at them and swerved and sped on, zigzagging all the way, hooting and cursing.

But Julius Monk was delighted. 'I feel immortal here! I will live forever and ever!' He shouted to the sky. 'I will never be lonely again!'

A wandering minstrel trio struck up a tune on trumpets and a small fire broke out in the Mama Africa kitchen, where a temporary kitchen-hand had forgotten to check the kudu kebabs and fillets of crocodile tail. Smoke billowed from the windows.

20

Mr Devilskein

Julius Monk felt thrilled with possibilities as he first saw and heard and smelled the life of Long Street on that otherwise ordinary Friday night. What others might have seen as imperfections, like the garbage, the crazy drivers, the tacky made-in-China trinkets of weary hawkers and the charlatan doctors promising quick riches and true love, appeared to him as evidence of a wonderful vibrant world, full of hopes waiting to be dashed, order waiting to be turned to chaos. It was a radiant place without limits; even a demon could appreciate the beauty of that. As they walked on, heading for the café where Erin had planned they would have pizza and milkshakes, every now and then Julius would halt and shake his head and say, 'Oh, but it is marvellous. I am fifteen going on centuries and I have never seen a night like this.' Nor a place more ripe for catastrophe, he thought. 'It's glorious.'

'Yes, it's a perfect night and a wonderful street.' Erin laughed lightly and pulled him on past the golden lights of an eatery with yellow parasols beneath Victorian, broekie-lace, cast-iron arches. 'Maybe it's the most wonderful street in the world.' And she felt at that moment that it must be, for she was in a state of rapture too on account of Julius Monk's great delight at everything. The wind had carried a blanket of clouds down the mountain, then died away, and the atmosphere was unseasonably balmy.

They arrived at the café opposite the Palm Tree Mosque and Erin directed Julius Monk to seats at the counter in front of the open window so that they could have a view of the street and the people passing by. People had stared as they'd made their way to that table, but Erin had ignored the looks that Julius hadn't even noticed. He found the menu a fascinating object, and she explained the dishes. When the waiter came, Julius Monk was enthralled because he spoke with a French accent and, when prompted by Erin, the waiter regaled them with tales of the Ivory Coast, the country of his birth, and then Nigeria, the country where he grew up. Of Nigeria, he told them horror tales of broad-daylight hijackings and government corruption. But he was a jovial man, who said he was writing a novel and that he was particularly fond of the work of Jorge Luis Borges. That led to series of further explanations, for Julius Monk was thirsty for knowledge, and eventually one of the waiter's other customers complained loudly because his food hadn't arrived and he could see the waiter was talking too much.

'I wonder if we shall see the stars you told me of,' said Julius Monk, craning his head to look out of the window and up at the sky between the palm fronds and the power cables.

'Maybe not tonight,' said Erin. 'There will be other nights though, I promise. The stars are always there, but not the clouds. When it's a clear night you can see the Southern Cross and Orion's Belt and – oh, there are so many and each one has a story.'

On this point, the talkative waiter concurred when he returned with two milkshakes and recommended that Erin's friend try beer sometime. He laughed to hear that Julius had never tasted or even heard of it and asked where Julius had grown up.

'In a cursed place,' said Julius Monk. 'And I lost all my memories.'

'Truly must be cursed, if there is not beer to be had.' The waiter chuckled at that and they all laughed together, before the waiter left to take other orders.

Above them black slits had opened in the clouded sky, and they widened from slits to almond shapes, and another hole appeared, like a gaping maw. When Erin looked up, she gasped. 'Look! The sky has a face and he is watching us.' Something about that made her anxious. She thought of Mr Devilskein, but did not want to ruin the mood. She unwrapped two straws and popped one into each milkshake and then showed Julius how to drink his using long sucks.

The taste of ice and milk and chocolate gave Julius Monk a pleasurable shock and made his teeth ache. 'Is this pain?' he asked.

Erin laughed heartily. 'No! Pain is a bad thing; milkshakes are good.'

'I thought you did not believe in good and bad,' said Julius Monk.

She sucked some more and thought about how to answer that. 'It's a different kind of thing,' was all she could come up with, but she felt a little caught out.

Swiftly, he changed the subject. 'That tree, the one you call a palm, is it old?' he asked.

'Very. As old as this street.'

'Not as old as me though.' He said it sadly, as if it was a cause for great regret.

'You don't look old,' said Erin, trying to cheer him up. 'Usually, old people have dry skin and wrinkles and thin grey hair and their bodies are tired. You look like you're fifteen.'

'Still,' he said, gazing at the palm. 'Those people with grey hair are alive and I am not.'

'Of course you are. I thought we'd covered this.'

'Indeed.' His eyes twinkled and he sucked very noisily on his milkshake.

And she took a long sip of hers, which was made with gloriously double-thick real vanilla ice-cream. 'Mmm, this is dreamy.' She smiled at him over her glass.

Inside Mr Devilskein's apartment, Kelwyn looked upon the fragments of some kind of exquisite ruin in awe – there were keys and artefacts everywhere and a tear in the ceiling revealed a heaven crowded with supernovas. 'What is this place?' he asked. 'And what has happened here?' Erin had talked about a garden being there, not a bomb site with an astonishing view of the Milky Way.

Zhou indicated a note nailed to the back of Devilskein's kitchen door. It read:

The occupant of this Company residence has been forcibly removed and remanded to indeterminate custody on charges of high treason, for breaking Company rules, for revealing Company secrets to a human and for daring to go against the Company policy to keep keys in desirable disarray. The occupant of this Company residence will be terminated further to a trial, the verdict of which has already been decided.

'And I am to blame,' wailed Zhou. 'If I had not befriended Erin then none of this would have happened. Julius tricked me into leading her to him. I'm a foolish cricket, foolish, foolish, foolish.'

'But what exactly has happened? Where is Devilskein?'

'They have arrested him.'

'Who are they? And who was the boy with Erin?'

'They are the Company and Julius Monk is the demon

boy you saw Erin leaving with just now. Only Devilskein has the power to contain him. She is in mortal danger.'

'We must find out where that Monk bastard took her.' But when Kelwyn turned around the front door of the apartment had vanished. An impossibly sweet mist filled the vestibule and Kelwyn, the white kitten, and Zhou were overcome by sleepiness.

Soon Kelwyn really was dreaming, a most peculiar dream, too vivid to bear. He was himself, but older.

He closed his fingers around something in his pocket – a very exceptional Opinel penknife. Its five-finger sharp blade – so named for its ability to effortlessly slice off all the fingers of a hand in a single slash – could never be dulled, and it possessed a frightful history… He was a young man, twenty-two and in Paris. He strode along the Boulevard Saint Germain. His eyes were fixed on the tips of his alligator-skin shoes as their brass tips clapped against the all-knowing paving stones. Under his arm was a fresh baguette – together with coffee and jam it would be breakfast. His fingernails were dirty with rich black earth. He wore a pair of Levi's 501s picked up at a vintage clothing stall in a famous flea market and an old Louvre Museum T-shirt. Between the threadbare cotton of that shirt and the warm, brown skin of his chest there hung, upon a fragile chain, a double-dolphin-headed key. No earthly locksmith would recognise the code stamped into its brass metal. Only Kelwyn knew this dolphin-headed key led to a door that housed a character simultaneously alive and dead and who dreamed in a language reserved for demons and fallen souls.

'Dreamy, perhaps, but it's no dream,' said Julius. 'I'm sorry Erin,' he said with sweet breath – invisible rings of a powerful intoxicant swirled from his belly through his mouth and up her nostrils to bewilder her brain. A tear shone in the corner of his eye, but he was looking outwards towards the passers-by and Erin could not see it. Nor did she realise that when that tear fell to the ground her view of reality would become his to command.

'No need to be sorry,' she said, and in the sky above her the wind had unzipped the clouds all the way down Long Street to reveal a channel of stars. 'Look!' she pointed. 'They're out.'

Julius Monk was dazzled. And dazzling.

'They're magic, aren't they?' said Erin. 'And free for all.'

'What do you mean by "magic"?' He did not turn from the stars; the tear ran down his cheek.

'You're magic too,' said Erin. 'And so is Mr Devilskein.' She had become a great believer in magic. How else could apartment 6616, with its six doors to an eternity of other doors, be explained? 'Magic is something beautiful, it is not part of the world, it is beyond, like the stars and like you. It makes life bearable. How else could you be so old and so young at the same time, if not by magic? It is the magic of Mr Devilskein that has changed me from being an ordinary, spoiled girl into something quite different. It is the magic of the gardens and zoos, all those six doors, that has made me able to draw and paint in a way I couldn't even of dreamt of doing before.'

And then the demon's tear splashed silently upon the plastic laminated tablecloth and fractured into a dozen tiny crystalline baubles.

Unlocking his gaze from the stars, Julius Monk turned towards Erin. His face was so gentle, it was impossible to believe he had ever been capable of the wrath she had once witnessed. In the warmth of the café lights, his usually pale skin looked healthy. He certainly seemed like a living boy of fifteen and nothing more than that. He reached out and touched Erin's cheek, very tenderly; his long nails felt no more treacherous than feathers. 'You are perplexing,' he said.

She smiled. 'I'll take that as a compliment.' At a table

nearby, pizzas and hamburgers arrived and their flavourful cheesy, grilled, and ketchup-covered scents wafted in Erin's direction. 'We should order some food.' She pointed to the menus. 'Have you decided what you want?'

'I am floundering,' he said, darkly.

'No need to flounder; it's not a serious matter; if you choose the wrong thing, you can always order something else.'

'Really?' That seemed to affect him deeply. 'This world outside the Haga is so contradictory. On the one hand you tell me there is no evil, and on the other you say pain is bad and gardens are good? How is that?' His tone was sharp. 'It seems you are deluded.'

'No.' Erin flushed. 'It's just how it is. And too serious to discuss over pizza on a Friday night. You should go to university and do a degree in philosophy.'

'What for?'

'Dunno.' She shrugged. 'Then you can discuss all these things. Talk about them.'

'What is the point of talking about them?'

'I suppose it disentangles them.'

The street was buzzing with life. Sirens from a fire engine wailed; it was on its way to Mama Africa, where the small fire had grown and was consuming the kitchen.

'So, this magic you talk about,' he said, 'is it good or is it bad?'

'It can be both.'

'But you said you don't believe in either!' he roared, causing people at nearby tables to turn and look at them.

'Shhh,' said Erin. 'You're not in your room now. In public places you have to keep your voice down.'

He apologised and they were quiet for a while.

In the doorless vestibule, Kelwyn was still deep in his Paris-filled dream.

He was still wearing Levi's and those crocodile shoes, but he had turned off Boulevard Saint Germain and was older by a decade. He shared a tiny plant-filled apartment with an ethnographer. She had coffee ready in the pot on the stove. Kelwyn placed the baguette on a breadboard, took his exceptional Opinel penknife out of his pocket, and began slicing the bread. The flash of the blade startled him.

Kelwyn sighed. He couldn't understand why he was in Paris. Even so, he continued to slice fat diagonals of the sweetly scented loaf, which would be slathered in slightly salted butter and black cherry jam.

His flatmate poured coffee into two cups. 'Looks like a storm is brewing,' she said.

Kelwyn nodded. 'Rain. Sun. Rain. Sun. Rain. Sun,' he said with some melancholy. 'And in between there is fresh baguette with cherry jam.'

The two dolphins hanging on the key on the chain around his neck did a one-hundred-and-eighty degree flip against his chest – they fluttered like that sometimes, as his heart might have done if he still had one. What? I do not have a heart? he realised with horror. Only then did he understand that his heart had been cut out. And in a fantastical garden, beyond a door only Kelwyn could enter, Erin was waiting for night to fall and dreams to come to Kelwyn so she could bicker with him in the language of pawned souls and complain about his unwarranted optimism and uncouth friendliness.

Kelwyn shifted in his sleep, but neither he nor his kitten woke up.

The moon rose over Long Street. It was a picture book slip of a moon, very yellow, almost becoming amber from the fumes at the restaurant down the road. The band of minstrels had moved along the street and was passing Erin and Julius; they played as they walked and the music was jolly. A breeze swirled through the restaurant and the tiny glassy beads of the demon's tear sparkled and scattered. The music would have made Erin forget Julius Monk's difficult mood had she not seen a fearsome face in the throng across the road.

'We are doomed,' she said in an alarmed whisper. 'See? Across the road.' She pointed, agitated.

Julius Monk, it seemed, froze at the sight too. 'He cannot be here, it is impossible.'

For there was Mr Devilskein, his visage more awful than ever, shaking his fist and glaring at them from beneath the palm tree.

'But he lives here; we should have gone to another street. How stupid of me. I'm sorry.'

Then Devilskein vanished. Erin blinked. Julius smiled.

'Just a last breath of him, no more.'

'What?'

'You shouldn't have trusted me,' Julius said in a low, cruel growl. 'You silly, silly girl, asking too many questions, poking about in places that are none of your concern.' He grabbed Erin by the throat, lifted her up and tightened his grip with menace.

'Where has Mr Devilskein gone?' Erin gasped.

'Pathetic, really.' And then he dropped her, as if bored by the ease with which he could snuff out life.

Around them people in the restaurant were staring and whispering.

'I think we should go back to the Haga,' she said, trying to recover her breath.

'But you invited me out, Erin Dearlove,' Julius hissed. 'And I am not ready to leave here yet.' Then he turned his glare on the people around them whose whispers had turned to concerned chatter. 'Quiet,' he commanded.

'Zhou was right. You're a beast,' she said, quietly.

Julius Monk's eyes had turned to misanthropic ice, his breathing had quickened and around him the atmosphere was turbulent. A chair quivered, glasses fell over. A wrath like never before filled him – a rage of volcanic intensity began welling up from his feet. He forgot that he was in Long Street, that Erin was beside him, that the stars were glittering overhead.

'I am not a beast,' he roared, with such force that the bulbs in the lights above him shattered.

Erin turned pale. 'No, no, you're not,' she said, her lip trembling. 'You're not; he's not, he's not, he's not,' she gabbled. 'I need to go back to Aunt Kate now.'

There was an explosion down the road, for the fire in Mama Africa had reached the gas bottles. The force of it caused the old mosque to shudder and plates fell off the walls in the café. Cars screeched to a halt. People were screaming and more sirens began to wail. And Julius Monk seemed taller than ever.

The waiter came to Erin's aid. 'Please, sir, leave the young lady alone.'

'Alone? Why? Look at me!' He grabbed the waiter's collar. 'Just look at me! Do I look like a beast?'

The waiter shook his head, terrified. The patrons of the restaurant were stunned; nobody dared speak or even move.

'He is more sweet-tempered than any normal boy,' Erin mumbled, trying to recover her calm. 'He likes music and chocolate milkshakes and stories. He is gentle. There is no such thing as evil.'

Somewhere along the road a woman screamed because the flesh on her arms was melting into flames. And in that scream Erin heard her mother, and she closed her eyes. Flashing in the grey of her memory a linen cupboard door was slammed shut. Erin was inside the cupboard, crouched beneath the middle shelf, breathing fast. To her left was a pile of towels washed many times too often, the cotton was hard; those were the towels they didn't use any more. To her right was a pile of old copies of *House & Garden* magazines: an annual subscription to the magazine was her mother's one indulgence. Erin took a magazine and paged through it even though it was too dark to see the images clearly. *Away, thoughts!*

Suddenly, Devilskein was there again, like a ghost. She was shocked to hear a strange gurgle and a choking sound as tears flooded from Mr Devilskein's eyes and poured down his scarred cheeks.

'I'm sorry, Mr Devilskein,' Erin said.

'Ah, Erin,' said Devilskein. 'The return was inevitable at some time or other.' Erin did not understand who Julius and Mr Devilskein were, why they had the powers they had, and yet she knew with a dreadful certainty they were her future; just as she had known that when she was pushed into the linen cupboard she would never see her mother again.

Silent as it was inside the café, outside it was mayhem; Long Street was burning. The wind had come up again and carried the flames from Mama Africa across the street and down the road. Cars were ablaze, people were panicking, running in all directions, hooters and fire alarms howled. Yet despite rescue workers' efforts the inferno would not be tamed.

Julius Monk dropped the waiter, who scuttled away.

'Erin,' said Julius Monk with startling loudness and an eerily calm voice that was as smooth as oleander nectar. 'Long Street, in fact all of this town, will burn to the ground tonight. The wind is strong, the flames are hungry; your aunt and your mathematics teacher are trapped.'

Erin's mouth fell open. 'Why?' She had been in trance-like state, focused only on Julius Monk, sitting with her back to the windows; she turned and saw a bank of flames. 'What is going on?'

And then she was back with her mother in the laundry room. Outside they heard shouting and gunshots, then silence, then her father – the sounds her father made seemed inhuman, more like a pig at slaughter. Voices came into the house. Her mother opened the linen cupboard. Hide in there. Her mother took off the brooch she always wore: a small but beautifully crafted silver owl. *This will keep you safe my sweet child. Don't come out. No matter what, don't come out. I love you, my baby girl. I love you. No matter what, don't come out.* Her mother shut the door.

Many hours later Erin pushed open the linen cupboard door, holding a magazine in one hand and the owl brooch in another, and clambered out of the cupboard. What she saw caused her mind to close down; she stopped crawling, pinned the owl to her shirt, piercing her skin as she did so, and sat there paging through the magazine. There was an article about a banker who lived in a mansion with a glass staircase and who had peacocks in his garden. By now Erin was dehydrated, hungry and overwhelmed; she soon became delirious. That is how the police found her, a full day later: covered with flies and babbling about the mansion with staircase and fancy birds. For months she had been unable to revisit that hell, but all the memories had come rushing back.

And now Julius Monk took advantage of them.

'You couldn't save your family, but you can save all these people and your aunt and Kelwyn,' said Julius Monk. 'You can stop the destruction now, but in return you must give up your soul.'

'But I thought we were friends,' she said, weakly.

'Friendships change like the seasons.'

'Maybe,' she said, so disappointed, but then defiantly continued, 'or maybe evil exists and you are it. Pure evil.'

'What a misguided cliché! Evil is never pure,' remarked Julius Monk. 'I thought you understood that evil is just a matter of opinion. Destruction is as natural, as necessary, and as good as creation.'

'Why me? Why is my soul worth all this?' She waved her arms desperately at the chaos in Long Street.

'Take the deal while it's on offer, foolish girl.'

'Why does life have to be so ugly?' said Erin, thinking of her mother. 'What did I do to deserve this?'

'"Deserve" has nothing to do with it,' snapped Julius. The windows across the road exploded, the mosque began to crumble, and a baby injured in the blast wailed.

'People are burning,' said Julius Monk. 'And soon your Aunt Kate and Kelwyn will be too.'

'No!' Erin cried. 'Don't let them or anybody else die. Take me and my soul or whatever you need and let the street and the city and my poor aunt and silly Kelwyn alone! Quick! Quick!'

With no more formality than that, the deal was concluded, and very quickly indeed.

Without so much as taking a step, Erin and Julius Monk were near the mountain end of Long Street. Then Devilskein's son looked up at the sky, so full of smoke and sparks, flushed with flames and flowing with wind.

'Stop the fire,' said Erin, desperate. 'Stop the wind, before it is too late.'

Since Julius Monk did not take orders, he deliberately paused for a few minutes, and in those minutes people cried more loudly, revellers burned, lives were altered. Then Julius Monk opened his mouth, flared his nostrils and inhaled deeply, drawing into his lungs the sparks, the billows of black smoke, the flames, even the furious South Easter. He breathed in deeper and deeper, swallowing every last bit of the turmoil, and when he closed his mouth, the street was silenced; the fire was gone, only ashes remained. Then thunder rumbled overhead and it began to rain.

'Come along, Erin,' said Julius Monk, grabbing her hand. She knew she had no choice but to go with him. 'It's over!' He laughed. 'The world, I mean, it's over! Your friends are safe, but the planet is not.'

At that moment the great prehistoric plates of the earth around the San Andreas Fault heaved and began to shift in a microscopic, but soon to be cataclysmic, fashion. The oceans around the Americas trembled.

Erin's hand was thin and small and cool in his. As they walked through the swirling soot and rain, Saturn was rising in the Southern night sky. Van Riebeek Heights was still standing, untouched, although some of the neighbouring buildings were close to ruin. And simply by willing it, Julius Monk took Erin into the Haga.

'Welcome to your new home, my little bird,' he said with a horrible sweetness.

21

Aftermath

Only a door away, Kelwyn was engulfed in a languid doze.

'Master Talmakies, I presume,' said a voice, and, in the dream, when Kelwyn turned, there was a monstrous-looking man behind him. 'My name is Albertus Devilskein; we have a friend in common.'

Kelwyn desperately wanted to wake up so that he could get to Erin, but sleep would not release him.

Devilskein glanced about anxiously. 'I don't have much time left in this existence. Guard this with your life.' With these words, he held out a key: a double-dolphin headed key hanging from a long loop of chain, which he placed over Kelwyn's head as if it were an Olympic medal. Then came an unearthly wail. And Devilskein was gone.

The white kitten hissed and Kelwyn woke with a start.

He was relieved it had been a dream. But when he looked down, he saw there was a dolphin-headed key hanging around his neck. The key moved in time with the breathing of the kitten, who had gone back to sleep inside his jacket. Still drowsy, Kelwyn looked around – he was in a dusty vestibule with six doors and on the stone floor was engraved a message:

The history of the world is a story in equal measures of wonders and catastrophes. Throughout time, there have been those who have believed in magic and those who have not; those who have faith in gods and those who do not; and there have been those who harness the power of will and those who do not. Miracles, magic, time travel, immortal souls and the multiplicity of adjacent futures are matters of choice and preference.

And snoring just south of the cryptic note was a large brown poodle. The appalling dust in the place tickled Kelwyn's throat mercilessly and after a fit of coughing he was fully awake.

'Zhou?' he called, remembering the cricket, but now unsure what was dream and what was real. The cricket scuttled out of Kelwyn's pocket.

The poodle did not stir.

Aunt Kate and Greg were still chatting and drinking; they had worked their way through another full bottle of wine and moved to the sofa. Greg was shifting closer and closer to her, while Kate was thinking how extraordinary life was, for just that week she had decided to quit worrying about finding a man and focus on her art instead. Men, she had decided, were just too much trouble, bringers of too much grief. Then, on that Friday evening, as Greg's lips brushed against hers in their first kiss, a divine certainty came over her: she knew without doubt that he was the one she would spend the rest of her life with. It was not a logical thought, it came from a place other than her brain; perhaps it came from her soul. Like Kate, Greg too felt a rush of love; cool as the air over the fjords of Norway, from whence his ancestors hailed. Before that night, a gloomy cynicism had taken hold of his heart, but Kate's touch reminded him of how lovely it was to be close to somebody.

'You're magic,' he said to her, between kisses.

In a realm of pain owned by the Company, Albertus

Devilskein, super-genarian, was being stripped of his particles, atom by atom, from the feet upwards. For his acts of treason, he would be eternally undone, erased both from the past and from the future. Not only would he no longer exist, but he would never have existed. He would be universally forgotten by all, his existence, in every direction, vaporised. As the Company deconstructor set to work on the fibres of his being, Albertus Devilskein closed his left hand around the small silver owl brooch on his lapel; in his last minutes, he connected with Erin through her mother's brooch.

Kelwyn studied the key hanging around his neck and considered the poodle, who he had seen around and about Van Riebeek Heights before.

Also awake and excited, Zhou waved his feelers in the direction of the yellow door. 'Don't worry, the dog's fine, that key is what you need to worry about, it belongs to that door, and it will lead us to the Haga,' the cricket said. 'I don't know how you got hold of it, but as it's in your possession we must act, it can only be that –' Zhou went blank; he knew there was a name he should associate with that key, but he simply couldn't remember and it was most disturbing ,that feeling of knowing he should know something but not being able to access it. 'Somebody… somebody very important is willing it.' Somewhat unnerved, he continued. 'That key will lead us to Erin and she is our only hope.'

The white kitten purred from inside Kelwyn's jacket and kneaded his soft paws against Kelwyn's chest; he had been thrown away at birth, left out in a cardboard box, and for the first time in his little life, he was blissfully content, oblivious to the impending catastrophe.

'Here goes nothing,' said Kelwyn, uncertainly. He fitted the key into the lock and pushed open the yellow door.

'Erin!' he said, surprised and delighted to see her before him. 'The cricket was right!'

Her skin was the grey of a person near death, she was on the other side of the room but facing him; Julius Monk had his back to the door, but when Kelwyn called to Erin, the demon boy swung around and was instantly thrilled by the prospect of taking out Erin's soulmate in front of her very eyes. He pointed a finger at Kelwyn and summoned an ice-blue flame to burn the life from Kelwyn's young heart.

It hit him like a volley of winding punches, knocking him backwards; almost right out of the Haga, but Kelwyn grabbed the doorframe and held on with all his might, his knuckles turning white from the effort.

On the other side of the room Erin was lifted off the ground, levitating.

But it was not Julius Monk's power that was doing this, it was the force of transference. For realms away, as Albertus Devilskein was rendered null and void, he concentrated his last act of will on sending all his knowledge, all his power and all his magic to Erin Dearlove. And then he was undone. One great iron key out of his collection of millions dematerialised; one room vanished from the labyrinth of sixes.

Erin knew instantly that she and Kelwyn must escape from the Haga.

She thought of getting to the door and then it was: she was on the other side of Julius Monk, her back protecting Kelwyn from the demon's ice-blue flame. The sudden absence of the extreme pummelling caused Kelwyn to fall to the ground. Exhausted from the assault, he sank back against the doorframe.

'Get up,' Erin commanded, with unexpected power in her tone. 'This is no time to relax.'

Kelwyn scrambled to his feet. He had tears in his eyes,

his neck was burned, his tracksuit top was blackened and he clutched his chest, sure that the white kitten could not have survived the demon's battering flame. Erin grabbed him by the hand and yanked him through the doorway, slamming it shut so quickly that there wasn't even time for the smile to fizzle from Julius Monk's exquisitely awful face. Erin kept her shoulder hard against the door.

With the rage of a tornado, the demon boy rushed at the door, and had Erin not been imbued with Devilskein's exceptional strength, the yellow door would have been ripped from its hinges.

It groaned, buckled around its edges, and the timber began to splinter.

'I don't know how much longer I can hold him back,' she said, breathless.

'Why don't you lock it?' suggested Kelwyn, who was close to collapse.

She pulled a face, and said, almost sarcastically, 'Well I would, if I had…'

'The key,' Kelwyn said, managing to hold up the dolphin-headed key.

'Where did you get that? Oh, never mind.' She snatched it and inserted it in the lock. With a quick twist of the key, the door was sealed shut for eternity – or at least for as long as nobody invited the demon back into the world. And the great plates of the San Andreas Fault were still again; the oceans drew back in relief; all disaster averted.

Erin and Kelwyn sank to the floor, Erin's arm around Kelwyn's shoulder.

'You did it!' chirped the voice of Zhou the cricket. 'You survived!'

'Not all of us, Zhou,' said Kelwyn, still holding his chest.

He did not want to say the words, but he feared the very worst for the white kitten. 'I failed,' he said to the little creature he dared not look at. 'I promised to take care of you.'

'Miaow,' a small voice piped up.

Kelwyn was astonished. 'It can't be…' He unzipped his jacket and the white kitten stretched and looked up at him happily.

'You don't think I'm that easy to get rid of, do you?' he said.

'But how?' He was gobsmacked and didn't know what was more extraordinary: the fact that the kitten was alive or the fact that the kitten was speaking.

'The key saved us,' said the kitten. 'You were wearing it around your neck. It shielded my heart – and yours.'

Erin looked up at the great key and one of the dolphin heads was indeed burned black. She realised she knew everything about that key, but she didn't know how, or why.

Then the kitten winked. 'I gave it to you in your dream, remember, Kelwyn? I looked a little different then and I went by the name of Devilskein.'

'Devilskein?' said Kelwyn.

Erin frowned. 'Who's that?'

'Nobody's ever heard of him,' said the white kitten and he trotted away in the direction of the kitchen. 'Wake up, Calvados! Come along, Zhou,' he called to the poodle and cricket, who were in equal measures surprised and comforted that the bossy little cat knew their names. 'I need a good strong cup of tea. What's more, Erin and Kelwyn have work to do: two million keys to sort, catalogue and pack away.' He looked over his shoulder. 'You'd best tell your Aunt Kate about it, Erin, because you won't have time to go to school for the next few decades. You'll find there are hordes of people who want their souls back – you're going to be very busy.'

Erin didn't mind about not going to school, but her head

filled with the volume of things that needed to be done.

'How will I manage?' she said, more to herself than anyone else.

She turned to Kelwyn, noticing for the first time the constellation of burns across his face. *Battle scars*, she thought. *Well, that's something I can relate to.* She smiled. 'I'll have to find a gardener. Kelwyn, you're good with plants – do you want a job?'

ABOUT THE AUTHOR

Alex Smith lives in Cape Town with her partner, their book-eating baby boy and their two dogs.

She has had four novels published in South Africa. She was shortlisted for the 2010 Caine Prize and won the 2011 Nielsens Bookseller's Choice Award. Her story *Icosi-Bladed Scissors* appeared in Arachne Press's anthology *Weird Lies*.

MORE FROM ARACHNE PRESS
www.arachnepress.com

BOOKS
London Lies, ISBN: 978-1-909208-00-1 Our first Liars' League showcase.

Stations, ISBN: 978-1-909208-01-8 A story for every station from New Cross, Crystal Palace, and West Croydon at the Southern extremes of the line, all the way to Highbury & Islington.

Lovers' Lies, ISBN: 978-1-909208-02-5 Our second collaboration with Liars' League, bringing the freshness, wit, imagination and passion of their authors to stories of love.

Weird Lies, ISBN: 978-1-909208-10-0 Our third Liars' League collaboration – more than twenty stories varying in style from tales not out of place in *One Thousand and One Nights,* to the completely bemusing.

Mosaic of Air, Cherry Potts, ISBN: 978-1-909208-03-2 Sixteen short stories from a lesbian perspective.

COMING SOON
The Other Side of Sleep ISBN: 978-1-909208-18-6 An anthology of narrative poems.

All our books are also available as e-books.

EVENTS

Arachne Press is enthusiastic about live literature and we make an effort to present our books through readings. If you run a bookshop, a literature festival or any other kind of literature venue, get in touch, we'd love to talk to you.

WORKSHOPS

We offer writing workshops, suitable for writers' groups, literature festivals, evening classes – if you are interested, please let us know.